DEEP PLEASURE

VOLUME I

SOFTER. DEEPER. WETTER.

CHERIL N. CLARKE

CONTENTS

SOFTER THIS TIME

DEEPER THIS TIME

WETTER THIS TIME

SOFTER THIS TIME

1

WARM RAIN

DECEMBER 31, 2025

Blindfolded under a crescent moon.

A slow touch from slender brown fingers grazed the inside of my ankle, circling.

The edge of her fingernail coaxed a shiver down my spine, and a warm Panamanian breeze swept a strand of my hair against my lips. I lay on my back. Eyes closed. Arms at my sides. Legs and feet together... *still.*

Save for my face, my body was completely wrapped in the soft grip of a sangria-colored muslin. My mind was amplified. And my body was... quiet. Trust. Lots of it—through months of expansion and evolution.

The bind was soft, but it held me tighter than any masked stranger's command ever could. I was encased in a protective womb.

Heat from her skin passed to mine as she slowly glided her index finger down the ridge of my nose. Her touch enticed an open-mouth breath out of me that landed in the palm of her hand. The muslin, warmed by my skin where it crossed my torso, carried a faint scent of hibiscus.

"Remember to breathe," she whispered.

I nodded.

A big inhale.

I was entranced by every moment of this.

A year ago, my heart would be pounding with the thrill of who might be watching. Now, its slow, bass drum rhythm was only for me. I didn't feel like I had to perform or give anything. The difference was ecstasy.

Ocean waves rolled forward in the cove below, loosening the humid air around our cliffside villa. I could hear her breathing. Softly. Deliberately. A touch slower than my heartbeat. We were nearly in sync.

"Do you need any more water?" She checked in.

"I'm fine," I whispered, tasting a bit of sea salt on my tongue. She'd checked in three times already. Water. Pillow under my knees. The safeword I hadn't needed to use. It was the safest I'd ever felt while being completely vulnerable. And in that security, a wilder truth finally had the courage to surface: I *needed* this.

She whispered something in Spanish.

I didn't catch it.

I only knew it made me feel like light had just shifted across my face. Then, a soft moan vibrated in my chest...

Her bare feet padded softly on the wood-planked floor as a distant timbre of joy emanated from elsewhere on the property. Other pleasure-seekers. I was still amongst my people, just in a different energy. A different season, literally.

This was what I chose. This was what I paid for. This was my magnificent *expansion*.

For the first time in a long time, I'd forgotten about my clinical to-do lists and schedules. I'd melted away from being always on. And I hadn't felt the urge to do anything erotically outlandish just to feel desirable.

For the first time, in a little over a year, my body was unequivocally *alive* outside of time. And... I was finally learning what it felt like to be cherished instead of consumed...

Six Months Earlier...

"I know how to hold you without taking anything from you."

That was the line that made me lean forward as I watched a micro-documentary on consensual touch. It made me narrow my eyebrows and put down my glass of wine. Who *was* she? And more importantly, could she teach me how to enjoy my body in deeper ways than I'd imagined?

She continued, "...it got to a point where I realized too many of us inhabit our skin as tenants, not dwellers. We pay the rent with function, forgetting the poetry of the place." She paused to gently run her hand across her neck and jawline. "We don't realize the immense pleasure possibilities in our being."

I liked the sound of that.

"Yes, I offer private sessions," she answered the interviewer. "To create a space where women can get to know the sacred side of sexuality and to not feel guilt for their desires."

The words seeped into me like warm rain.

Fetlynne Cadet. I scribbled her name down on the back of a nearby paper scrap, knowing I had to research her the next day.

Dignified. Bold. Majestic. Fetlynne captivated me in a way that made my half-eaten bag of pretzels and crumb-filled lap feel like a personal failing. *I need to be more mindful of my appearance,* I thought. My friends had been telling me that for years.

I continued watching as she conducted the conversation with her hands and smile, gold bracelets shimmering when the sun hit them. Fetlynne was draped in a white Ankara robe. Her bald head framed her face with breathtaking focus. And her cheekbones had just enough blush to look like sunset on bronze. Her brown eyes were strong enough to pull you under.

The documentary was filmed in an old church.

Fetlynne moved down a carpeted aisle inside the medley of stained-glass light talking about reclaiming touch from shame. About letting it be sacred by our own hands because, "we can sanctify touch without a saint. It's our birthright," she finished. The whole thing ended with her standing with her arms wide open near a decommissioned baptismal pool. Her words ricocheted off the walls and landed in my chest.

"I need to find her," I mouthed to myself as I clicked off the video. The visual of her adjacent to an empty stone basin meant for rebirth stuck with me for days. Weeks. Fetlynne's movements were deliberate and elegant. Unmistakable. Unforgettable. Echoing... especially her slow-blinks and easy smile.

Though I wanted to start digging immediately, I talked

myself out of it. "She might be too serious." "Aren't your annual Halloween parties enough?" "What if this is just some overpriced 'wellness tourism' bait?" But I couldn't help myself. I Googled her at 2 a.m. two weeks later, my laptop balanced on a stack of unread veterinary journals.

Mr. Pickles, my beloved French bulldog, grumbled at my feet for taking too long to give him his bedtime walk. But he'd have to wait just a little longer. I was on to something.

Fetlynne's social media presence was light. Just a handful of black-and-white stills from past workshops and two *very* artfully produced videos from eight months before. She was nude—so were the women under care—but every camera angle ensured nothing R rated was revealed. Just gorgeous brown skin on even more brown skin.

I was intrigued. Fetlynne also had a newsletter and recurring article publications. I clicked through to the archive, scrolling past essays on consent, on the physics of breath, on the geometry of touch, and the forces of energy and emotion.

"Sign-up." I spoke aloud while not wasting any time subscribing. "It took you too long to admit you want this, girl. Something different. Something *meaningful.*"

When the automated reply arrived, it was nothing more than a subject line and a single sentence: *Welcome to Bliss.*

"Okay! And... *okay*, Mr. Pickles. Let's go out!" I nudged the petulant pup with my foot before scooping him up for a cuddle. He snorted. Such a dorky diva. *Just like you*, I chuckled at both of us. But on that SW Atlanta night, Fetlynne's lingering grace made me swap my wine-stained sweatshirt for a linen tunic I'd bought but never worn. Two blocks in, however, the humidity had it clinging to me like a damp paper towel. Wrong choice.

I made a mental note to look up "breathable fabrics" right after I finished researching "sacred touch" when I got back inside.

Days later, I was stuck in after-school traffic feeling my car's AC drying out my lips.

Just as cars started moving again, my phone buzzed with an incoming video call. Precious. My half-Dominican, all-Brooklyn friend whose life had been a whirlwind of job changes and dating chaos since we'd had our last girl's trip in New Orleans. We'd kept up through texts and memes, but actual face time had been scarce.

"Angelaaaa! Hey, girl!" she beamed.

"Hey, friend! You're in a great mood! Love the hair color." I glanced in my rearview mirror, then at the road, and then at my phone screen. Her smile was contagious.

"Thank you! It was time for a change. Okay, now—" she pivoted abruptly. "Don't hate me, but..." her voice trailed off.

"What?"

"Well, listen. I know a guy—an accountant who seems boring as fuck by day, but who is also a big freak at night—very connected. And he's respectful. I vetted him." Precious nodded positively. The last time we'd been together was partially because she'd been burned by love and running from her own tears. "He's chartering a sixty-foot catamaran out of Miami for Halloween," she added.

My eyebrows popped up. I hadn't even thought of Halloween yet but instantly remembered the last two I'd experienced. Adventurous. Hedonistic. Mind-blowingly intense.

"It's a four-night *Sensory Drift* with only eighteen spots. Chef, mixologist, a DJ who only plays on vintage vinyl," Precious yapped.

"Miami?" My mind jumped to our other friend: Jasmine, whom I hadn't laid eyes on since we shared a sexy cowboy. The memory still sent a warm shiver through me—less about him, more about who I'd been bold enough to be that night—that I'd actually had a threesome with one of my fucking best friends! *Me*. Nerdy me! But we didn't get weird about it. Just moved on like schoolgirls taking a secret to their graves.

I pressed down on my brakes as traffic stalled again.

"Matter of fact, let me get Jasmine on this call." Precious read my mind.

Jasmine's face appeared in a box below Precious' a few clicks later. Her pink hair was gone, replaced by a chic, closely-cropped natural cut. "Hey, ladies!" Jasmine's voice was a smile. A South Florida beach curved wide behind her.

The next five minutes were a rapid fire overlapping of excitement and catching up at once—Precious pitching the *Sensory Drift*, Jasmine asking practical questions about cancellation policies, me barely contributing. It would be easy to say yes and fall back into the rhythm of us. But something strange had opened up inside me, right in the middle of their noise.

"So, are you guys interested in another Halloween girls' trip, or not? Precious looked at me.

I opened my mouth, but the automatic "Hell yes" sat on my tongue. It wouldn't budge. I thought back to Fetlynne and the energy she gave off. Jasmine's eyes narrowed slightly, studying me.

"Ang, you okay?" Precious quizzed, her tone impatient. "You've been floating through this whole call like you're not really here."

I half-smiled. "Just a little tired." I fed the easy lie even though it did not fit the opening of our call. "Long day at the clinic."

"Well," Jasmine chimed in. "...if Angela is in, so am I."

A silence.

"I need to check my calendar." My hand tightened on the wheel. "The holiday is a busy time for... pet boarding. I'll get back to you soon?"

"Okay, so, that's a no," Precious clocked me. "It's all good, girl. If you don't want it, don't do it. Because I can tell you don't."

"Wait. What? No!" Jasmine protested.

No, no, no. I didn't want to go into why. I wasn't even sure.

Awkward silence.

"Angela?" Precious pressed.

"Uh..."

"You're an animal doctor, not a babysitter."

I grumbled under my breath. "I know," I finally said. "I just feel like I don't want to be a character in someone else's fantasy this year. I want to be in my own." I felt a shudder at a memory from last Halloween where I rode the face of a handsome stranger with a pup mask until I came. Until I squirted and he actually liked it. Thinking back, I wasn't sure if I did. It was weird.

"What does that even mean?" Jasmine cocked her head. They both looked at me.

"I don't even know, to be honest. All I know is I think I want to learn more about myself this year." *God, am I just being boring now?* I wondered, stopping short of telling them that I was intrigued with something else.

Jasmine huffed. "I guess I get that."

"Same," Precious added. "But we should still get together for something else. Anything else. I miss y'all!"

"Me too," I finally spoke again. "All good. Let's set something up."

The call ended with promises to link up later that summer either in New York, Atlanta or Miami if even just for a concert and a spa weekend. By the time I pulled into my driveway, I realized I'd just said no to a fantasy to make room for an inquiry.

I grabbed my laptop and went back to Fetlynne's newsletter archive, following a few links until I found it: "Begin Your Journey." The path was clear, professional, and immediately intimidating.

Step One: A free 15-minute discovery call to check for synergies.

Step Two—*if* one went well—was a 90-minute conversation to discuss boundaries, history, and intentions. In-person. The investment for this step alone was listed as $300. Non-refundable.

Step Three: A segue into sessions with names like Pleasure Mapping, Sanctuary Holding and Deeply Penetrating Somatic Experiences.

"Whoa," I grumbled, rolling my neck as I took it all in. This was nothing like what I'd been used to in this realm. It seemed so... clinical, but in the most intimate way possible. To get to the bliss Fetlynne promised, I would first have to walk into a room and use my voice to ask for it. There were no velvet ropes, costumes or secret codes to get in. Just a calendar link.

I read it again, noting how it was all phrased in a language of gentle authority. I translated it in my head: Pay $300 to talk about your feelings, then maybe later, pay more to let her touch you while you try not to do anything awkward or goofy. All one on one.

The exclusivity was based on my own courage, I realized.

My index finger hovered over the "Book a Discovery Call" button. To click it was to see if I had the right vibe to advance to the 90-minute conversation. Because that's what I wanted, I clicked. And hoped she wouldn't call me back right away.

2

JUST CURIOUS

"I don't kno—" Delete.

"I would like to—" Delete.

"I'm curious about..." Pause. "...what touch feels like when I'm not trying to be unforgettable."

There. I finally answered the first question on Fetlynne's intake form. Of course, I'd procrastinated until the hour before our call. That's what emotionally evolved adults do when asked direct questions about intentions.

It was my day off, and I sat in my usual corner table in a tiny Vietnamese restaurant. It was the kind of place where the server never wrote anything down but never got my order wrong either.

Fish sauce permeated the air. So did the distinct crackle and pop of something deep fried in oil. An untouched bowl of *bún chả* sat in front of me. The noodles had congealed around grilled pork patties while I contemplated the next question: "Describe your current relationship with your body."

"Hmm." I ran my hand from my chin to my jawline, up towards my ear until finally stopping at the back of my neck. Squeeze.

"Everything okay?" My server stopped by. Her eyes flicked from my face to the still-full bowl. "Food no good today?"

"Oh, no. It's fine. Just taking my time." I nodded and smiled.

She refilled my water and disappeared.

Yes.

Just fine.

"I think..." I began typing again. "My current relationship with my body is healthy. I'm comfortable with how I look and—" Pause. That was a lie. Sort of. I *was* okay with my height and weight. By no means was I a gym rat, but I was physically fit with some muscle tone. But the question wasn't about how I looked. It was about an *association*. And I had no idea how to answer that. What kind of link was anyone supposed to have with their body? It functioned, right?

I hadn't thought about myself in ways that would tell me if I had areas that could "hold specific memory." Or, what I hoped to "make space for." The language felt too floral and emotional. I couldn't joke my way through them and that made me uneasy. A little self-conscious. But I still wanted to know what Fetlynne knew, so I did my best.

Twenty minutes later, I pulled into a mostly-empty lot at Cascade Springs Nature Preserve—another one of my favorite day-off locations because of the waterfalls and streams inside. A few birds shrilled in the background, and I could feel the soft sigh of my car once I parked in the crunchy gravel lot and turned it off. The plan was to soldier through this initial call and hit a nature trail to debrief afterwards. Alone.

At exactly 2:00 PM, my phone rang with a local 404 number.

I took one last breath and exhaled it through a tiny gap in my lips before clicking accept. "Hello?"

"Hi. Angela?" The kind voice was instantly recognizable, yet more real. It was a bit deeper than I recalled, but there was still a smile in it.

"Yes, it's me." I adjusted my seat to give me more room, but I left the sun visor down so I could glance at myself even though this was not a video call.

I heard her typing halt, creating a completely silent background. "It's Fetlynne Cadet. Thank you for carving out this time."

"Of course. Thank you for... making the time." I rolled my eyes at my own echo. I was already mimicking instead of trusting my own thoughts. My eyes went still, staring at the dashboard and trees beyond my windshield.

A soft chuckle. "So... how did you find me? I'm always curious."

"On YouTube. Well, TikTok, first. I'd seen a 30-second clip and followed the trail to a short film on YouTube."

"Mmm," she sounded delighted at my extra effort to seek the source. That relaxed me. "I'm glad. And I'm happy you booked this consultation. The right people always find their way to me when it's right for them." A beat. "Now," she pivoted, picking up the pace. "Your answers had a lot of curiosity in them."

"I realize they weren't as certain as they could have been."

"That's fine."

"But I've had a few experiences that opened me up, uh..." I paused. Bounced my knee until it hit the steering wheel. *Ouch.* "Erotically. But nothing that was deep or penetrative in a way that could make me feel more." Terrible phrasing, but it was too late.

"Aha... That might explain the small note of sadness I sensed."

"Sadness?"

I heard a few clicks of her typing again. "Yes, when you said, 'What touch feels like when I'm not trying to be unforgettable.' That's actually a powerful starting place."

But how was it sad*?* My mind was stuck on that word. "Oh." I gripped the phone tighter. "Well, I didn't mean to be down."

"Not like crying or in pain," she clarified. "Just... unwittingly disconnected."

"I'm not sure I follow." I sat up straighter. Glanced in the mirror with furrowed eyebrows.

"When I hear someone say they're trying *not* to be unforgettable, I know that there's a pressure to perform for others, even if it's self-imposed. It tells me their actions are usually gifts for someone else," she explained. "That's not inherently bad. It's an act of giving. But it can also be draining," she paused. "So that line alone tells me you're ready to experience *intimacy*, not just sex."

I no longer heard the birds outside. The temperature in the car seemed to drop. Everything went still.

"And maybe you're actually tired from constantly holding too many things together, but we'd need more time to go deeper into that," Fetlynne finished.

I looked down at my free hand in my lap, staring at it as though it were someone else's. Now I *was* starting to wonder about my "relationship to my body."

"You there?"

"Well, there was one person I—" I caught myself. Too much, too soon. My voice felt naked.

Fetlynne didn't fill in the silence. She let me decide, and then I abandoned it.

"Okay." I focused. "I'd like to understand more of what you can glean from me. Of who I am and who I could be," I continued honestly.

Maybe I was a fraud who had been faking her own pleasure for years. Or maybe I was a normal person enjoying the hell out of life until I started feeling a little lost. I had no idea. But even if disoriented, I appreciated feeling *seen*.

Was she right or distorted? I didn't know. But it was the first interesting diagnosis I'd gotten in a decade. I wanted to keep listening.

"That's what the next conversation is for," Fetlynne picked back up. Her voice was rich honey again. "To see what's under the costume through a deeper, in-person conversation."

And just like that, the separateness between us seemed to dissolve. Along with my angst. *Vibe check passed.* There was no doubt I wanted to explore more with her. Somehow,

Fetlynne's questions made my confusion feel valuable instead of shameful. I wanted to see what was in the hollow place she'd named. Find out what I might have been carrying around. Plus, she didn't seem worried about it.

THE WOODS FELT different when I got deeper into the trail. Determined to still take my walk and process what I was getting myself into, I suddenly felt every brush of leaves from trees that hadn't been trimmed. The cool mist from the waterfall. And the creaky bows and rebounds from the wooden planks underfoot. Everything felt *loud,* but not overwhelming. My mind was spinning with questions. "What if I'm thinking too hard and should just stick with what I know?" "Should I tell Jasmine and Precious?" I kind of wanted to, but it felt premature.

By the time I got three miles in, my legs were loose, but my thinking was clearer. My clothes were also damp from a slight drizzle. Still, I stopped in front of a small stone structure tucked into the hill. It was enclosed by moss-covered stone and a spray of multi-colored leaves, looking like a dollhouse church. Flowers, old fruit and hollowed coconuts now faintly filling with rainwater sat inside its little arched opening. *So Atlanta.*

I lingered long enough to consider what wishes, spells, gifts, or other offerings people had left at that spot. *Gifts.* The word thrust me back to Fetlynne's interpretation of me on our call. *What might a gift to* myself *look like?* I had no idea. That was the most exciting part. Unnerving, too. Because it meant I'd need to do more work to find out what I actually desired.

"I got this," I smirked. If I can venture into kinky cabins sex parties alone and watch shibari shows while flirting with all genders in previous years, surely I could handle the next step.

My walk back to the parking turned into damn near a skip. Back at my car, I did it—calendar blocked, confirmation received. As I drove home, a group text from Precious exploded on my screen: "SO. I put the down the deposit for the Halloween boat. It's happening! 🎃⚓ " Angie, just including you in case you change your mind. No pressure."

My gut tightened. *Nope. Not doing it.*

A second later, another email from Fetlynne tumbled in. The subject line read: "Preliminary Audit: What Have You Been Using Your Body For?"

I was a doctor. I knew how to audit a body. I just never imagined being the subject.

3

JUST NOTICE

"What do I even wear?" *Not these scrubs.* "What if I'm not good at opening up? Or at being quiet?" Questions trampled my brain as I prepared to meet Fetlynne in person.

A week had passed. An unusually heavy one. I'd guided three families through the final goodbyes of their beloved pets and the sterile scent of the euthanasia room swirled in my memory no matter how many times I tried to forget it. "Shit. What if I cry?" The professional compartment in my brain felt cracked. I was experiencing more feelings than I wanted to, but didn't dare cancel my appointment. I'd been looking forward to this.

"Keep it casual," I told myself while thumbing through various shirt options. "Don't overthink it, girl." I chose a charcoal tee and dark jeans. A black jacket for the inevitable Arctic AC. Bam. And, juuuust for the hell of it, I pulled on a pair of socks with Mr. Pickle's little pudgy face before sliding into clean white sneakers. My version of a lucky charm.

Fetlynne's studio was in her home, which made me nervous at first, but I'd checked out the street view as soon as I got the address and was put at ease. The house was a classic Craftsman bungalow with a wide porch wrapped in pristine white trim. It wore its age in a few places—paint peeling softly near the roofline, a single loose shutter—but the lawn was sharply edged and the hydrangeas were explosions of blue. As I followed my GPS down the street that mirrored what I'd seen online, the abode looked more like a favorite old robe that had been stitched and restitched with care.

"Hi there!" She greeted me. Fetlynne was *much* shorter in-person than I expected but still felt monumental in presence. Her cobalt sundress almost swept the porch when she extended a hand. "You must be Angela," she smiled gracefully.

"I am," I reciprocated the warmth she offered.

"Welcome. Please, come in."

Fetlynne seemed to be late-40s or early-50s, not much older than me. Her practice was in the formal parlor. High ceilings and antique crown moldings. In the center was a low wooden table adorned by a heavy crystal decanter with water and two lowball glasses. It was all cushioned by a giant Persian rug.

"Make yourself at ease," she told me. "This is our space for the next hour and a half. Nothing enters or leaves without your consent."

Lemon incense and soft ambient music filled the air. Fetlynne slid out of her slippers and stepped forward on bare feet.

“Okay, thank you.” I took off my shoes, following her lead.

Even if she hadn’t retreated to bare feet, I would have asked. The place was not the kind you’d trample through with sneakers on. It was too thoughtful. Too...sacred-feeling. Fuck. My socks. They felt like a scream as we walked toward a spray of floor cushions near the centerpiece.

“You have a beautiful home.”

“Thank you so much. It’s been in my family for a long time.”

I noticed an abstract floor-to-ceiling tapestry on one wall. It swayed from the breeze of a small open window, adding decoration without hiding what was behind it. The one formal piece of furniture was a plum-colored chaise lounge pushed against another wall and adjacent bookcase. It was one of those look-but-don’t-sit pieces. Above it was a conspicuous painting of an open mango dripping at the slit while showing off its blazing orange heart.

I blinked. There was a cluster of paintings, actually. All fruit. All tastefully suggestive, but the juicy mango sat centered. Unmistakable, just like her.

“Would you like some water?” Fetlynne clipped my observation.

“Yes, thank you,” I answered, not knowing which pillow to sit on. “Oh wow.” I couldn’t hold back a gasp when I saw a gigantic raw geode cracked open. Its crystals looked magical, glowing from within under a small hidden light.

"That's my pride and joy. I found it in a dusty little rock shop in Arizona twenty years ago." She handed me the water and then gestured to floor cushions.

"Please, choose where you'd like to sit."

Don't overthink it. Don't overthink it. I picked one facing the couch that anyone older than us would have covered with plastic.

Fetlynne sat at a slight angle from me, taking a sip of her water before speaking. "You noticed the mango and the geode. What do you think they have in common?"

Aw, shucks. We're diving right in. "Uh..." I was not prepared for an art interpretation. "Femininity? But also masculinity—the geode. I don't know; they're both split open but one feels much softer than the other." I paused, craning my neck to look harder. "They both also hide a lot inside. Life. Light. Maybe unknowns?" That was the best I could do.

"Life inside. Light inside," Fetlynne reiterated, her wooden bracelets sliding against her forearm as she took another drink. It was then that I noticed a small tattoo of two fish that looked like yin and yang on her right wrist. This woman was quicksand. Everything about her pulled me in. "You recognized life and light in them. Now... let's find yours."

The next hour followed a conversation that felt like being gently turned inside out. We talked a little bit about my day-to-day life and profession, then on to my perceived stress levels, friends and any other community support—and finally, what intrigued me about intentional touch. I told her about my previous experiences and then expressed that seeing her triggered a desire for slowness and deeper sensation.

"To be honest, I'd never thought of pleasure outside of intensity." I glanced around to fill in the gap until my eyes landed on a small, stuffed anatomical uterus nestled between two books: *Slow Love* and something else that looked like it was written in French. My head cocked to the side in interest.

Fetlynne listened and followed my gaze before bringing me back. She disarmed me with a question: "Where in your body did you feel the most alive during previous encounters?"

My mind went blank. I'd never thought to map it.

"Try to think about the moments or day after an encounter. What tingled at the memories? Your chest? Your legs? Your bones? Your throat?"

"My... legs," I answered, fidgeting with my necklace.

We moved from memories to present activities and rituals —the latter of which I had none. She showed me how to audit my body. What to look for when a pleasurable thought caused a physical ripple—a softening in the belly, a warmth between the shoulder blades. How to identify areas of holding—the clenched jaw, the raised shoulders—and breathe into them until they softened. And when to say "softer" or "slower" or "not there" without needing a reason. The whole experience felt like clearance to recognize the sheer amount of communication from my body I'd been ignoring.

"Thank you for this," I couldn't help but show gratitude as we moved through the 90 minutes.

Fetlynne eventually asked if I was okay with a "touch exercise," leading me through a sunroom to a surprising private garden when I agreed.

“Can I grab my shoes?” I was overdue for a pedicure and didn’t want to take my socks off.

“Of course,” she chuckled.

Her backyard was a contained choir of greens, yellows, and hints of purples. A stone bench sat under a magnolia tree. A small fountain added a water element.

“It’s just a different kind of room,” Fetlynne grinned, still barefoot and free. Her dress lifted slightly with the breeze. Strong legs. Moisturized skin. Liberated stroll.

I want to be like that. The thought zipped through my mind just as fast as the birds flitting by. The air was humid and sweet, begging me to breathe slower and take it all in. But then a fat bumblebee lumbered past my ear. My first instinct was to duck. My second was to laugh. I had no idea what to do, so I stood still. Then I followed Fetlynne to the stone bench.

She took just a moment to light two small urns with copal before returning to me. The smoke created an ethereal boundary around us.

“Sit here.” She placed a hand on the bench’s sun-warmed surface. “I want you to feel the support. This is your anchor, okay?”

I nodded, and sat, noticing the difference between the concrete and the flutter in my chest. The magnolia leaves rustled. Fetlynne then moved behind me.

“Now, I’m going to place my hands on your shoulders,” she spoke calmly. “My intention is for you to feel the weight, heat, and support. Your only task is to notice what happens in your body, alright? There is nothing for you to do in return," she assured me. "And if at any moment you want to stop, just say 'pause.' Are you ready?"

I gulped. "Yes." Then, I instinctively closed my eyes.

Her hands were warm, solid, and utterly still.

And off my mind went. "Should I relax more?" "Arch my back less?" "What does she want from this?" "Will this turn into a massage?"

I waited for the next part—the squeeze, the travel, the signal—anything to tell me what we would graduate to. Nothing came. Her hands just rested. They held. Their ardor seeped through my t-shirt. My mind, armed with a thousand scripts for this moment, found none of them fit.

Oh.

This is just... happening. *To* me.

My shoulders, which I hadn't realized were hunched near my ears, began melting because it felt like more work to hold them up. A slow breath escaped me as my entire body relaxed more. I even felt the subtle warmth from her abdomen behind me.

After a few minutes, she lifted her hands. I immediately felt the cool garden air rush to meet the places they'd been.

"Now, hold your palms up. Face them towards the sky but fingers toward me." Fetlynne came around to kneel in the grass before me.

Our positions sent a shiver up my spine. Uncertainty. New territory. But I did what she said. Fetlynne then cupped her hands beneath mine, supporting them despite my thinking she'd hold them. It was the way you might hold a baby bird.

My own hands felt strangely heavy and light at once. I

watched them resting in hers, and felt a bizarre, tender welling in my chest. It wasn't arousal, but I didn't know how to describe it. *Dis...arming, maybe?*

"Just notice," she whispered, her eyes on my palms.

And I did. I noted the vibration in my skin where we touched. I saw the give of the grass under her knees. I felt the staggering novelty of receiving a gift that asked for nothing back. And that the gift was the simplest thing in the world: human touch. That it was the first one like this that I had known.

I wanted to lie down. My body felt slightly inebriated, but in the precise, shimmering way of heat rising off asphalt. By the time our session was over, I had learned that my body kept a frantic ledger of give-and-take, and that lying down that burden felt like waking up from a lifelong cramp. It was unnecessary.

"Take this feeling with you, Angela," Fetlynne said as she walked me to the door. She clasped one of my hands in both of hers one last time, gently grazing up my forearm before thumbing my wrist. "The body remembers. You've given it a new memory."

"I will. Thank you." My voice was softer than I'd heard it in years. I pulled on my sneakers, already wanting to book another session.

"I'd be happy to see you again whenever you'd like," she said. "I think you have a wonderful journey ahead of you."

"I'm very interested in coming back. I'll schedule another date soon," I told her. "Thank you so much."

"The pleasure's all mine." She smiled. "Safe journey home."

. . .

THE WORLD BLURRED on the road. Fetlynne's touch clung to my skin like the steam from a too-hot bath—soothing, but revealing little places that were tender. It also embarrassed me because I didn't know it could feel like that without sex. And now that I did, I wasn't sure what I'd do with that knowledge.

"I need to journal," I spoke aloud, craving a way to capture and dissect everything I had just experienced. It felt too simplistically incredible to be real. Or for me not to have already known it was possible. I kept thinking of a question she'd asked me before we left the garden: *what would it feel like to touch yourself without a goal?*

I didn't want these discoveries to end.

4

ECHOES DON'T KNOCK

I didn't even want to go to the dog park. Not after volunteering all weekend with rescued circus animals. But Mr. Pickles had been whining at the door like he had somewhere to be. Which, I guess he did. Pee on a tree. Bark at clouds. Make sure the other dogs knew he still ran this shit.

I threw on some soft shorts, slipped on a tank top, and decided not to overthink it. Zero makeup and no jewelry. Just a clean face and SPF. Oh, and beautiful hair. I had gotten my tresses done that week.

Almost ten days had passed since my first real session with Fetlynne and I was still integrating what we'd uncovered. I was eager to go back, but existing obligations kept me away. Bills and things, pesky fuckers. But August in Atlanta had no business being so beautiful on that day. Still humid, still sticky, but the breeze was flirting again.

I walked Mr. Pickles to a shaded park near my clinic—

quiet enough for a day I wasn't ready to meet people. He was in full gremlin mode, though, already dragging the leash toward the gate before I could finish my iced coffee.

"Go, go." I unclipped him and stepped back toward the fence.

I half-watched my pooch while scrolling social media. On one of his manic laps around the park, I looked up. That's when I saw it.

My mouth went agape. I swallowed hard, breath speeding up at the sight of familiar black ink on brown skin. I knew those forearms. My stomach flipped.

He bent down to pick up a scuffed, muddy ball. And just like that, the rest of him slid into view. Shoulders. That jaw. And a very specific, deliberate way of moving his hips that reminded me of one of the wildest, most risqué nights of my life.

Rich.

Or "Cowboy" as I remembered him from two years ago. A leash hung loose in his hand. And some grinning brown mutt with too-big paws trotted alongside like they belonged to each other. He hadn't seen me yet, but I knew it was him. There was no way on Earth I could forget the sexiest man I'd ever entangled with. *What was he doing in Atlanta?*

For a second, all my progress stuttered like a raggedy car trying to front like it was a collectible. The air in my lungs felt thin and my heart galloped towards memories that made my thighs clench. I stepped back into the shade.

Jesus. Jesus. Jesus. I felt a throb. Didn't want that. Not here. Not now. Too late. Rich straightened up, wiping his thick hands on his dark jeans. He scanned the park in a lazy sweep. It passed over a yapping terrier, a man on the bench, a cluster of kids by the water fountain... and landed on me. I could see his brow furrow and lips bend inward to a soft bite. Recognition was a slow dawn in his eyes, followed by a flicker of something hotter, more immediate. Amusement. Interest. He started to say something, then stopped.

He doesn't remember me, I thought. *Good.* Well, maybe not. Being forgettable might hurt more. He ambled over. *Shit. Shit. Shit.*

I became acutely aware of my bare legs, soft shorts, and the not-so-new tank top. And it was at that moment Mr. Pickles chose to barrel into my shins, snorting and demanding attention. The physical jolt broke my trance. I looked down. Fumbled for his leash, buying myself a second to gather the pieces of myself that had just scattered. When I looked up again, Rich was coming over with the mutt following, tongue lolling.

"Angie?" he called, stopping a respectful few feet away. His voice was exactly as I remembered: a low, gravelly baritone that felt like it was rubbed in honey and bourbon.

"Uhm..."

"Holy shit. Cat woman! It is you!" He laughed. "Meoooow!" recalling the Halloween costume I'd worn that night.

"Mr. Cowboy. Rich," I cleared my throat. "Wow. Small world."

"No kidding." His eyes traveled over my face, quick and assessing. "You look... good. Really good."

Likewise, I thought. *You look like trouble.* He was dressed down—an aqua-blue tee stretched across his chest, those jeans, and scuffed boots. The tattoos on his veiny forearms… ones I'd once traced with my tongue, seemed to pulse in the dappled light.

"Thanks. You too. What are you doing in Atlanta?"

"Visiting my sister. She just had a baby. I'm the fun uncle, dog-sitting this menace." He nudged the brown crossbreed with his boot. The dog wagged its entire rear end. "You live here now?"

"For years," I told him. "I'm a vet. My clinic's a few blocks over."

He looked impressed. A slow smile spread across his face, transforming it from handsome to dangerously appealing. "Sounds amazing."

A silence.

MORE FLASHBACKS of rooftop lights on our entangled bodies flooded my mind. The reckless, exhibitionist thrill of him watching me with Jasmine in the hotel room before claiming his own turn. It had been a masterpiece of mutual consumption. A performance for an audience of each other.

And now, here he was. In my quiet, post-Fetlynne state. A souvenir from a museum of a former self.

"Yeah, well," I shrugged, aiming for breezy. "It has its crazy days like any other job, but I love it."

"I hear that. Good for you, doctor…" He shifted his weight, the leash swaying. "You here with…" He glanced around, a subtly pointed question.

"Just me and Mr. Pickles." I patted the bulldog's head.

He snort-laughed. It was the name, I was sure. I always

got that. "Cool. Cool." Rich's gaze settled back on me with more intent and the park sounds all faded away. "Listen," he picked up again, leaning in slightly. "I'm in town until Sunday. My sister and her husband are begging for a night out. I'm supposed to be on babysitting duty, but they've got a backup." He paused, licking his lips. "It'd be good to catch up —properly."

The invitation was a test. A direct line back to a version of Angela who would have said yes before he'd finished the sentence. That Angela would have already been planning the outfit, anticipating the thrill, the validation, the certain, sweat-slicked conclusion.

But Fetlynne's hands were a new celebration on my skin. Sparklers in my brain. My body hungered for that path. But God, I felt the pull—a seductive, nostalgic gravity and chance to be the unforgettable Angela for one more night. I also felt the new, fragile thing inside me—the possibility that had softened under a stranger's still hands in a sun-drenched garden. And I wanted more of that. *Then say that*, my mind goaded.

I took a slow breath and offered a genuine smile. "You know, Rich, that's really nice of you to offer." My voice was steady. "And it's wild seeing you. But... I'm actually in the middle of something. A personal... project. It's taking up a lot of my headspace."

He blinked. Confused. I hadn't said no. I'd said something else.

"A project?" he echoed.

"Yeah. Just... learning some new things about myself." I bent down to clip the leash back onto Mr. Pickles, who was now sniffing Rich's mutt's butt with intense diplomatic interest. "It's not really a good time for catching up like that."

For a long moment, he just looked at me. Then a soft smile returned to his face. More curious than conquest-oriented. "A project, huh? Okay. I can respect that." He reached down to scratch his dog's ears. "It was good seeing you, Angie. Really."

"You too, Rich. Take care."

"My number's the same. Just to say that if you ever want to catch up with no pressure, I'd love to hear about any and all self-development you're into." He winked. And with that, he turned away. "Come on, Rocky. Let's go."

I watched him leave with the same confident gait carrying him out of the park. The bubble popped. The sounds of the world rushed back. My hands were trembling. I clenched them around the leash. Mr. Pickles looked up at me, as if to say, "Well? Are we staying or going?"

"We're going, buddy," A taste of triumph was on my tongue. "We're going home."

As I walked back to my car, the spirit of Fetlynne's touch settled over my shoulders again, lighter than memory, warmer than the sun. And suddenly, the realization that I listened to my body and spoke what it really wanted versus what I thought I should do with a ridiculously handsome man in front of me. The awareness was quiet but absolutely seismic.

5

THE UNVEILING ROOM

I was early. Glancing at my watch, I decided to idle up the street rather than sit in Fetlynne's driveway like a thirsty pigeon. When the time drew nearer to three minutes early, however, I proceeded.

"Angela," she greeted with a full smile and looked me directly in my eyes. She wore her hair in a fresh cut, crimson romper that showed off toned arms, and a cowrie-shell necklace that glimmered against her silk-brown skin. Fetlynne was yet again an energy and a *vision*. "It's nice to see you again," she added.

"I'm happy to be here." I'd gone for tomboy cute: green cargo pants, a fitted white tee, a single perfume spritz. My hair was in a thick ponytail that reached my back. Dresses were never my thing, though I'd put on a little makeup to brighten my face.

"Come on in."

The front door clicked gently shut and the first thing I noticed was the smell of vanilla.

"I was thinking we could try talking in a different room today," she announced. "Or would you like to keep the same session space?"

"Whichever's easier for you." I gestured vaguely.

Fetlynne looked at me with a raised eyebrow.

"Or...We can try another room." I smiled. *Choices*. Mine to make, always.

She winked. "Alright. Follow me."

I trailed her down a new hallway to a room with no garden view. No windows at all, actually. Just wall sconces, candles, books and flowers on shelves, and a low bench to anchor the room. Carafes of rosemary, strawberry, and lemon water were on display. And a beautiful birdcage chair hung in one corner. The space was quiet enough to hear myself swallow, but alive with the perfume of wood, wax, and earth.

"Now, I've been meaning to update my service offerings online—one thing I'm terrible at, honestly. But I do have a short list right here and I can tell you about some bigger events I have coming up in the fall and winter if you're interested." She handed me a brochure from a shelf.

"I'd love that." I liked following her lead and intuition but felt better knowing there was a pre-determined variety of things for me to experience.

"Perfect. We can do any of them except the 4th today. That one requires advanced planning on my part."

I scanned the menu and read:

The Flirt Lab

Learn to navigate the Yes/Maybe zone through the art of tease, the build and the enticement. Interactive testing and learning in a low-pressure environment.

The Professional Cuddle

A pleasure-focused immersion in warmth, stillnesss, and breath. Clothing-optional.

The Unveiling

A ritual of release. One item of clothing at a time. No rush.

Tantric Massage (90-minute)

A practice of extended sensation. Where touch is not a means to an end, but the destination itself. Time vanishes. Pleasure magnifies.

There were more, but I stopped. My eyes kept drifting back to "The Unveiling." Fascinated by it. A faint, familiar heat prickled under my skin.

I looked up to see Fetlynne now standing by a chest of drawers. She rolled her wrists and flexed her jaw, giving me time to choose. "This one." I tapped the page. "I'd like to know more about this one."

Fetlynne smiled mischievously. "Fantastic choice."

"How so?"

"Well, this ritual is in your own hands—literally," she explained. "You remove one piece of clothing at a time, with all the time you need between. There is no goal of nudity. It's to discover what you want to reveal or show off—because most of us want to be marveled at, right?" She smiled, a knowing glint in her eye. "To be truly seen."

Did she just dig into my subconscious? I chuckled a little.

I hadn't even been aware of that desire in this context, but once she said it, something clicked. I *did* like being watched. I also had a nice physique that no one ever saw because it was usually covered by scrubs and animal fur.

Fetlynne kept explaining. "The aim is also to feel the sensation of fabric leaving your skin. It can feel like claiming your own spotlight. And you're in complete control."

"Let's do it!" the words burst out.

"Uh huh...already excited," she giggled.

Suddenly bashful, I felt the heat flood my cheeks. "Yes."

"I can see that."

Fetlynne pivoted to turn on faint music before saying, "You can stand or stay seated. Eyes open or closed. The only thing that matters is your comfort. So...when you feel ready to remove something, you do."

My body went stiff with attention. I remained standing, staring at my sides. I noticed how clenched my fingers were. Then let them go. Felt weird. Fetlynne then walked to the corner where the cute birdcage chair hung. With one gentle pull on a rope cord, she revealed a floor-to-ceiling fabric. The clink of rings on rods dinged like a start timer. Ivory linen bisected the room, softening the light and separating us at once.

Then, she turned on a track with delicate, floating sounds that drew at something deep inside me. Vulnerable. Aching. It held me in place.

"I'll be here," she said, moving behind the veil. Her outline was now a blurred silhouette. "And you'll be there."

A beat.

"Ready?"

I exhaled slowly. "Yes."

"Wait. What is song is that?" I couldn't help myself. It instantly relaxed me. "I'm sorry. Don't mean to interrupt the exercise."

"You're not." I could hear her grinning through her words. 'Hold Me As I Land' by... Seinabo Sey. And good. It's doing exactly what it should be doing."

By the time the last word left Fetlynne's lips, the sound shifted—Sey's voice entering softly. I felt it in my sternum, tender and intimate. "Okay," I mumbled, making a note to look it up.

Watch. I decided to remove my watch first, then, my t-shirt. Nothing happened. Fetlynne didn't move. Didn't react. Didn't even shift her weight. She was just... there. Witnessing. I stopped to pour myself a cup of strawberry water. Unsure. Scared. This wasn't the "being seen" scene I was used to.

After a long moment, Fetlynne's soft voice came. "Angela. Take a breath and tell me one thing you feel right now. Just one."

"Cold," I whispered. "The air on my shoulders... it's cold."

"Good," she said. "Thank you for telling me. Now feel it."

Alrighty. I let the cold be cold. Allowed it to pebble my skin. My breath began to deepen and heat the air in my lungs. The frigid feeling soon became a sensation, not a shock, and I felt less frantic. More present. I was getting the hang of this, but my breathing still ticked up as I stood there in my bra and pants. Shoes and socks.

"Feel everything," she whispered. "*Experience* everything." She got up again and fiddled with something on the wall across from her—still behind the veil.

Then, the music crossfaded into "Loving Me" by Janine—I recognized that one from TikTok, ironically—it made me smile. This track was enveloping, guiding me to slow down and think about myself against the lyrics.

I paced a little. Stopped and closed my eyes. I touched my widow's peak and dragged my fingers down the curve of my hairline before exhaling. Then, I stepped out of my shoes and unzipped my pants. I felt more warmed up and calm now. Instead of tugging my pants off, however, I let them fall in a pool around my ankles and stepped out. Then I stood there in a white bra and panty lace set that I'd worn for no one but myself.

The room felt cool again.

Just for a moment against my thighs and chest, hardening my nipples. Made my legs tense a little. I had not expected that. The shocking intimacy of it all.

My shoulders tried to hunch forward, but I forced them back. This wasn't the time to shrink. "So…" I spoke again to give myself something else to do. "What are you doing?" I quizzed. The question sounded more accusatory than I meant it to. I guess I did feel exposed.

"Marveling. Can you feel yourself?"

Marveling? I liked that! "Yes, I can," I told her.

A shivered breath tumbled its way out of me as I halted further undressing. Suddenly, I was more aware of the architecture of my own body: the cut of my hip bones, the line of my quads. And how gorgeous the snowy lace lay flat against my dark brown skin. I smiled broadly; very happy I chose this experience. But I didn't know what to do with my hands, so I just let them hang.

Finally, the room warmed up again. *Maybe it was a thermostat she'd fiddled with earlier.*

Fetlynne then stood and walked toward me from the other side of the fabric. She paused just far enough away to not be inside my reach. Her eyes were gentle. Her voice, lower than before. "Would you like me to come closer?"

I nodded, forgetting she might not see it clearly. "Oh, yes. Yes, I would."

She advanced into my space, but still behind the fabric. So close now I could feel the warmth of her skin in the air between us. But I didn't move. We locked eyes and I held a tender gaze, even if mildly distorted. The stare sent electricity through my entire body, and my mouth fell slightly open again.

Almost imperceptibly, I felt her fingers brush upwards against mine through the linen. The touch feathered up to the back of my hand and sent a shiver down my spine. I stepped closer, my toes now against hers. One more inch, and we'd be lips to lips, but she shifted, gently placing her forehead against mine.

A soft, high-pitched moan instantly escaped me. The whole world *narrowed* to this point of contact and my shoulders fell. Eyes closed. I felt my body try to shift toward seduction despite the fabric, or flirtation, or shame. But nothing but breathing came. Ours, syncopated.

I didn't know what time it was. I didn't know if this was halfway through or already over.

But I knew I wasn't being impulsive. I wasn't running from partner to partner. I wasn't trying to be unforgettable. I was being *held*, without being touched. And when Fetlynne finally pulled away—slowly, so slowly—I knew I'd just been attuned to a different kind of yes. But what on Earth was this new frequency? And why did this tingling connection—through a veil, not in someone else's arms—feel more like a homecoming than any thrill?

6

HOLDING

Being watched without being wanted is a hard experience to describe. Yes, I was in my own spotlight, but the light wasn't warm or bright enough at first. I hadn't felt the adrenaline or satisfied bruise that usually came with being exhibitionist. But as the days after went by, I felt an aching for more of this kind of attention. I wanted to talk. I wanted to share. Be noticed, touched, held, heard, and acknowledged again. I even wanted to try hugging because I knew I didn't have to be so awkward at something so simple.

No matter where I went in the days after my last session with Fetlynne, I was haunted by that veil on my skin and her breath on my lips. In my clinic. In the lab. At home. At the grocery store. I could still feel the delicate pressure of her forehead on mine, a phantom touch. It made me hyper-aware of my jeans, wishing for softer sweatpants or nothing at all. I could still see her as she got on her knees in front of me in the garden. A reverent yet empowered position I'd never been able to experience as the one who was being honored. It was an offering that demanded nothing, yet gave me everything. I craved more.

My physical desires seemed to be reorienting.

The whole journey with Fetlynne made me start journaling again because I suddenly felt random arousal throughout the day. Quieter nights that found me dissecting my past sexcacades like an artist studying early brushstrokes. I allowed slower moments without feeling guilty about them. But wild daydreams about what her touch really felt like crept in. *Tantric Massage.* The choice on her menu boomeranged into my mind. I initially hadn't known much about that.

Bzzt. My phone vibrated just as I finished up a journal entry—Jasmine.

"Hey, girl!" I answered, genuinely happy to hear from her.

"Hey, friend. It's been a while. What's going on? How are things?"

Where do I begin? I'd been self-conscious about sharing my new journey, fearing judgment. "Things are going great."

A silence.

"That's it?" she laughed, knowing there was more.

"Oh! Girl!" I had something for her. "You will never, I mean never guess who I ran into at the dog park a few weeks ago."

"Then don't make me try. Who?"

"Rich."

"Rich?"

"Yes. Sexy cowboy from the NOLA Halloween party two years ago!"

"What?!"

"Yes, girl. Felt like a real ghost of booty calls past. But he was cool. Cordial and respectful, actually."

I told her all about our run-in and my turning him down to meet up again. She couldn't believe it. Though not her fault, Jasmine had an older version of me in her head. A goofier, more awkward and most-likely-to-fall-over-a-handsome man, Angela. Sure, I was still clumsy and could use a personal stylist, but all of that wasn't me anymore. And the changes started before Fetlynne. They'd begun a year ago and slowly led me to someone like her.

I tip-toed into telling Jasmine about Fetlynne.

"You're seeing a sex doula?"

"Well, I don't think that's her title, but I guess you could say that. More of a somatic pleasure coach."

"Fancy schmancy. Whatever. A sex worker. You're seeing a sex worker."

I didn't like the spice on the way she said the title, even if it were true. "Friend, I hear the judgment in your voice, and I need you to check it. This work is important to me. She's a professional who's helping me in ways I asked for."

"But Ang—"

"I mean it. I'd never dismiss what you do for your peace of mind; please afford me the same respect. Because if she were a trainer at the gym, you'd call it self-care. She's a trainer for my nervous system and my pleasure. The equipment is just... more intimate. And the results are changing my life."

"Well, damn. Alright. Since you put it that way."

A silence.

We picked back up, and I teased out a little more info but kept the massage a secret. That didn't need to be her business if sharing it would taint the experience with negative energy.

I TEXTED Fetlynne the next day. "Hi…" then got pulled away for an emergency with a frantic dachshund parent. By the time I got back to my text, thirty minutes had passed and she'd responded: "Hi Angela. How can I serve you today?"

Jesus Christ. How does she always know what to do and say to make me feel open? I bit my bottom lip and smiled before typing back: "I can't stop feeling that veil on my skin. It's distracting."

An hour later, she responded. I imagined her smirking with pride when she typed: "That's just the work waking up. Don't ignore it. Feed it when you can. You don't need me to recreate the feeling. Have you considered creating an altar for yourself?"

"Myself? Not at all."

"It doesn't have to be as self-absorbed as it sounds," she typed back. "Think of it as a sensory charging station. You don't need any statues of deities. Just…" Her message ended abruptly and I noticed the 'recording' microphone icon pop up. Fetlynne finished with a voice note instead of typing a paragraph.

"Good afternoon," she began. I could hear wind chimes

in the background and imagined her sitting on her wrap-around porch. "So... what I'm suggesting is just a dedicated space for your own attention. It could hold a stone that you found on one of your hikes. A scrap of fabric with texture that makes you want to sigh. A photo where you see your own power in your eyes. Maybe just a single flower you like the smell or shape of." She paused, the chimes dancing in the silence. "The only rule is that everything there must make your body say a tiny, 'yes' when you touch or look at it. Spend time there. Breathe. Let it remind you that you are the source of your own marveling." She paused again, her voice softening. "You have a very intelligent body, Angela. It knows how to speak, if you listen. That's a gift."

I blinked, hand on my chest after hearing her compliment. I didn't have the language to respond in a way I thought adequate to meet Fetlynne's energy, but I tried with a voice note.

"That might be the most beautiful thing anyone has ever said to me," I paused. Took another breath and let the words tumble out. "It feels true. And a little scary. But...thank you. That means more than I know how to say."

THE TIME COULDN'T PASS FAST ENOUGH. At $300 a session, I couldn't see Fetlynne weekly, but boy did I want to. In the meantime, I joined some of her online workshops and popped into one lower-cost group coaching session. Our next 1:1 was for a professional cuddle session. It was one of those ideas that I thought was ridiculous and only for losers or people who had money to waste, but with her offering it changed my mind. Besides, since when was I a stranger to being "weird?"

When I arrived, Fetlynne had a tray of fresh fruit available. Vegetables and a bowl of popcorn, too. She was relaxed, in a cozy cardigan and French Terry sweatpants, white socks on her feet. After pleasantries, we went into her main parlor with the ground full of pillows and don't-sit-on-me chaise. Fetlynne positioned herself on the floor by a window near the trays.

"Come," she beckoned, outstretching her hand to pull me towards her.

She guided me to lie with my head in her lap and stroked the hair at my temples at first. Okay... I seriously started to wonder if I was an idiot for paying for this. But then she began tracing the outline of my face. Sometimes with the pads of her fingers, other times, letting her nails gently scrape my skin. Slowly. Curiously. Fetlynne explored every contour of my appearance before stopping to feed me. Grapes first. Then strawberries. Blueberries.

"Breathe with me," she whispered, wrapping her arms completely around me.

And we rocked and swayed. Inhaled and exhaled. No eroticism. No unveiling. Nothing but holding each other and space for whatever came up. She massaged my scalp.

Using the front, back, and sides of her hands, she caressed and gently gripped my neck. Then her hands moved to my collar bones. Gently tracing, scratching.

I could feel her breath on my earlobes, in the shallow dip where my spine met my skull as she intentionally moved.

Fetlynne managed to make me feel completely surrounded with just her breath, hands and intention. She slowed. Holding, gently squeezing, and humming against my shoulder so her voice vibrated through my bones.

My body jolted. A full-body flinch, and seismic *yes*. The tremble of her vocal cords on my skin was so unexpected yet overwhelmingly familiar. *Don't stop*, was all I could think. *Don't let go*. I didn't know where I ended and she began, and it didn't matter.

Fetlynne continued for what felt like eternity, stopping only to feed or offer me a drink. She wrapped her arms and legs around me and turned us into a soft pretzel. We breathed as one organism. And just when time was winding down, she hummed us to a stop again. In utter silence, I lay against her chest and felt a single, hot tear slide down my cheek. Shock was all I could chalk it up to.

My breath caught in my chest and the weight of my head gave way. I sank deeper into her skin, into the safety and revelation that no one had ever held me like this without me having to instantly *be* or do anything for them. It was impossible to describe level of disarm and calm I felt when it was time to leave. Fetlynne had given me the discovery of deeper water in the well of intimacy. I was thirsty for more.

7

THE MISALIGNMENT

"Girls!" Precious called Jasmine and me through our group chat. "I know we said we'd get together again, soon, but we didn't put a date on it, and I need it *neow*. A quick weekend wherever is best for y'all. But something!"

"Okay, well, damn," Jasmine responded.

I love my friends, but wish I hadn't answered. Their high-energy chatter immediately sliced through the quiet I wanted to sink into after being with Fetlynne. "Everything okay?" I asked. I'd been preparing dinner for myself and Mr. Pickles.

"Work stuff. I'm sick of it. Stupid corporate politics, KPI fuckery, and dumb ass quarterly goals."

"I hear that," Jasmine chimed in. "I can make a weekend happen if it's here—can't really travel this month. Mid-summer slowdown at my studio and I need to watch my spending."

"I'm in the same boat," I added. My clinic was doing well,

but I hadn't planned on adding the investment that was Fetlynne. "But..." I picked up. "I can probably tolerate one of those budget flights since it's a quick hop from ATL to Miami."

We went around in a circle deciding details and the plan congealed with the comfortable ease of habit: a long weekend, a chic hotel, great food. Jasmine was already texting links to a new boutique spot in Wynwood with a rooftop plunge pool. She knew the city better than all of us.

"Perfect," Precious said. "I need to just check *out*, okay? Spa, pool, room service. And maybe we finally do that wine tasting."

It sounded lovely.

It *was* lovely.

It was the script that had soothed us for years. But as I heard their excited voices, I noticed my mind was adrift. My enthusiasm was a beat behind, and I was merely mimicking. The problem was I didn't *want* to check out. I wanted to check *in*. To myself. But that sounded boring when said loud. And I didn't want to get into what I had going on again.

"That pool looks amazing," I pushed myself to contribute. "I'm just... honestly, I think I'd rather skip the wine tour this time? Maybe just one long, lazy dinner where we finish all our sentences?"

"Angela, this is a trip. The tour is an experience! It's something to do." Precious pushed back.

I could have dug in. Could have tried to explain the unexpected revolution happening in my cells. But I didn't. "You're right. Ignore me. I'm just in a weird headspace. The tour sounds perfect though. Let's do it!"

A part of me thought Jasmine might blurt out my personal business, but she didn't. At least for now. Thank goodness.

We hung up and the planning surged forward with a wave of emojis and logistics through text. I sent a heart-eyes emoji and muted the chat. I was desperate to savor the energy I'd built with Fetlynne. Wouldn't allow it to get swallowed by my friends.

In fact, I had an altar to set up. The first item I chose was a framed photo of me from a fitness competition years before. I didn't think I would place, but I did. Third, which was just as good as first to me considering I'd done all the training while running my practice.

"Looking like a fucking goddess," I smiled at the picture and set it down.

I didn't yet have a rock from a hike, but I did have fabric and flowers to add. And... I added a mirror. Its reflection was the one guest of honor I was eager to meet.

A WEEK LATER, I was rolling clothes to slide into my travel duffel while running through a mental checklist on autopilot:

Mr. Pickles at Happy Paws Inn, check.

Dr. Walker covering emergencies, check.

Out-of-office reply set, check.

The logistics were seamless. I packed an emerald-green jumpsuit that made me feel like a superhero, a retro swimsuit, and a pair of jeans with two tee options. Simple. Easy. Ready to head to the airport for our girls' trip.

But just as I settled into my seat and swiped my phone menu to switch to airplane mode, an email notification slid in: Fetlynne Cadet.

Subject: NYE in Panama: Bring the New Year In With Your Whole Body.

I couldn't resist opening it after skimming the preview: "This year, I am hosting a very small, curated retreat in Panama. The event will center Black women and our birthright to pleasure."

"Hello Beauties," the body read. "If you're reading this, you're already on a courageous path of reclaiming your pleasure and presence—one that doesn't shy away from the juiciness of women's pleasure, of the embodied, or of the fully erotic. Maybe even the taboo, depending on where you are in your journey.

I'm inviting you to a sanctuary to welcome the new year from a place of deep somatic sovereignty. This experience will be hosted by myself but also include two other practitioners. It will take place over four days in the lush privacy of Playa Morillo, Veraguas, Panama with sweeping views Pacific Ocean. Fully catered and vegan-friendly, our offerings will include guided sensory journeys, non-sexual cannabis cuddle puddles, suspension rigging for those who yearn to fly, tantric touch, and advanced rituals including erotic mummification and rebirth."

I stopped reading. Almost forgot I was on a plane until my seatmate wedged into his seat smelling like Subway sandwiches and Doritos.

Damn it.

I wanted to read the next paragraph but didn't want to chance my nosy neighbor peeking. I swiped my phone to a black screen but couldn't help but wonder: What the hell was *mummification*?!

My mind was a tornado. I mean, I knew what it was, but had no idea how it lent itself to anything erotic. Just how advanced was that? And who on Earth would pay to look like King Tut?

I thought back to the other activities mentioned. The cuddle puddle. Imagining it with others and on THC made my skin prickle with an urgent, dizzying heat. My mind dilated.

I thought I was exploring a serene forest with Fetlynne. But her email was a map showing I'd only been at the clearing the edge of a wild, vast, and extremely eccentric rainforest of possibilities. *What have I walked myself into?*

The aircraft's usual noises surrounded me. Dings and safety announcements alongside the chatter of other passengers, but I felt it again. The same dizzying pull I'd felt clicking "Book" for my first session with her thrummed in my veins. It was ten times stronger this time. *I need to learn more about this*, I thought, as the plane began taxing down the runway. For now, however, it was time to focus on my friends and a weekend of sisterhood.

TWO HOURS LATER, moisture beaded on the windows as we descended, blurring Miami's palm-tree sprawl into green and concrete streaks. I was in an Uber thirty minutes later—traveling light has its perks. The ride to Wynwood was short. As I stepped out of the car, I smiled. Jasmine.

She opened her arms before saying a word. "Hey, friend," she whispered in my ear.

"You look amazing," I mirrored her decibel, but meant every word. Jasmine's body was a sculpted work of art. For as long as I'd known her, she was disciplined about fitness. She owned pole dancing and aerial fitness studio in Ft. Lauderdale, so it was kind of her whole life.

"Thank you. And who taught you how to give better hugs?!" she joked.

"What?"

"I don't remember you ever giving a good squeeze—just usually a half-assed grazes."

I shrugged. "Would you prefer the old way?"

"Not at all." She stepped back and smiled at me.

I could feel the faint warmth of her breath leaving my space. Without warning, a flashback me taking both her and Rich back to my hotel room from a rooftop New Orleans. I felt the pierce of her nails later digging into my skin. I couldn't forget it because I'd gone into the rendezvous completely sober. But Jasmine had started it. I had no idea until that night that she'd had a budding crush on me. Had no idea the weird tarot card lady at the party would be right about that night being the start of a phase of excitement and spontaneity. I wondered, now, if she would "see" that I was slowly falling under a different kind of spell. One of devoted to myself.

"Heeeeyyyyyy, friends!!!" Precious's boisterous voice karate chopped through the moment. If Jasmine and I were embers and coals, Precious was a wildfire. "Ain't seen you bitches since Angela got us hemmed up by TSA with that that bag of sex toys."

Oh Jesus. I couldn't help but laugh sheepishly. "Shut up! Both of you, just shut it up!"

We were back in flow. Already.

"Come." Jasmine took the lead. "Let's get checked in and put our stuff away. We have all weekend to catch up." She started walking ahead of us. "I can't believe we let so much time go by without a reunion."

"Same, girl," I chimed in.

"I really missed you ladies," Precious added. "All jokes aside."

Once we were all settled in at the hotel, we debated grabbing a late lunch at a nearby burger joint called Skinny Loui.

"You can't be serious. The menu is nothing but grease." Jasmine was offended at the suggestion. She'd relaxed a little on her rigid diet, but not so much she'd down fatty burgers and fries.

"Okay, so, no to the soul food joint. No to burgers. And no to Cuban Sandwich shop." Precious wanted pleasure food.

"Why don't we do this place," I point to a spot on the maps that bragged a "lengthy selection" of all kinds of items —including healthy options.

It worked. And we were off.

The first night was easy. We quickly caught up on work and life, Jasmine even sharing a bunch of pictures from her recent trip to Ghana where she'd visited her grandparents who still hassled her about finding a husband. But after just one round of drinks, we'd had enough liquor for the night.

Our crew had clearly matured and recalibrated over the last two years. Well, mostly.

"Alright girls, I'm exhausted," Precious announced. "And that bartender bitch got one more time to look at me like I ordered and didn't pay."

"What?" Jasmine and I giggled in unison.

"I don't know but every time I glance around, our eyes lock, and I don't like that," she added.

"Yup," I signaled for the check. "It's time to go!"

We wound down the night at our hotel's pool. Swirling in my mind, however, were thoughts on my new path. Was it weird? Was I stupid for paying for intimacy when I could clearly attract it for free? Would my friends judge me hard if they knew the full extent of it? But then a reverie of Fetlynne's soft fingertips kissing the hollow between my eyebrows warmed my body. The ways she gently massaging the hairs back and forth before smoothing them back out and then using her fingernails to gently scrape at my skin. She knew how to unwind me. Attentiveness. Calm. Devotion—to *me*. I'd never felt anything like it from anyone in my life. How could that be wrong?

8

THE DECISION

I skipped my daily acts of admiration and gratitude the next morning. It felt too out of place against the backdrop of my friends. I also forced myself not to re-open Fetlynne's email and risk the temptation to start researching everything. Patience.

That day my crew enjoyed beach time, the wine tour, and an evening of live music and more catching up until late in the night. Precious admitted she was ready to restart dating because she wanted a partner eventually to come home to. Jasmine still had no desire and was content with work and someone to scratch the occasional itch. Occasionally, she'd flirt with someone. Male, female, it didn't matter. She enjoyed the thrill of teasing. And then there was me—actually reminded of Fetlynne's flirting menu option *because* of Jasmine. I could lean into the energy right now or wait to pay for it with Fetlynne. There goes that word again: pay.

Tension started to tighten my shoulders and jaw, but I

wouldn't let it to take over. That night, I took a long shower, vowing to relax more the next day. Maybe sharing a little so it didn't feel like I was holding in a dirty little secret. And just like that, I realized what I'd been feeling: shame, guilt, and maybe a little fear. There I was with my best friends and all I kept feeling was the weight of a hush-hush investment in myself that wasn't dirty at all, just... different.

As the water slid over my shoulders and down my sides, I turned to face the tile wall behind me. I closed my eyes, braced my hands on either side of me and pressed my forehead into the cool ceramic. My breath fogged a small circle on its surface.

With droplets bouncing off my back and legs, it hit me: I was protecting something new, fragile, and so *meaningful* I couldn't translate it into our old gossipy lexicon. But I had nothing to be ashamed of! Seconds later, I turned around and switched off the shower. My negative thoughts evaporated.

Our final morning found us lounging at the Venetian Pool in Coral Gables. We were supposed to hit up a drag queen brunch afterwards but decided to keep it tranquil and enjoy the fresh turquoise waters instead. Once our conversation turned to rest-of-the-year plans, but I didn't mention Panama. Hell, I still needed to get more details on that. But when Precious sighed and said, "I just want to feel *seen*, you know?" I met her gaze.

"I do know," I told her. Finally, I felt more honest with them. Because I was finally truthful with myself.

Precious shot me a curious look but didn't press. I smiled at her, grateful. The time for me to share more with them would come, I was sure. It just wasn't right now. I still enjoyed our time together and meant it when I said we shouldn't let so much time go by again. We might have all come from different worlds, but over the years we'd built a sistership that held a unique comfort: the ability to witnesses who each other used to be, and be guardians of who we were becoming.

I FINALLY RE-OPENED the Panama email on my flight home. I read every word about the weekend and was eager for privacy to research more. I knew a little bit about suspension rigging but not the mummy business. I thought I was leaving Halloween ghouls behind. And there was the price. The weekend would be $3500.

Thirty-five HUNDRED dollars.

It gave me pause. *I could replace the aging ultrasound in Exam Room 2 for that. Or finally upgrade to the digital X-ray system I've been putting off for a year*. The responsible vet in me immediately drafted a polite mental decline. *Maybe not this year*.

I loved the idea of it, but it felt too irresponsible to drop a thousand dollars a day. *Applications are now open. Space for 12.* But...before I could type out a real response, the other part of me remembered a line from one the articles I'd read on Fetlynne's site. It was single, stubborn question: *What is an investment in your own transformation worth?* Damn it.

I didn't have an answer. I closed the email without responding at all, neatly shelving the conflict for now. Meanwhile, I knew one thing that I wanted right now for sure.

"Fetlynne. The Tantric Massage," I texted her within hours of arriving at home. "I keep circling it in the menu, and I think I'm ready to 'not have an end goal'. I want to know what it feels like when touch is the destination." I was speaking her language more.

"Okay," she answered. "I think you'll enjoy that. It does require a specific kind of surrender. If you have a few minutes now, we can chat about it. It's not a session you just walk into."

"I do," I texted back, then called.

Fetlynne told me that her tantric massages were incredibly sacred to her. They weren't thoughtless rubdowns with happy endings. They were to honor the temple that is the female body and give her clients a taste of what it felt like to be adored. Possibly worshipped...over time. They were fully nude on the client side and hers.

"The first one wouldn't go deep but would still give a premium value," she told me. "Everything progresses on our comfort levels." She cleared her throat. "And if you let yourself go in the moment, I think you'll find that it heals you long after you leave the massage table."

I breathed into the silent phone. Fetlynne had reframed it entirely. This was a treatment just as much as it were a treat. For the weariness I carried in my shoulders, for the static in my mind. "Thank you," I finally spoke again. "For saying that. I—I want this. I do." It felt dangerously intimate, yet I said, "Let's book it."

"Wonderful!"

We chatted more, her asking me explicit questions about boundaries and clinical questions about trauma before giving me specifics of what to expect along with locking in a date and time. By the time we brought the call to a close, she chuckled and said, "Don't worry. We'll go slow."

THE NEXT TWO weeks at work were busy. Gratifying one day. Draining the next. I'd performed a delicate, life-saving surgery on a pet iguana for some kid who'd saved her allowance all year to buy the scaly little thing. I'd also had to console a woman who sobbed uncontrollably while her ancient, peaceful cat slipped away in my arms. Her grief wasn't just for the feline; it was for her last connection to her late husband. Holding space for her loss with professional calm had me absorbing the shockwaves of her sorrow until my own back felt like cement. All this on top of the typical administrative and operational work of running the place.

By Friday, my nerves were frayed. The thought of ninety minutes with Fetlynne sounded like a dream. By Saturday afternoon, I was on her doorstep ready to be anointed by her gifted hands.

9

THE FIRST TOUCH

The house was warm and quiet—just the soft sounds of the room. And the lights were soft. Easy for me to drift away from visual distractions. Fetlynne wore a flowy, sleeveless tangerine dress that brushed the floor. Her skin was oiled. She wore minimal jewelry. And incense wafted through the air.

"Hey, Angela." She greeted me with goddess energy.

We hugged, full-bodied with no space in between. Fetlynne smelled like pomegranate blossoms.

"Hey," I whispered, nervous.

"I'm glad you came." She rubbed my back, as if I were an infant needing soothing.

"I've been looking forward to this," I confessed, following her into the parlor where we'd had our first session.

A massage table, oils, a feather, and a few other things awaited. Fetlynne offered me fresh cucumber water and my choice of cushion to settle in. We chatted for ten minutes to ease into things. She shared a few details of how she knew she was called to do this work—a little about her own nerves—but not too much. Just enough to break the glamour-aura about her. I was grateful for a peek behind the veil.

"I think I was looking forward to this just as much as you were," she confided.

"Oh really?"

"Mm hm." She did not elaborate. Instead, she led me to a magnificent indoor/outdoor shower off the side of her sunroom. I hadn't noticed the extra ingress the last time. It felt like I'd stepped into another world. One that was even warmer, with a wood-clad bathing space that opened straight into the other side of her private garden—rainfall shower, stone basin, brick underfoot, and a cedar tub waiting just beyond the threshold. A small, bronze singing bowl and striker sat next to the sink.

"You can get undressed in here. I'll step outside," she told me.

When she mentioned the shower before the massage, I had *not* imagined a space like this. I wondered if she'd intentionally downplayed it because wow – it was a showstopper. We wouldn't use the tub, but its presence still charged the air. Because now... I wanted to get in it.

Focus, Angela, I scolded myself. *Take off your clothes.*

Minutes later, Fetlynne reentered the space—nude.

I expected this. I did. But the moment she stepped in, my body tensed. I became self-aware. I wondered what the hell I was doing. My mind ran 100-meter race on me.

"Close your eyes," she instructed, and I obeyed. "Right

now, I'm going to tap the singing bowl just once to ground us, and then I'll step in, okay?"

"Sure," I whispered.

A beat.

I exhaled, and then... she struck the bowl.

The sound reverberated, instantly relaxing me. She then guided me under the warm stream of water. A light steam quickly built up but it was never too hot or too cool. Plants on either side of us made the space feel like a living cocoon. For the next few minutes Fetlynne bathed me with a milky soap that smelled like lavender and bergamot—from behind—so I felt her more than I saw her. She used a natural sea sponge to rub my shoulders, arms, belly, back, legs, and then turned me to face her while repeating the cleanse.

For a moment, we locked eyes and she said, "You have *beautiful* definition in your back and shoulders."

One hundred butterflies took flight in my stomach. "Um... thank you. Thank you so much." My breath was jagged.

"You're welcome," she spoke softer this time. Turned me once more so weren't facing each other. Fetlynne cleared her throat once more and rinsed me off.

I was completely relaxed by the time I stepped into the brown pedicure flip-flops she gave me. We toweled off and I followed her back to the parlor. The blinds were closed. All of the candles were on. And ambient music already floated through the room. She slipped out for a moment only to return wearing red waist beads against her soft tummy.

I eased on to the massage table, face down, trying to hold the relaxed feeling from the shower. I could feel the faint heat of Fetlynne taking a walk around the table. She stopped only to rub her hands together and energize them before slowly moving them over my body. But she didn't make contact with my skin right away. I just felt the staticky warmth from her palms moving over me like gentle clouds.

She lingered at the soles of my feet, the backs of my knees and the side of my glutes, the only cool spots on my body. Then, she gifted me the first touches of her oiled hands.

"Are you comfortable?" she whispered in my ear.

"Yes."

"Alright. I'm going to climb on the table and start now." And those were the last words she spoke for the next hour and fifteen minutes.

Fetlynne gently wedged my legs apart to make room for herself as she massaged my back and sides. My neck. My shoulders.

She used open palms. The sides of her hands. The backs —her nails to gently scratch. She engaged her forearms and elbows—her breath, nose, and her breasts. Fetlynne intuitively moved around me, sometimes allowing her warm body to kiss mine after certain strokes. Sometimes not. I was surrounded by her touch and didn't know what to expect next. Her using more of her body was a delightful surprise as it gave me so many new sensations. It felt more *whole.*

She spent time on my legs and feet. My toes. The entire outline of my body all the way back to the top of my head and then down again from my shoulders to my arms. My hands. Individual fingers. She massaged my glutes so slowly I thought she'd stopped—but she hadn't—she just given me a few seconds to breathe before using her thumbs to carefully press the creases beneath each of my butt cheeks. Again, deeper where it was close enough to the bottom edges of my labia that I trembled and groaned and gyrated in ecstasy. There was no inch of my backside that she had not touched.

At the halfway point, I was in a half-awake, half-asleep in her heaven. Sedated by her touch and strokes.

It was only warmth and moisture against my earlobe that woke me. "Turn over for me, please," she instructed. She was so close she could have nibbled my earlobe. The energy Fetlynne gave off made me weak. It made me wet. It made me *want*.

I took my time repositioning, inebriated from her attention. This time was more intense. She was above me. Naked. Oil-slicked brown skin. Slow-blinking with a slight smirk on her face. *Gorgeous*. And tending to me. From this vantage point, I noticed she had another small tattoo—some kind of music symbol and notes—just under her left breast on her ribs. I studied it while she started with my chest and abdomen, spreading the energy in all directions.

She spent several minutes doing this before carefully getting off the table and standing behind me. There, she softly...so...very...softly, began massaging my breasts. With more oil on her hands, she moved around them in a circular motion, careful around my nipples. Unhurried. With focused intensity. She rubbed and stroked and cupped. Fetlynne's breathing sped up as her own breasts hung over me. It felt so good. Too good. A light moan escaped me as she softly thumbed over my nipples until they stood erect. She kept this up for a few minutes before moving on to my arms. Kneading them, one small area at a time until she reached my hands.

A heavy sigh. I couldn't stop my audible expressions.

Fetlynne rotated my wrists before gliding to my fingers, gripping and stroking each one the way you would if you were giving a hand job. My body trembled and my breath caught.

She climbed back on the table, pressing her full body onto mine but at an angle so our private areas didn't touch. She did a few slow glides back and forth, almost belly to belly. Almost nipples to nipples. *Almost...* pussy to pussy. I could feel her wetness on my inner thigh and my own pooling on the sheets beneath me. *Oh my God.*

I had no idea how long this went on before she got off me and moved downwards to bring her hands from my lower abdomen to my quads. Squeezing intermittently.

With her face close to my skin again, Fetlynne moved her nose up and down my legs and around my center in such a slow, fluid manner, I was hardly ready to feel the heat of her breath on my yoni. Just once. And then she pulled back, resuming with her hands in the creases around my most sensitive areas. Pressure. She applied sweet pressure.

And I dripped.

Fetlynne was delicate. Spontaneous. Watchful. The moment I tensed or squirmed or moaned she adjusted appropriately—with more or less. It was like she was dancing with me except I wasn't moving. Just her and my energy. She didn't spend a lot of time in my groin area, but it didn't matter. I was throbbing. Leaking. And a bit self-conscious of how wet she got me with little focus on my genitals. When the time drew down, she focused on my face and head—brushing into the tiny half-moon below my earlobes. She touched my lips and made tiny circles over my cheeks. This woman even swept her fingertips against my eyelids and lashes.

Then she massaged my temples and scalp. I fell asleep.

"Angela," she murmured into my ear.

I stirred.

She gave me a moment before speaking again. "Our session is over now."

10

THE DRUG

Fetlynne was crack—she was *cocaine.* For the next week, I could think of nothing but her touch.

In all my forty-five years of living, I could not think of a single moment with any lover that made me feel so adored. And she did it all with no expectation for me to do anything but lay there and receive. To enjoy without performance of any kind. What kind of witchcraft was this?

I loved how present I felt when I was with her. How much I learned about my own body when I was around her. Until that last session, I had no idea my ankles were sensitive. Or the narrow bridge where my thigh met my hip. *Or* the slight indentation of my hipbone. I'd never had anyone journey the contours of my body like that. It made me slow down in every way when I was alone again.

My showers were different. How I moved around the house changed. How I masturbated and made love to myself at night was *highly* impacted. I'd just had a sampling of bliss and wanted another helping. But I had to pace myself.

I knew my personality and realized too much of this might not be good for me. Not because I thought she had any ill intentions, but because I didn't want to get addicted. Fetlynne wasn't a wild fling in another city. She was a wellspring of selfless attention less than 30 minutes from me. That felt risky. Add to that she felt like ecstasy with just her introductory touches. What would she feel like when we weren't "going slowly"?

Three weeks later, I was back on her table. Couldn't help myself. She'd sent an email for a summer special: 50% off for existing clients on a specific Wednesday. It was an impulse buy—a treat for having otherwise resisted the urge, I rationalized.

"Welcome back!" Fetlynne wore a rose-colored maxi dress. Bare feet. Big hoop earrings. Gold dusted shoulders. "It's good to see you standing in my doorway again."

"Well, every time I see you, my week gets better."

"The whole week, huh?"

"The whole month!"

"Careful, Angela. Talk that gets you the good oils," she held my gaze then smiled.

A bashful silence. I blushed. Shrank a little.

"I'm teasing. Come inside and cool off. It's way too hot today."

We ran through the usual chit chat, and this time she offered me a slice of still-warm almond cake.

"You bake?" I asked incredulously.

"It's a hobby. And I made too much this time. Was

expecting nieces and nephews this week but my sister canceled." She shrugged. "I made the cake anyway," she giggled.

"Sure, I'd love a slice." Her energy was magnetic.

I learned Fetlynne was Haitian-American. Originally from Birmingham, AL, she had also lived in New Orleans and various parts of Mexico. She'd been in Atlanta, for the last twelve years, however. Like me, it was now home.

Soon enough, we had a repeat of the previous session, but this time she prompted me with a choice. "Do you want to go deeper today?" There was no expectation in voice. Simply neutral.

"Um..." I thought about the effects of the last one and bit my bottom lip. My fingers drummed at my sides before I finally answered. "Yes."

And so it began. But she was more playful and talkative this time. I could tell she was receiving just as much as she was giving because her touch felt like self-expression for her. Everything was going as expected until she ran the tip of her nose down the bone of my right forearm to the tip of my thumb.

That's when I felt a graze of her tongue against my finger, a slight suck on the tip, and a gentle bite in the curve between my thumb and index finger. She let out a warm breath to immediately counter the cool moisture her tongue had left, and that sent my body into a tailspin. I tried to hide it.

As she worked her way around me again, I felt myself losing track of everything but pleasure. I thought she planted a few kisses on my calves, but I wasn't sure. Her touch was too delicate to tell. This went on for another hour until my entire body vibrated with heat and hunger. I created a puddle on her sheets, and she kept bringing her face close... so close. But didn't touch the obvious with her lips, although she did cup it with her hands when she was done.

"Mm." I whimpered. The heel of her palm put gentle pressure on my clit and I just wasn't ready. I'd never had foreplay—because that's what it felt like—for over an hour before genital touch and it was body-quaking. "Oh my God..." I breathed.

"He's not here," she winked. "Just me."

Touché. Her quip put a much-needed pin in the room's tension.

"You have more tightness in your quads this month," Fetlynne mentioned casually.

"I've been in the gym more," I managed to breathe and follow her pivot.

"Don't forget to stretch." She rested her hands on my knees and looked me in the eyes with a smile. Fetlynne opened and closed my legs one last time just because it amused her, I think. My heartbeat raced.

"I will." I felt a strong pulse between my legs. Felt it in my belly.

I wanted run but stay at the time. Because a part of me began wondering what she was like as a lover and not a service provider. I couldn't afford to think that way. It was dodgy to even consider blurring the lines and I had to avoid that at all costs. Still, I wanted to stay in her care forever.

I swallowed, trying to find something professional to ask. A joke to make. Anything. But my mind was blank. All I could do was breathe and feel. There was nowhere to hide. Fetlynne had me open.

"Remember to notice everything," she told me as she walked me to the door. "You should never be a stranger to yourself. Should never be unfamiliar with your body."

"It was hard at first, but I am. I've been learning," I told her, proud of myself.

She chuckled at my earnestness. "You know, I just love, love, *love* that you're leaning into this. You have remarkable courage, Angela. Watching you blossom is beautiful to witness."

"Thank you," I blushed.

"Until next time..."

I REVELED in the aftershocks for the next month.

I found myself journaling more. Singing along to music more. Even cooking elaborate meals just for myself, following a recipe to the gram, then eating it straight from the pan in glorious solitude.

One afternoon while eating, I decided to research the activities for Fetlynne's NYE event. The cuddle puddle looked exactly how I imagined, just that hers would be a pod of Black women only—most likely, knowing her. I then read more about consent-based group intimacy and had my biases challenged on some things and confirmed on others. It was a lot.

The cannabis infused meal excited me. It seemed low pressure, high awareness. I liked that. But when I searched, "erotic mummification," I realized I wasn't ready. Not one bit. Some of the content was clinical—on *Psychology Today*—other parts were part education, and lots of porn. The latter was too dark. Too kinky. Very intimidating. Weird—not for me.

While a little bondage piqued my curiosity, the extremes of it did nothing. There was too much to worry about from a safety standpoint: body temperature, circulation, breath, claustrophobia, panic, needless delay in case of emergency. I flagged it as not a low-risk activity with too many opportunities for things to go wrong—fast.

"Probably not worth going if I'm only interested in a few of the activities," I said to myself.

But then I remembered Fetlynne's attentiveness. Her professionalism. Her care and love for this work. She wouldn't put other women in harm's way, I felt certain of that. And there was no clause that said attendees *had* to partake in every activity on the menu. I closed the tab. But another one was behind it with a video showing a more artistic and intimate mummification scene—I had opened so many tabs I didn't realize this one lurked in the background.

"It's still odd though," I murmured. But a part of me was curious about the intention behind it. In her setting, specifically, what was it for?

A WEEK LATER, after hiking through a deep, sandstone gorge, I found myself thinking about the invitation again. Time was going by and not many spots were left. I hadn't talked to

Fetlynne again since our last session—restraining myself—but I wanted to. Simultaneously, I started looking at all the money I spent, the time I invested. I wondered if I were lowering myself into a beautiful, expensive fantasy that it might be too hard to climb out of if I went any deeper. Taking a six-week break from her gave me clarity. I also hated not being able to share with my friends. In fact, I felt a little isolated from their day-to-day concerns as a whole new universe had opened to me.

Every time I asked myself, "Do I want to continue?", the answer was yes. But isn't that drug addicts say? And every time I asked myself what I was doing for NYE, I couldn't think of anything that didn't feel cliché, boring, or unfulfilling in comparison. With Fetlynne, I *knew*, I'd get to new erotic heights. Knew the way she caressed the underside of my jawline or brushed her lips against mine would make my body expand like nothing else could. I knew that each new session went just a little bit farther. A little bit deeper. Got a little bit more oceanic. And that's when it hit me. Jasmine was right. I *was* seeing a sex worker.

Shit.

The realization had bubbled up so organically. It was true. And that stung. What did that make me? Suddenly, I felt embarrassed. Ashamed. I'd never thought of myself as someone who needed to pay for sex. But was this even sex if there was no orgasm? *Of course it was!* In fact, it was better than sex. It was deep intimacy.

The more I thought about everything, the more confused and self-punishing I became. The moment I got back inside my car, my body slumped forward, my head resting on the steering wheel. The air in the car felt too thick to breathe.

Tears of frustration pricked my eyes. What was I doing? Why was I doing it? What was I chasing? Before I could stop myself, my phone was in my hand, Fetlynne's contact pulled up. I pressed video call. Instantly regretting not giving her a heads up first.

She answered on the third ring. I apologized immediately. She sensed my energy. Calmed me.

"It's just I keep worrying... that's why I haven't been back. I've also been thinking of your event. What if I go and it's too much? What if I love it too much and the real world feels gray afterward?" I crashed out while she sat calmly in her studio.

"Everything your feeling is normal. There's nothing wrong with you," she told me.

Fetlynne encouraged me to ask any questions I had about our 1:1s and the upcoming event. There was one break in tension when I laughed-stated that I was "afraid to even ask about the mummification."

She took it all in stride, explaining vulnerability, trust, rebirth, and desire in one scene. "But don't even think about that if it makes you uneasy. As you already know, it's not a requirement." She took a beat and looked at me with complete focus. "Angela. None of this work is about leaving the real world. It's about building a better one inside yourself. Even if you never see me again, I'd like to think that you're more confident and know yourself better than you did before we met."

"I do. And I thank you for that."

"Think of New Year's Eve as the most advanced practicum for everything we've done. You're a student who's earned her place in the room—*if* that's what you really want. There's no rush. Heck, I don't plan on retiring any time soon. There will be more. I wouldn't be offended in the least. And as for the activities..." she leaned into the camera slightly "...the most important skill you'll practice is curation. Your 'no' to one thing is a sacred 'yes' to your own sovereignty. That's the whole point. The choice in anything in this life is yours. Always."

And just like that, I felt like I was talking to an elder, not a woman just a few years older than me. In less than 15 minutes, Fetlynne assuaged my fear of the unknown, addiction, and validated my desire for transformation even if that meant through the lesser-traveled path of eroticism.

Later that night, I left my deposit.

11

THE OTHER SIDE OF THE VEIL

Fall came and went with a much-needed crispness in the air, a sharp relief from the muggy summer. The change in the leaves. The addition of more clothes. It was all a welcomed transition to the deep quiet of December.

Business stayed busy but manageable. I'd finally told Precious and Jasmine what I'd been up to and the tight knot in my chest loosened.

Precious hesitated, then slowly smiled. "A retreat in Panama? Angela, that's...actually kind of iconic."

Jasmine nodded thoughtfully. "It makes sense. The way you've been talking lately. Seems like you've found a lot of peace and sense of belonging in it."

They'd asked questions, of course. But they were questions of curiosity, not judgment. *What will you do there? Is it safe?* I assured them I had no safety concerns and told them a few things that were on the agenda. Explaining it all without a flutter of shame made me feel solid in a way I hadn't anticipated. I had let them in, and the world hadn't ended. It had quietly enlarged.

"Shit, girl, maybe I would have went with you!" Precious said. "I wish you would have told me, but I get why you didn't. Some things we need to keep just for ourselves."

"True, true," Jasmine echoed.

Correct.

I'D ALSO SEEN Fetlynne a few more times since summer. Exploring different menu items. Light bondage. Sensory play. Flirt sessions. Even attended two group events to get a feel for how it might feel when it wasn't just me in the room. I enjoyed the fellowship and community of other likeminded women more than I thought I would.

I'd found a new local tribe. Not to replace Jasmine and Precious but to build a new connection in the same frequency. I felt more equipped to navigate my body and desires than ever and that clarity felt like a superpower.

As the time drew nearer for my flight, I looked over the final outline for the weekend, from the location to the activities, to the other facilitators and supporting crew. My fingers absently traced the neat rows of my new braids—low-maintenance, and just enough to feel like a reset. December 28th couldn't come fast enough.

~

Playa Morrillo is a superb beach on a winding, unpaved road in secluded Veraguas. Our villa was a few minutes beyond it, in Mata Oscura. Sharing transportation wasn't normally my thing, but I opted to lean into the communal spirit and rode with a group of four others from Atlanta. We hired a private car for the six-hour journey from the airport.

Inside the van was a couple and two other singles. Small talk, jokes, and expectations filled the first half; intermittent sleep took over the second. Our driver navigated the cliffside slowly, tires softening dirt as jungle pressed close on both sides.

The goal was to arrive well before the sun set, and thankfully, we did. My eyes widened, and my heart smiled at the purple-orange streaks in the sky. I'd been holding my breath for this moment.

Though in a small, gated community, the house itself was large and on an acre of land. Elevated above the beach, its entrance was framed by lush, tropical florals and gleaming white stones. The location dropped us all back into warm, humid, skin-blooming weather.

We were greeted by a long table under a canopy, laden with glass dispensers of cucumber-mint water and bowls heaped with mango slices. A volunteer smiled at us like she already knew our names.

"For your brow, Angela" she said, placing a cool eucalyptus towel in my hand. Holy shit. She *did* know my name! Fetlynne must moonlight as event planner—or hired one with impeccable attention to detail. "The journey is over.

You've arrived," she continued. Cold and fragrant, the cloth startled my skin.

"Welcome, Terry," the volunteer then greeted the woman behind me. And on and on.

After the chilled towels and beverages, we were all cleansed with sage by another one of her volunteers. Then, we finally all filed into the home. Bright and spacious with high, polished hardwood ceilings. Afro-Panamanian art adorned the walls.

"Hello, ladies!" Fetlynne appeared in all white. Radiant. Jubilant. And oozing gratitude, she welcomed us all with hugs and a gesture toward the laden table. "Grab a snack if you'd like. The others will arrive like waves. For now, consider this your first practice: settling in."

She gave a brief tour of the main floor—a giant open kitchen overlooked the ocean. A terrace-infinity pool seemed to vanish into it. Then, she showed us to our rooms. The system was simple: find the door bearing a calligraphed card with your name. My room was spare and perfect, a white mosquito net cascading over the bed. I'd already sprayed myself with citronella—prepared for the jungle.

I dropped my bag and ambled back to the deck. Two hammocks dangled between coconut trees, and a mischievous monkey swung from one citrus tree to the next.

Back in the common area, more women trickled in, each greeted with the same deliberate calm, until the villa finally felt full and charged with a collective anticipation.

Evening one was curated for relaxation: a four-course, cannabis-infused meal designed to open our hearts and minds for the days ahead. Energized laughter pulsed through the room as we got to know each other better, along with the scent of smoked paprika and roasting mushrooms The attire ranged from soft rompers to silk kimonos and linen palazzo pants, to bras and panties, and waist beads only.

Fetlynne introduced her crew: A Panamanian Chef, two earthy volunteers, and two co-facilitators. She also had us all introduce ourselves to feel more familiar. The ice melted by end of the first course: a chilled avocado-ginger soup to the ambient sound of steel drums.

"I'm so grateful all of you decided to bring in the new year with me, truly. To turn away from the glitter and big balls dropping," she paused, just on time for a childish snicker to ripple throughout the dining room. "Ahem. Choosing the grain of your own skin is a revolutionary act. This table is your proof. Let's begin."

A voluptuous dancer entered for a short, ritual performance, then the next course arrived: spiced pumpkin fritters with tamarind drizzle that made my toes curl and release. The cannabis buzz rose like a slow, green wave with each bite.

"So," Fetlynne spoke again, "I want us to each share one sensation we're grateful for in this room."

Answers floated like fireflies. "The breeze."

"The sound of the ocean outside."

"This cool floor on my bare feet. It feels so good in the heat of this room."

As more time passed and more clothing came off, and I caught a lingering glance from Fetlynne. She'd noticed the lace, ruby bra and panty set I'd had hidden under my clothing. I'd unzipped my hoodie but still had my pants on. We'd had enough 1:1s for her to *know* what was under them based on the parts that were exposed. I never mismatched my lingerie. Blasphemy.

Fetlynne's lips parted for a moment, before she caught herself and closed them. But it was too late, her recognition and awareness of me sent a full-body tremor through me. I kept eating. Leg slightly shaking under the table. I had an inkling of what she was thinking...or what I *hoped* she was thinking.

COCONUT-CURRIED JACKFRUIT on a bed of forbidden rice was the main course. Followed by a dessert of dark chocolate pot de crème crowned with a crystallized violet. It was so much and so good I could barely finish. After the final course and a champagne toast, we dispersed for showers before regrouping in the cuddle puddle room, which was wrapped by floor-to-ceiling windows.

A gigantic, sunken square lounge pit dominated the center. Its thick, tufted, cloud-soft cushions formed a low wall around the edges. Small pods of bean bags and a fortress of pillows also dotted the room. In that moment, I realized why the retreat was for women only. I could not imagine being relaxed enough to be high in such comfort with strange men. Granted, I'd only known a few of the

Atlanta women casually, but it still felt safe enough to try. I trusted Fetlynne's vetting judgement.

"Find a space." A volunteer's voice guided us. "Your body knows what it needs. A connection, or an island. Both are perfect," We all knew the rules around touch, consent and boundaries already. Most immediately stepped into the main square and started laying out or stretching before caressing countless of hands.

But I couldn't sit still. Not yet. I needed to move. Get blood flowing. Feel the night air on my legs and belly. The THC made me chattier than usual. I found myself talking first, with a woman named Chrissy who flew in from Philadelphia, then another from Vegas named Yolanda. Both of whom didn't sink into the cuddle puddle right away either.

Chrissy was a ball of kinetic energy. "Can you believe that big ass sofa thing? I was expecting, like, IKEA faux fur. This is next-level, and I am here for it, girls!"

I burst out laughing, then muzzled myself. "Same. I've never seen anything like it. Looks amazing though. I'll join later!"

"Cheers to that," she said, raising her glass before floating off to go journal.

Just then, Yolanda appeared leaning against a doorway with the easy grace of someone who knew how to be content alone or with a crowd. A slender Latina with a bone-straight black hair save for a blue streak. She had an androgynous edge to her.

"Hiding from the pile?" she asked, her voice warm.

"No. Just...circulating."

She smiled. Glanced out at the dark sea. "Smart. Gotta

survey the territory." Yolanda looked down at my hand. "May I?"

I was confused.

"Touch."

Of course. The rules. I'd completely forgotten about them amid small talk. "Sure," I smiled.

She grazed the edge of my fingers first, gauging me, before enveloping my hand into a soft clutch. "So, what life did you leave back at home?" she asked.

"One of saving animals. I'm a veterinarian," I told her. "And you?"

"¡Qué padre!" she exclaimed, slipping into Spanish. "How wonderful is that? And me..." she hesitated. "I'm a... performer. Showgirl, actually. I have my own cabaret show in Vegas."

I hadn't seen that one coming. "Sounds like so much fun. And work!" I laughed. She smiled and agreed. In that moment, however, she was just a stunning woman in a villa who made my pulse trip over itself.

Thick raindrops soon began falling in fat splashes outside. We retreated indoors. Finally, I was ready to join the cuddle puddle. My heart rate had slowed dramatically and I felt light—euphoric even—as I sank into a corner of the giant square. Yolanda stayed with me for a bit, asking if she could lay in my lap. The simple act of stroking her hair against her temple proved incredibly relaxing for us both. She closed her eyes, squirmed; and the edge of life and time seemed to dissolve.

I had no idea how long I was caressing her before segueing into giving her a shoulder massage. I don't know why I did it, but it felt natural. Before I knew it, a subtle, smile settled on my face. Apparently, I'd learned some skill from being on the receiving end of massages from Fetlynne, and now, I got to experience the joy of giving.

"That feels so good," Yolanda whispered. "Thank you," She looked like she was fighting a tear from falling from her eye. Her vulnerability sobered me in a good way. A load of oxytocin washed over me.

I almost asked if she was okay but decided it was better to leave it be. Touch was enough of a response to what her body and energy had shared.

A few others eventually laid down next to us, and we all just held, pet and caressed each other. It was a new experience of platonic touch, even if there might be something simmering with Yolanda. I didn't know. It didn't matter. The point was experiencing so many pairs of hands caressing me while still high from dinner felt like some magical other world. Rain came down harder outside, beating against the windows and adding its own sounds to the intentional micro world Fetlynne had created.

The ebb and flow were perfect.

We moved as needed. Had tea, water, or snack breaks as desired and by the end, those who were still awake sat together and shared their thoughts on the experience. It was a gift. That's all I could add. No other words were needed.

12

DOWNPOUR

Rain hammered night. It was when I woke up to use the bathroom that I found myself alone in the dead of a stormy evening with Fetlynne, dressed in an oversized t-shirt and short shorts. I'd gotten so used to seeing her in bright summer dresses at home, that the casual domesticity of her pajamas was a jarring intimacy. She was still working, but unarmored.

Before I could speak, a facilitator joined her. They were setting up for suspension rigging the next day. Not wanting to disturb, I slipped into the hallway shadows and retreated to my room. I was still quite tired and high from the night before.

By morning, the torrent had calmed enough to allow for our sunrise yoga session on the sun deck. We broke for communal breakfast, then spent a few leisurely hours at the beach. The ocean front was so devoid of people that we were the only ones there. A cloudy, humid day made the air thick and still, amplifying the surf's roar.

We got a surprise while out.

"Wow!"

"Look at that!"

A massive, leatherback sea turtle, heaving herself up the gold sand in the dull morning light to nest. Awe swelled then quickly dissipated as we formed a more quiet, respectful semicircle around it. We didn't want to frighten her. I was utterly fascinated by watching its labored digging and slow release of glistening eggs. They were like falling moons.

When she finished and the nest was covered, she lumbered back into the crashing waves. "I've only ever seen them sick or stranded," I murmured, almost to myself. "I forgot they could be this mighty."

"That must have been something for someone like you." A warm shoulder bumped mine. Yolanda.

It was lovely to see her up close again.

"She makes it look so graceful," Yolanda whispered, her gaze still on the retreating turtle. "And so… determined."

Before I could answer, a battalion of red rock crabs erupted from a hole nearby.

"Look at these little side-steppers," I quipped. Our solemn spell broke into soft laughter. We chatted and snacked on frozen pops for a bit longer before heading back to the villa for the afternoon event: suspension rigging.

The facilitator was a gender-queer person whose presentation was too eclectic to box into masculine or feminine. They'd erected a tranquil corner into a shrine of soft light and woven hemp. Purple uplights and the thrum of ancestral drums soundtracked the scene before giving way to spoken word poetry. I was transfixed, my own breath syncing with the slow movements on display. Though I was curious about this experience, I'd ultimately felt better being a witness than a participation for it.

The first person to be suspended was the full-bodied beauty who had danced for us during the opening meal. We watched as she was meticulously wrapped in beautiful patterns of jute. Then, she was hoisted to hang upside down, bound at the hips and angles. Her breathing was slow. Certain. Welcoming of the touches from the rigger against her thighs and the slight curve of her waist up towards her ribs. She let out a soft moan.

The rigger stood below her, one hand on the line, watching. A wash of indigo light now bathed her limbs as she drifted into a dreamlike rotation. This was one of the few moments when photography was allowed. A few flashes and clicks captured her silent, inverted flight.

Three other attendees opted for this experience and the afternoon unfolded into a breathe-held gallery. The whole scene brought to the front of my mind what I *did* agree to for this trip. Mummification. But not in any of the ways I'd seen it done online. And in no way that would make me feel claustrophobic or powerless. In fact, Fetlynne and I had done two test runs a month before in Atlanta—starting with just my lower body: from feet to waist with linen and wide, breathable elastic bands for stability to see how I experienced the sensation Then, including my torso.

"Are you sure?" she asked, shocked about my interest about it.

"I think so. Something about being swaddled appeals to me. I'm surprised at myself," I'd admitted. Maybe the old me wanted a wild-Halloween remnant to make an appearance somehow.

"Well, it is a wonderful way to explore trust without fear, but it is advanced. Lots to consider ahead of time."

"I know. I read all about it. Watched a ton of videos too."

"Of course, Dr. Greene."

"Not you calling me by my daytime name."

"If anyone would thoroughly weigh the risks, it would be you."

"You are correct."

It was late summer. Just as the leaves were starting to signal fall. We were in her parlor with the air condition on high. She began with a more traditional massage to relax me after our shower—hot stones, a twenty-minute foot rub. Breathwork. Stillness. Trust. Fetlynne explained everything thoroughly before and again while she did the first wrap. "Are you comfortable?" "Can you still move each toe?" She kept constant eye contact with me.

"Yes, thank you." Grateful for her constant check ins, I sank as she wrapped my legs over three minutes.

Fetlynne worked in almost a meditative state while still watching for any changes with me. A nearby table held scissors and everything else she needed in case I did *not* enjoy the sensation.

In the quiet, I got used to the stretch and contract of the

linen with each breath I took. I leaned into it, relaxing, enjoying the psychological tide of surrender. When she'd finished, she lay alongside me, arms draped over me and in that moment, I felt held so completely that my mind went absolutely quiet.

It was only when a soft beep went off and she ran her fingers against the base of my throat to let me know the 10-minutes were up that I resurfaced, blinking, as if from a deep sleep. We'd agreed on a very brief trial-run and she honored it to the second. The woman was an artisan of trust.

FAST FORWARD TO TONIGHT, December 30th: my thoughts buzzed about doing my experience tomorrow. I was still a little nervous about doing it again, especially in front of onlookers. But I knew I could back out at any time; I still had control.

When the rigging portion of the current evening ended, we had dinner and then gathered for goal setting and manifestations for the new year. She wanted us to do it early so we could do a rebirth ceremony in the sacred dark of the coming night, to be unwrapped and renewed before the year turned. We all wrote our thoughts down on slips of rice paper and were on our own for the night.

The next morning, rain came down in sheets. The air was electrified. It was the 31st and I was a wild mix of readiness and terror. After a light breakfast, Fetlynne pulled me aside. "Your time is after lunch. The space will be ready." She ran her thumb across the ridge of my collar bone and adjusted my shirt. Then, looked me directly in the eyes with a gentle smile. "Are you?"

I exhaled and nodded. The nerves were still there, but they were bowing beneath a deeper current of readiness. I'd spent most of the year learning to listen to my body and today, it spoke in a clear, single word: Yes.

The Wrap

Narrowed. My world contracted to the pressure of the wrap, the sound of my breath under the rain drumming the awning, and the scent of hibiscus dye. Outside with the expanse of the ocean and ruggedness of cliffs and jungled Earth, I lay still while time changed states from a river to a lake.

There was no "next." There was only a deepening of now as Fetlynne's hands smoothed down the feathery tensions. The muslin held my shape like memory foam.

"Breathe in for me, Angela. And hold it," she instructed.

I did.

She then secured the final band around my chest, so my lungs had enough room to expand. The layers she built felt like an embrace from the inside out.

"Now exhale." Fetlynne's check-ins felt like vibrations. Her fingers caressed my neck and earlobes—my face was not covered—serving as the only tether to a world outside of our nest. I didn't think of onlookers. I didn't worry about goals. I was a verb, not a noun. And the verb, I realized, was *resting.*

Not the noun rest, but the active, profound, and long-forgotten act of coming to a complete *stop*.

My body went weightless.

I couldn't feel my bones.

I didn't know if I was here or there.

I no longer braced for anything.

Fetlynne caressed the inner curve of my arms and used the tip of her nose, then lips, to brush the shell of my ear. I felt like I levitated. Her body's warmth radiated into mine and I felt loved. I *was* love.

She moved around me with a fan and small bowl of ice before crawling around me on the large massage bed. The line of her thigh was a solid warmth against my hip. Fetlynne traced the path of a single melting ice drop down my sternum—keeping me cool—and I suddenly felt a range of emotions. Excited. Anticipatory. Afraid. Vulnerable. Exposed. Eager. The intensity shook my body, but she held. I could not move anyway. I could not run from myself. I had nowhere to hide. I was all emotions. Pure vulnerability.

"You're safe with me," she whispered in my ear. The edge of her teeth and tongue nibbled my earlobe as the last word left her lips. An action only the two of us knew happened.

The secret lick brought me back into my body—my thighs clenched. Rain came down harder beyond us, and a fresh wave of heat bloomed in my chest. I squirmed, feeling an intense wetness between building up between my legs. The sweet torment of surrender rocked my body from within. I was suspended in ecstasy and my heartbeat galloped again. My mouth fell open with a loud moan.

Release.

Fetlynne began unwrapping me piece by piece. Fast at first to give me an immediate sense of freedom, and then slowly. The night air touching my skin was the first moment of me expanding back into myself again.

"Oh my God..." the words slipped out of me on their own.

"He's not here," she whispered playfully. "Just me."

Her voice was even softer this time.

13

AFTERCARE +

"Coming to" was the sonic boom I never knew I could experience.

For at least thirty minutes after our scene, Fetlynne sat with me privately. Holding, hydrating, and talking with me. She wiped my unexpected tears. But she couldn't stay for hours. There was still more to the event.

As we regrouped for the goal-setting portion, she caught my eye from across the room and offered single, slow nod. It was a private assurance: "I see you...it's okay."

Gratitude warmed my face at her wordless recognition, and I spent the next hour in a daze. Only half-into the goal-setting portion. Fetlynne briefly whispered something to a facilitator while nodding for me to join her alone again. I wandered to a corner in the back by a large window.

"Hey." She reached for my forearm and searched my eyes. I could hear the other woman leading the rest of the group from the other room while Fetlynne served as my rescue breath.

We chatted for a few minutes, and she put her hands on my shoulders like she did on the very first day I sat in her garden. We didn't share many words, but there were enough to guide me.

"Just breathe from here," she touched my belly. "With me."

Inhale. Exhale. I followed her lead.

"Now...just let it land, Angela. I promise, the work is done. Just let it be."

And I did.

She stealthily rejoined with the group and in a few more minutes, so did I. As the night crept closer to 12:59, a beautiful surprise of fireworks in the distance captured our attention. With the shimmering lights landing over cove, their muffled booms reached us as soft thunder. I appreciated the beauty even if through a subdued lens. It was a perfect wind down.

Surrender is not *the opposite of strength.* I scribbled in my journal later that night. Almost everyone had gone to bed by then, but I had become reenergized. *I just can't believe how such a strange activity showed me that I could stop everything at any moment and still be fine. I didn't have to manage everything. And most importantly, I didn't have to perform.* I put my pen down.

Tap. Tap. Tap.

A delicate beat was at my door. I glanced at the clock. 3:34 am.

A beat.

There were no more knocks, but I didn't hear feet padding away either.

I opened the door. "Fetlynne?"

"I know it's late," she whispered, but I saw that your light was still on. "I just wanted to check on you."

"Thank you." I stepped aside and gestured for her to come in.

She hesitated. Gulped.

"What's wrong?"

"I um...I want to. Trust me," she said, still hushed. Then, she paused to look around. "I do." Her right leg shook.

"Are *you* okay?" I asked her.

Another hesitation. "Yes." She sighed and came in.

"But—"

"I just wanted to let you know I wish I could have spent more time with you earlier. And I'm still available to talk through your experience. To help you process anything. That scene was intense. You might have emotional reactions surface even days after."

"Okay. I appreciate that." I sat on my bed.

"Okay." She didn't leave. I didn't want her too.

Fetlynne rubbed her forehead and leaned against the door. I went over to her. And in this moment, we embraced. Neither of us were eager to move our hands or explore like lovers. But...the hug lasted a long time. When she began retreating, I held her in place. "Stay..."

"You're amazing," she said.

"Is that right?" The compliment was a butter knife through my emotions.

"Yes!" she relaxed a little. "And thank you for the hug. I guess I needed one too."

"Healers also need healing. This I know." I'm not sure what compelled me to say that, but I couldn't stop it.

Fetlynne's eyes glistened. I moved closer. Her breath became jagged. Our faces hadn't been this dead on since we stood on opposite sides of the veil. And tenderly, so...so... tenderly, our lips touched. My body damn near exploded. Fetlynne kissed me deeper. Deeper. DEEPER. Her tongue was heaven. Her body was nirvana. After six months of the most intimate work, we connected in a more primal way. Breaths became rapid. Hands hungrily explored. The boundary had been crossed.

"Mmmm. Angela," she moaned. The vibration of her utterance rocked me to the core. I had to step back or collapse into her.

In that gap, we stood there looking at each other wide-eyed and stricken. We stopped.

"I don't usually do this, Angela. I can't. Especially not now while you're in such a vulnerable state. I'm sorry." She looked regretful. Maybe a little pained.

"It's okay." I wanted to keep going.

Fetlynne searched for the words. "At the end of the day, it *is* okay, if you want it to be. But I have a responsibility to you. And no matter what I feel, I need to honor that."

"What you feel?"

Her face said "shit", but she uttered nothing. She looked down. And then up. "I want to give you time and space to recalibrate from tonight. What just happened...that was real. For me. Very real. But it's my job to protect the integrity of our work, and right now, that means stepping back so you can integrate your experience without this...complication."

I listened.

"Please know that I'm not pushing you away. I should have followed my gut and not knocked on your door. I'm sorry. I should have waited until you came to me because it's right now the most crucial thing is holding the space we built," she rambled.

My body relaxed, and I smiled. "I get it. I do."

Fetlynne reached out, her fingers just brushing the top of my hand—a professional's touch that now carried an even more electric history. "Get some rest, Angela. You were magnificent today."

"Thank you....so were you," I smiled. "Good night, Goddess."

She beamed and then turned to walk out. The door clicked shut behind her, leaving me with the ghost of her touch and the weight of her confession hanging in the humid air.

The End.

DEEPER THIS TIME

1

ON MY KNEES

FETLYNNE

My first teacher told me the space between practitioner and client is sacred ground. You do not walk through it with muddy boots. You kneel. You become the perfect honeycomb for the spirit to move through.

For six months, I was that golden nest for Angela. Open. Present. Serving. Then, in the throbbing silence past 3 a.m., I *felt* the questions she'd been wading through after our session. I remembered the vulnerability, gratitude, and trust in her eyes as she looked up at me under that moonlit sky. I tasted remnants of her skin on my lips. And I debated.

Her light was still on in the villa—the only one. And in that moment, I chose to rise from my knees. I went to her door, but not as the keeper of the veil. I went as a whole, aching woman. My feet were uncertain with each step, yet I kept going until I reached her room. Three taps.

A smile.

Deep, penetrating eye contact.

"Fetlynne?" she'd answered, her expression an elixir of shock and delight.

I hesitated. Second guessed. Thought more.

I felt my body rattle with internal warnings to stop. But then, I ignored my boundaries and crossed the threshold. Sweet, sweet nectar, she was.

"Stay..." I could still feel the warmth of her breath when she begged me not to leave. It weakened my knees. It melted my resolve. I searched for strength and discipline, but her, *"it's okay"* destroyed all control. And I committed to submitting... to her pull this time.

Our lips meeting was a merging of currents: the clean, channeled energy of our work and the saccharine underground river of my own want. I knew the rules. I had personified them. But in that moment, my body wrote a new truth over old text.

When the door clicked shut and sealed us apart, I felt a haunted expansion in my chest. It was now a sanctum vacant of its goddess, occupied only by the reverberation of soft moans.

Why had I let my power unravel?

I didn't know.

"Mmph..." The savor of her lips still gave me a naughty audible reaction. But it was also tangled with the sharp ache of complexity. It's bad for business to mix personal and professional. It's dangerous for a woman like me to want more with a woman like her. It's also a road I didn't want to stop traveling.

Shit.

Angela had a way of flirting with edges even though she was visibly uneasy. That was magnetic. The way she'd use humor as armor but quickly put it down because she hungered to stop hiding. It was courageous.

I was charmed by her curiosity. Her voice. Her scent. Her intellect. Her pleasure-filled groans. And there was something about how easily—*too* easily—the frequency of her breath synced with mine. It made me want to sigh for her.

"Fetlynne..." I heard the echo of my name slipping from her lips. It reverberated in my ears as I'd tip-toed back to my room, grateful that no one else at my retreat knew what had just happened between us. But I was nervous that *that* 30-seconds might be the wrecking ball to half-a-year's-worth of work—that it had opened a trap door to a toxic power imbalance, or worse deeper feelings.

A WEEK HAD PASSED since our time in Panama, and I found myself thinking about her more during my daily orgasms. How slippery she felt on my fingers. How sweet she tasted on my tongue. The way her body quaked when I caressed her ankles, how her skin was always warm was in that shallow dip at the base of her spine, and... her specific scent when she was fully aroused. All of it made me drip. All of it made me throb. All of it made me cum.

"This wasn't how you were supposed to bring in the new

year, Fet," I exhaled the words too loudly in the silence around me. Talking to myself as I groomed in the mirror.

It wasn't raining anymore. We weren't at the gorgeous cliffside villa anymore. I was back home in Atlanta with three clients to see today, and none of them were her. So unfortunate.

"I'm fine." I lied and smiled before turning off my personal life and answering the front door.

"Hi, Fetlynne!" Melissa, my new-year-resolution client greeted me. Bubbly as ever. "Welcome back!" Medium height, average weight, and full of rebellious tattoos, she was a once-a-quarter client who swore, every year, that she was going to start coming monthly to explore more. She didn't. She was there for her usual chit-chat and massage.

"Thank you, darling!" I gave her a warm hug.

After hot chocolate and catching up, we moved into our session. Shower. Heat. Music. Oils. Skin. Just like always, I was able to dissolve time and space in my massage room. With each knot I removed from her shoulders and intentional pressure I put on the bottom of her feet, I felt my assuredness come back. Uncomplicated. It felt good. Felt affirming. The more Melissa relaxed on the table under me and the more her body unfurled like a flower into the sun, I knew I was still a goddess capable of bringing a pure heaven to women on Earth.

Yes, I moved us into a sensual space and stimulated her to the point of dripping excitement, but there was no graying of boundaries. No confusion of why I was touching specific places. And explicit places I didn't touch at all because I rarely did—except lately with Angela. This was my usual meditation on the mind of skin; one I could interpret with more than twenty years' of experience. This was work. It was the bedrock.

As our hour came to a close and I walked her out, I cleansed my space with sage and lit a few candles. My rituals of conclusion were complete. But when I stared into the blue bottom of one of the flames, a spark from across time lit up in my mind. The light was history—decades of it. Mine.

2

700 HOURS +

Somatic bodyworker. Intimacy coach. Sex worker. Sex doula. Healer. Goddess. Witch. Fast. Whore. I've been labeled many names over the years. They've become kinder as time has gone on. The first time I heard the last one, I was seventeen. It wasn't from a boy in a hallway. It seethed with contempt from my religious aunt. She bristled at the way I effortlessly magnetized the male gaze. She misread how this energy flowed through me without my rousing it. And she couldn't bear the idea of me being "one day open for business," as she put it. She didn't see innocence or even a gift. She saw sex. Corruption. Sin. In a child.

"You will draw nothing but problems if you don't control your behavior!" she scolded.

But I hadn't even been intimate with anyone yet. What behavior? I was still just a kid worried about prom and graduation. About my swim meets, because I loved the water. And maybe even college. I'd never even seen anyone but myself naked. It was such a bizarre introduction to how others would define me solely based on the innate power of my womanhood.

A Black girl born to Haitian parents who lived in the deep south, my journey to the present has been anything but smooth or predictable. We started in Alabama and I hated it. Eventually, we moved to New Orleans, where I adored it. I never did go to college, but I did attend a culinary arts institute. I survived one grueling year before changing my mind and enrolled in massage school. Touch was the only thing I loved more than baking.

By then, I'd noticed the effect I had on my lovers and friends. I was aware of how much people consistently relaxed around me and always want to lean into me. It was more than physical contact. It was with talking too. But the former took the lead. I had no desire to go into official psychology. In fact, I felt they were two sides of the same coin. My somatic and tantric work probes the corners of human emotions just as much. The only other profession in the world that got this close to people's true feelings was bar tending, and I'd spent a few years doing that too. My life has been of service to human desires. Embraces to lonely souls.

Going to massage school and learning real techniques unexpectedly made me the default one to lead the intimacy in every relationship I had. And because I was never good at monogamy, I juggled *lots* of relationships back-to-back. Sometimes simultaneously—I'm not proud of that—and I also had lots of sex. I *was* proud of *that*. Maybe my pious aunt was right. Maybe I was destined to become a whore. Or maybe she planted that seed in me by making me even wonder what it meant. It sounded like a woman who had a lot of freedom but suffered the judgement of other, more dead-inside people. People who couldn't fathom that kind of liberation. I wasn't sure, but there was a rebellious streak in me that was dangerous when combined with my ability to light a match under the hidden hungers of others.

Much of what I learned about sexual pleasure came from personal experience. Various partners. Being fearless with having open conversations about wants, fears, curiosities and needs. I was naturally inquisitive and always found a way to get my lovers to confess what they secretly craved. Then we tried them. Meanwhile, I read books and magazines to privately discover what I wanted—then experimented voraciously. Again, with various partners.

"I just love being around you." I'd hear the expression all the time. From women and men. "You make feel safe" or, "so relaxed." "I feel like I can tell you anything."

All of those words told me that in a painfully cold world, *I* was *warmth*. I was shelter. I was nurturing. The phrases were addictive, and I got hooked on making people fall in love with me. Maybe *that* was my true original sin? I wasn't sure.

Add the 700 hours of study on touch, human anatomy, and better understanding my own effect and yearnings, I'd found my calling: giving. Because it also gave so much back to me. And that felt damned good.

But after working strip mall-based massaged businesses for a while, I felt restricted. I also bore the strain of paying off my school loans. The paychecks didn't match the bills. And sometimes I struggled with the jobs.

When you don't own the practice, you can't be discerning of who lays on your table. Some clients arrived reeking of sweat or smoke. Some were unaware of the gross sounds they made. Others, of how bad their breath was. There were too many days where my stomach clenched and cringed in the dark while clients lay oblivious. And too many men sought happy endings the moment the door closed even though that was clearly against policy.

It wasn't until I had a session with a woman who noticeably needed to cross a sensual line that I reached a fork. My oiled hands had slipped a little too low from her shoulders to her chest, grazing the top of her breasts. The barely audible whimper she let out—and the slight adjustment of her torso—begged me to keep going.

It felt so natural and so right to help her *feel* the touch she wanted, but I had to think twice. I couldn't risk my job. I *needed* that paycheck, whether it was too little or not. But she needed *me*. Nervously, I allowed my palms gently caress her once more. Slowly. Thoughtfully. Cupping. And with a thumb graze to just the right spots. Then I stopped. Common sense and the law prevailed in the moment. Still, her exhale turned into a full-body shudder, and she tipped me 30%. We didn't say much after the session, but when she was fully dressed again, I could see gratitude and grief in her eyes.

"Thank you," was all she murmured before ducking out.

That session kept me up all night. I began realizing how much physical contact in society had been walled off to those with licenses like me. To doctors, hairdressers, barbers and maybe tailors. While my hands worked within the legal lines, I could tell by the way people responded to the mere *permis-*

sion to be touched that they yearned for more. Their body language told me what they would never dare say out loud.

I had no plans of going to into sex work back then, but I knew I didn't like the bind of "professional" licensure. I hated the state acting as chaperone for two consenting adults. People were hungry for more than crumbs of affection. And I was tired of being the one who had to say "no" when everything in my body, and theirs, screamed "yes." Especially for those I could hand pick.

3

INTEGRATION

Angela returned. A solid fact on my doorstep two days later. She'd booked an "integration session," which was a standard post-retreat offering, but she set it for 8:00 p.m. on a Friday. My calendar system shouldn't have even allowed anything after 5:30. In the comment section, she noted, "I'm still working on the surrender part." I let it slide. Didn't cancel or reschedule.

Otherwise, we had not spoken much since Panama. I'd seen her messages in the trip's group chat that she'd gotten home safely, but she hadn't been back in my parlor. And I hadn't pressed. I had responded with a heart emoji to her message and left it at that.

Now, a silhouette against the southern sun, she stood before me holding a potted orchid.

"Hey there," a smile bloomed on my face.

She was nervous. I could see it in the way clutched the

plant and bit her bottom lip. "I tried to wait the recommended month but—"

I grinned. She was following the rules while her entire being clamored to break them. Too familiar. Angela was *perfect.* "The recommendation is a guideline for average connections," I told her, stepping back. "I don't think ours is average." The orchid in her arms was proof. A client sends a gift card. A lover brings flowers. A woman caught in the riptide of transference brings a living, breathing metaphor.

"Oh?" her voice was soft. Her eyebrows lifted just a hint. "Well...thank you. Oh!" she perked up. "This," she chuckled, and thrust the plant toward me. "It needed a home," she finished. A peace offering. An excuse.

I took it from her. My fingers involuntarily brushed her cool skin. "It's beautiful." I was already calculating the light in my sunroom. The care it would need. "Now come. Get out of the cold." I stepped aside to allow her in.

My eyes admired Angela from the top of her head to the bottom of her feet as she slipped out of her boots. "Here," I offered my hand after putting the plant down. "Let me take your coat."

The biting of her bottom lip changed now. It wasn't anxiety. It was excitement. "Thank you," she smiled. "And you..." She looked at me slightly puzzled.

"Have a little more hair," I helped her. "But I'm not sure how long it'll last. I'm itching to shave it back off," I laughed.

"You're very attractive either way."

And just like that, two weeks of silence disintegrated in the satisfying click of understanding: Angela hadn't come for integration. She came back for more.

. . .

For the first fifteen minutes, we reviewed her thoughts and feelings of being bound and released. Of everything that led up to that scene.

"I learned that there is a body inside my body that only the most patient lover will find," she expressed. "And I'm not calling *you* my lover," she doubled back, unsure of the correct language.

"I know what you mean. Go on." We shared a pitcher of hot apple cider and relaxed on a chaise I'd recently moved into the parlor.

"It's hard to describe but it's there. Also," she pivoted. "One of the biggest things I needed to admit was that I thought I had an amazing sex life for all the wrong reasons. I just didn't know any better; I thought intensity signaled a skilled lover...but after working with you, I realized intensity alone becomes the easiest, most lazy way to make love to someone. Again, I don't mean *we* actually 'made *love*' but—"

"I understand. Verbal language is limited. But I get it. Fast. Hard. Pounding. Rushing to climax—not inherently bad, but not even close to the most expansive experiences possible."

"Exactly!"

"With you...I mean...*whew*. My body is just in full bloom. Ripe. Everything is open. My mood is better. I'm solving problems faster. I'm more creative. I'm slower to get annoyed. It's a complete and total shift. What is this, witchcraft?" she joked.

"Not quite," I chuckled. The word didn't hurt coming

from her. "But some do consider it sex magic. I don't. To me, it's just reclamation work."

"Reclamation work?"

"Yes," I leaned in. "Most people live on top of a buried self that knows how to want and feel pleasure without shame. But that self can barely breathe under the rubble of everyone else's opinion on sex and intimacy. My job is to help you clear the debris so you can find what's always been yours. The body inside your body, I guess you could say," I winked.

Angela anchored a hand on her hip and released a deep, satisfying laugh. "Tuh? Well, I'll be..." she whispered. "That... sounds right."

I placed a hand on her knee. "Exactly. And you, my dear, are a vein of gold. I love the way you glisten." I cleared my throat, catching myself. *Keep it professional, Fetlynne. Keep it professional!* "So... you experienced a bit of an awakening."

"Indeed. Thank you for that." She rested her palm on top of mine, both now on her knee.

My heartbeat sped up. Gently, almost untraceably, I withdrew my fingers from under hers. "Did you ever dream you'd be the one asking for an erotic mummification?"

"No! What? It sounds crazy as hell. Weird. Foolish. I'd never even *heard* of that before! But...here I am, post-mummy wrapped and feeling more alive than ever."

I smiled and stood. Space between us was necessary. "That's the goal. To feel more alive *in* your vessel."

"To dwell in it and not just be a tenant?" she teased, repeating a phrase I'd said once in an interview. Angela got up.

"I can't believe you remember that!"

"You're hard to forget." She winked back.

I blushed and gestured toward the hallway that led to my second treatment room. "Shall we? The conversation part of our integration is done. It's the body's turn."

Her eyes followed my gesture, then returned to my face, a flicker of that old nervousness—or was it anticipation?—crossing her features. "Right. Of course."

Angela hadn't actually selected a type of service from the menu that day, but the familiar ritual began: the warm shower—inside this time, the low purr of the furnace, the scent of orange citrus oil I'd already diffused into the air. The room was a temple I had built with my own hands, and now the most complicated offering I'd ever received lay on a table in its center. She pulled the sheets closer to her chest. It was time to turn up the heat.

4

RIGGED CARD GAME

We started on the table but ended in a pillow-laded corner on the floor. The massage itself felt mild until the very end—I'd used a soundtrack of ocean waves layered under instrumental R&B to guide my strokes on her arms, legs, shoulders, back, breasts, and feet. I even added a little pressure in the crease where the back of her thighs met her ass. I knew that compression would push through her skin, and she'd feel it deep inside.

My goal was to bring us both into a state of deep relaxation and awakened senses. The rhythmic movements of the ocean were the perfect pilot. But as I caressed her quads, I found myself yearning to kiss the narrow bridge where her thigh met her hip. To lick the entire length of it. So, I did it. Without subtly, but no over-eagerness, either. Meanwhile, I ran my right hand up the side of her thigh.

She moaned and dragged her nails across the top of my shoulders, the only part of me besides my head that she could reach. Then she used her other hand to caress my crown. Nudged me closer to her swelling yoni.

"Please," she begged, as I breathed over it with warmth.

I nibbled her inner thighs. Used the tip of my nose to tease her clit and then, finally, I planted a warm kiss. "Mmm," I moaned with my mouth still over it. She was exquisite.

The vibration from my groan made Angela instinctively gyrate into my face, spreading her wetness across my lips. I'd been wanting to taste her for more than half a year, and she was worth every second of the wait.

"Fetl..." she could barely whisper my name.

The tension was high. We'd danced around this for nearly seven months now. And this wasn't foreplay for anything else. It was a precursor to pussy worship all on its own. That was the only thing I wanted to do that evening: devote myself to giving Angela the greatest sexual pleasure she'd ever had in her entire life. And to allow myself a little rope to enjoy it without guilt. Practicing what I preached for once.

As the music and ocean rolls continued filling the space, I focused on the motions of mouth, my tongue, my entire head. Slow. Explorative. Intentional. With an adoring and patient tongue.

It didn't take long to learn that Angela like broad circular motions over her glans and long licks up and down the sides. She loved tongue-led clit kisses that pulled back with a little suckle. That's what made her breathe the deepest. What made her squirm the most.

I loved the feel of her gripping my shoulders. Scratching

at the sheets. Spreading her legs wider to beg for more but struggling to keep them open there when I gave it to her.

I held Angela's thighs apart. I needed room. I longed to go down on her with reverence and savor every drop. Moans and growls soon coated the soundscape. We were two rushing rivers crashing into each other. I could feel my own wetness making a mess of my thighs as I buried my face between hers.

"Yes..." she panted, as I used a finger to spread her lips open for better access.

I licked and I kissed and I sucked. I stuck my tongue inside and pulled it back out. I interlocked my fingers with hers and we clasped hands before I stuck my tongue back in and moved it from left to right against her inner walls. She squeezed my hands, snapped her legs around my head and locked me in. This just made me thirstier. It made me inch away from slow and tender to a more hunger-driven desire to build pressure. To build sexual energy that would radiate from her pussy to the rest of her entire body.

Angela held on tight, bucking and rocking against my face. The large massage table groaned under us. I kept lapping up her juices, inhaling through my mouth so she could feel the alternate sensation of warmth and coolness. I don't know how long I ate her out. It didn't matter. It was well after hours and I didn't have any more clients. My only thought was pleasure. A groundswell of it.

When we released hands, I nudged myself free so I could move up her body. Kissing the softness of her belly. Nibbling at her sides. Making my way back to her breasts, gently taking one into my mouth while cupping the other. Her nipples were so hard they made the throb between my legs build to a thunder. I was equally as turned on as she was, intoxicated by how everything about her responded to my attention. I loved the feel of her nipples between my lips.

I sucked more. Licked more. Kissed more.

Delicately, I grazed them with my teeth.

Her breathing fluttered. Her body moved in a gentle wave. Angela loved this. She held me tighter and then kissed my forehead—a reciprocation I hadn't anticipated. My muscles tightened unexpectedly. I slowed down.

Go back down, I told myself. *Give, don't receive.*

Moving with my hands first, I slipped back down to below Angela's waist and opened her up again. But this time, to rub my thumb against her clit then slide a finger inside. She was so wet I easily inserted a second.

She screamed. High-pitched. Pleasure-filled. She gripped my wrists then released them.

I intentionally eased off with my tongue because I wanted to edge her rather than give her an orgasm. Slowly, I moved my fingers in and out.

Very, very, slowly.

I needed to decrescendo in a way that didn't make her feel cheated or disappointed. Slow strokes. A few light kisses. Sluggish, but still intentional strokes... One or two more light kisses.

I rested my face on her inner thigh. Inhaling. Exhaling. Syncing with her. Bringing her heart rate down. But once again, I gave a very measured push inside of her with my fingers, and then... an incredibly sloooooooow pull out. On that last one, I sat up and we locked eyes.

I held. She didn't flinch. A passionate penetration of solely eye contact. And then I seductively put my fingers in my mouth, letting her see how enthusiastic I was to taste her. I closed my eyes and savored.

"Oh, my fucking God..." she moaned breathlessly while watching me swirl my tongue over the fingertips that were just covered with her juices

I smiled. She already knew what I was going to say. "He's not here."

"Just me," we laughed in unison. Her voice was a playful mimic of mine, and the chuckle that followed was the perfect moment to pause.

At this point, it was an ongoing joke. I will never let a man take credit for my skills with women. Not even "God."

"How are you?" I asked, resting my hand over her yoni to help calm her body down even more.

Angela looked at me like I was stupid. She braced herself on her elbows and cocked her head to the side. "How do you think?"

Bashful, I looked away.

"I feel amazing," she confessed. "There's no other choice with you."

Her response hit like an ecstasy pill. The base of my neck tingled. I had to gulp a big breath to pace my *own* absorption of it. "You make it easy," I complimented her back.

Beautiful beads of sweat decorated Angela's stomach. Streaks rolled down mine. I straightened up on the table, sitting more upright between her legs by using my knees for support.

"What?" She quizzed, catching me admiring at her.

"You have such a *beautiful* pussy."

Her eyes widened. Mouth fell open. Angela was stunned. "Um." Her voice cracked.

"Never heard that before?" I continued like I'd just complimented her smile.

"No. Never," she stammered. "I—I don't know what to say."

I eased off the table. Walked around back so I was behind her head. "You don't have to say anything. It's true."

She craned her neck to follow me until she couldn't anymore. I wiped my hands on a clean, moist washcloth, then settled on a stool behind her.

"Oh, I get a scalp massage?" she looked up with glee.

I nodded. It was time to guide her back to a state of neutral relaxation.

Angela's body shimmered with residual massage oil. Her nipples were still erect. There was still a miniature puddle glazed over her pussy. But a few minutes later, she calmed. I moved my strokes to her neck, then down to her shoulders again. Kneading away any lingering pent-up tension.

Everything was going to plan. She'd even dozed off a little in the final minutes, allowing me to whisper in her ear. "Angela… we're at time."

Somehow, I managed to not go over 90 minutes all while not paying attention to the clock. Maybe I'd been doing this work for so long, I knew the rhythm of hours without having to watch them.

"Mmph." Was all she could grunt. And then she smiled. "Okay."

"I'll get you some tea. Or water, if that's what you want."

"Tea, thank you."

I grabbed a silk robe and slipped out of the room like I always did, expecting her to be mostly dressed by the time I returned. But instead, Angela was sweetly balled up in fetal position on the table. The sheets clutched in her hands under her chin. She was on the edge of sleep again. I glanced at the clock: 9:28 p.m.

"You know," I told her. "You'd warm up faster if you put your clothes on."

She blinked. "Of course, but that would deprive you of seeing what I had on under my outfit earlier."

She was right. Beforehand, I'd stepped out to let her undress and missed our other unexpected, shared moment: me admiring whatever lingerie she hid under her jeans that day. It was becoming a game to me at this point. Guess the color. Guess the texture. Guess the design. Because Angela never repeated and made each one more of a jaw-dropper than the last.

A part of me wanted to freefall out of facilitator mode and just be more of myself with her, but I couldn't break the illusion. Couldn't crack the fantasy. It wasn't that who she was used to experiencing wasn't real. Just that there was more. A lot more. But that "more" had flaws no one wanted to see in their bodyworker. Better to keep it away.

I watched Angela step into a strappy, fuchsia bra and panty set that melded perfectly to her body.

"You like?"

"I *love*," I marveled.

Instead of putting her jeans or sweater on, she leaned against the doorframe. Long legs. Sparkling skin. Dark brown complexion. Easy smile. Shit. Now *she* was the danger. Angela brushed her braids away from her face and rolled her neck with a moan.

"Did I miss a spot?" And now, I was the one using humor as armor.

"No. And thank you," she reached for the tea. Angela didn't break her gaze though. She had a mountain of confidence now. I wasn't prepared for it but didn't want to stifle it. It was gorgeous even if chancy.

"You're welcome."

She inched down to the pillows on the floor in the corner next to her—opposite me. Angela sat casually, as if she were fully dressed. Legs slightly apart, arms slung across her knees. If a tomboy were recruited for a lingerie ad, it would be that pose. For a few quiet moments, we sat opposed each other. She studied me.

"What?"

"You have an interesting way of hiding right out in the open," she called me out.

I touched my throat. Felt a tingle in my skin. I laughed nervously. "Um…"

"What—never heard that one before?"

"Touché." I grinned and went over to her.

By now, my playlist had switched to a completely new one. Masego's "Tadow" rocked the room with an easy jazz vibe. Angela put her cup down the moment I entered her space. I outstretched my hand to help her up. Thankfully, she took it. I had to end this night. Right *now*.

"Look, I'm glad everything is working well for you. I hope you can see the difference in yourself. I sure can."

"I think I do. I'm grateful for you."

I slipped a hand in my pocket, warming my fingers from a chill that suddenly passed through me. With few words left, I nodded positively. Angela got dressed now. Gathered her things. And we headed to the door.

Cold night air rushed in the moment I opened it. "For our next regular, *daytime* session," I said, "should I book you for the usual, or for something from the *advanced* side of the menu?"

Angela shrugged, looking guiltier than a rigged card game in a backroom hustle. "Whatever you want. Good night!"

5

INSIDE OUT

I'm pretty sure my new, nosey neighbor caught me hula-hooping at sunrise. She'd only lived there a month and was already grating my nerves. Always looking. Always noting. Always waving with that over-bright, performative smile. But it was my house in Grant Park. And I had my reasons to maintain my hip stability and bathe in sunshine—to outrun the creeping stiffness of a life spent bending over other people. In fact, I was overdue for laps in the pool. *Soon,* I told myself, yet again putting off my old, beloved activity. It wasn't warm enough outside yet anyway. By the time I finished hooping, my body felt great but I'd somehow managed to slip back into the house with a slight headache.

"Oh, come on," I grumbled when I realized I was out of ibuprofen. I was running low on coffee, too. "Hot chocolate it is." I needed something to smooth the start of my Saturday.

I'd already woke to a barrage of family texts for a summer reunion that would once again not happen because everyone waited until the last minute to book their tickets and couldn't afford them. I'd procrastinated on sending invoices, so that task loomed over me as well. I didn't see clients on the weekends. I was just...me. Living.

A glance across the room showed the orchid from Angela. Needed to water that too. *Angela*. Before I could think about the last night with her, my phone pinged with notification from my "Fetty," inbox. It was the one I used for close friends and family. The only one that I allowed real-time notifications for. Otherwise, I'd go crazy from constant alerts.

Being in this business for decades meant that I'd seen hundreds of clients in various time zones over the years. Many of them still stay in touch. That doesn't even count those who *want* to be clients and those who just want to waste my time. I had a virtual assistant who helped manage my calendar and initial inquiries, but I could easily see the notification numbers rise into the high hundreds daily. The documentary that put me on Angela's radar had also brought me to thousands of others. But she was local. She could show up.

The weekends were my cherished personal time, and I spent most of it in the kitchen. Once settled in from my morning exercise, I dumped a cheap Swiss Miss chocolate powder out of its packet, enjoying a moment alone that allowed me to admit that I really didn't like the taste of more "real" chocolate or cacao. The latter never dissolved right and formed a gritty sweet sludge at the bottom.

The thought of the revered cacao though, reminded me of one of my first times having it—along with access to shamans. Years ago, I'd gone to Mexico on a whim after burning out at my first spa job in New Orleans. I was chasing an ancient wisdom I thought I needed and landed first in Guerrero, then Puerto Escondido, then Puebla. It was dry, dusty, and surprisingly much cooler than what I was used to. It was there that I drank more of the grit than I wanted to. My two-week trip stretched to two years as I wandered and learned, labored and absorbed. If anywhere in the world felt like a second home to me, it would be Mexico.

I became a collector of experiences there. I sat in the dark, sweating in the womb of a Temazcal. I learned the slick, deliberate strokes of Ayurvedic Abhyanga. I let old women sweep my aura with bunched herbs, while barely understanding their spoken language. I understood their bodies though. And that information helped me understand the spirit just as much as the physique.

All of it was probably another 100 hours of personal study—maybe 200 by the time I synthesized my old knowledge with the new to create completely unique techniques of my own. My flavor would include sacred touch that embraced lingam and yoni massages.

That phase feels like a lifetime ago, but every client who lies on my table now is touched by it. Hell, I wish *I* could be touched by it. I was yet to find anyone local who could turn me inside out.

I finished my drink, savoring the sweet film it left on my tongue. My headache was a dull anchor now, grounding me in the kitchen and the day's chores. It was time to run errands, which meant I needed to call Jules. It was easier than calling a rideshare, and far more reliable.

"Good morning, Goddess," she answered cheerfully on the second ring. Attentive. Clear. Grateful.

"Hi there. I need you to come pick me up in an hour."

"Of course. From home, right?

"Yes. See you then."

The call ended in less than fifteen seconds.

I never had to ask if Jules was free, give an address, or explain what 'pick me up' entailed. She knew. It was our arrangement. The ease of it relaxed my jaw at just the right moment. I had built a world where my needs were simple, direct, and met without a ripple. It was a different kind of sacred ground, and I was its sole architect.

AN HOUR LATER, a pearl-gray SUV glided to the curb. Jules was always exactly on time, which meant she was always five minutes early, waiting around the corner. The passenger door was already open by the time I locked up behind me. Jules was poised behind the wheel with her hands at ten and two.

The SUV's cabin was a perfect seventy-six degrees—the vent on my side closed. My seat was warmed and adjusted, the lumbar support set just so. I smiled and slid in, appreciating the low-volume 90s R&B drifting from the speakers. Jules' gaze remained forward until I was settled. Then, she turned.

"Hello, Goddess." Her smile was a private crescent that complimented her soft, fluffed afro.

"Morning, Jules. Let's hit the Pastry Depot first. I need semolina flour." I noticed the smooth slope of her shoulders under her cream sweater. "That's a nice color on you. I like it."

"Thank you!" Was her only reply before we pulled away.

Then, silence. I needed it. Relished in it. Jules' car was a safe space. Navigating Atlanta's unpredictable traffic was a problem that wasn't mine. The quiet between us was deep and expected. Habitual.

From the pastry shop to the farmer's market, and eventually to the pharmacy, Jules waited in the car while I strolled in and out of each spot. If I had more than two bags, she took them. By midday, my errands were done. While Jules loaded the last bag in the trunk, I stole a few moments to admire a small cluster of bees work a flowering bush. They were fascinating.

"Thanks, Jules. I'll see you tomorrow at home."

"Um...you told me to remind you to hit the Y. For a swim morning."

"You are correct. I appreciate that. Then we'll do that in the morning."

She nodded, that delicate smile returning. Then I watched her SUV ease down my residential road. The afternoon sun felt warm and sweet on my shoulders.

Back inside, my phone pulsed on the counter. A text from Angela. I opened it.

Angela: *Been thinking about Panama and last night. A lot.*

I read it three times. A dozen professional responses

came to mind, yet I ignored them all. Instead, I typed four words and hit send before I could stop myself: *Me too. Been thinking.* I put the phone down with its screen against the table. My hands were clammy. A part of me wanted to flee.

6

MINGLED WATERS

I didn't check my phone again until after I'd swam a few laps and enjoyed the massage bed at the gym. Until after I had a reflective breakfast and cared for all of my houseplants, new orchid included. When I finally flipped went back to my cell, Angela's reply was buried amongst 62 others. It wasn't at all what I'd expected. Her text read: *Good. I'm glad I'm not the only one.*

I froze. Grasped the back of the chair next to me. Lost count of the next few minutes that went by. I put my phone down and shifted my focus to preparing for the week ahead.

Days went by. Then, a week passed. Just as I was wrapping up with one of my regular, overworked corporate clients who wanted an escape from his family and job, my phone lit up. Angela: *Was your advanced menu a real offer for our next session or just a professional tease?*

The question stopped me in my tracks. Made me smile.

Angela knew damn well that advanced was really on the menu.

It's real. I shot back, feeling my eye twitch. Because this time it would just be us. No audience or rigid agenda to stick to.

She sent a thumbs up emoji. The next day, Angela booked a 90-minute impact play session.

"Oh reeeaallly?" My eyebrows rose, intrigued. Thrilled. Eager. "This will be fun," I mused, already mapping the restraints and toys I would use with her.

The rest of my day zipped past. So did the week.

ANGELA WAS NEW TO KINK. That much I already knew to be true. I didn't need an intake form to gauge what would work well with her versus what would overwhelm. I read the ridges and curves of her body. I knew where she was most sensitive and most craving. Even sensed her ticklish spots.

Floggers, paddles, various restraints. Wands, whips, whisks. Gloves, dragon tongues and tails. I had an array to choose from. Floggers were the most obvious for someone like her. Teasing. Delighting. Frightening. I picked one up, feeling its suede tassels. I dragged them over my own forearm to test the sensation and feel what she would feel—as her—and a shudder rippled through me. *Mmm.* I sank into it...

"Beautiful."

I decided to delve deeper into sensory play than physical impact to ease Angela in, selecting a horsetail whisk for its thousand points of contact. It would confuse her in the most delightful way. I also picked a jade roller for a cool shock if her skin got too hot. Raw silk for friction and sound. And for memory recall, I pulled leftover muslin from our Panama session. She would see that first.

That should do it. A perfect, escalating journey for a novice. I glanced at the fabric—*but she wasn't a novice was she?* The thought hit me. Angela already had an extreme taste of surrender and then asked for the expanded menu.

An hour before Angela was due, I felt a lightness bubble in my chest and constant urge to smile. I also detected a little sweat on my neck. Just nerves. Professional anticipation. I rinsed off again, restless, but also to ensure every inch of my body was pure. I repositioned the bottles of oil on my side table three times. The tops must all face the door.

When her blue Audi rumbled into my driveway, I took a deep breath and willed a warmth through me. Angela's *everything* was mine for the next hour and a half. The knowing pricked at my spine.

"Hello there!" I greeted.

"Good afternoon," she smiled.

I could already see a merlot-blushed strap peeking from beneath her sweater. The warm plum hue kissed the slopes of her skin before I could. My knees wavered a little, but I held them straight.

Angela's braids were gone. Her hair was straight now. The

change startled me initially—my first time seeing her this way.

"Look at you!"

"Needed a change," she grinned.

"I like it. Honestly, you could rock anything and still look amazing."

She blushed. I caught her fingertips tapping against her leg. "Thank you."

WE CONDUCTED our usual ritual of talk with me threading in questions to assess how her week went and her current mental state.

"Any new stresses? Or old aches flaring?"

"Nope."

Stable. Good. This was necessary before taking her to a subspace. And she hadn't even noticed the queries. Guard down. Perfect. I even offered her a slice of warm apple crumble that I'd baked while delicately quizzing her to confirm her comfort and boundaries.

"Oh my God. This is heaven." Her eyes widened on the first bite.

"It's what I'm here to deliver."

She nodded, mouth full. Aura open.

It also felt good for me to be praised for something other than my paid work. Baking was my mediation in between bodies.

"By the way, do you have any food allergies? Just curious."

"Why, are you planning a dinner?"

I chuckled. "No. Literally just curious...peanuts, shellfish, corn, just asking?"

"No. And who the hell is allergic to corn?" she asked incredulously.

I burst into laughter.

I lead her to my garden shower where a steam bath awaited. She began undressing and exposed a body clad in peek-a-boo style of undergarments including a garter. *My God.* The steam curled around each strap and fastener, the garter biting into the sweet, strong curve of her thighs. I noted the topography: Long legs. Sweet hips. Toned arms. Strong shoulders. Not-so-innocent eyes.

"Wait," I told her. "Can I just...admire you for a minute?" I rubbed the back of my neck. Squeezed it.

She mirrored me, adding a slight nip to her bottom lip and gaze that locked on mine. "Sure," she breathed. Angela slowly trailed her fingertips from the back of her neck down the side, to the front, past her clavicle stopping at her chest.

My eyes picked up where her hands stopped. Observing down her body all the way to her pedicured toes. "Mmph." My gaze completed a journey back up to her bashful smile. "Every inch of you is a deliberate provocation."

"It is not," she shrugged but a devilish smile still escaped. The steam condensed between us.

Every word Angela uttered, every movement she made, prompted me to keep this going. The sponge bath was my countermove. A quiet, methodical re-establishing of the frame. My touch was clinical, thorough, and inevitable. By the time I guided her to the sanctuary, her skin radiated from the certainty of my hands.

"That's new," she gestured to a single, dramatic piece of driftwood on a shelf.

"Like it?"

"I do!"

I winked. The room was still and humidified. Low, honeyed lights glowed from two paper lanterns I placed just for her. They were in corners—not overhead. Traces of sage filled the air and a small, black stone basin with towels rested on a side table next to a dimmable salt lamp.

"Oh my." She noticed a low platform table covered in cream-colored linen. My tools were arranged atop. She pulled her robe closer to her chest. Stepped closer to inspect. Her inhalation quickened. It was subtle, but I noticed it.

"Breathe," I intoned, my voice low. "You know this. We're just going deeper."

She spun to face me. Surprised. "Wait. Is this from...?" Angela picked up the muslin fabric.

I smiled. "It is. Please," I motioned to the table. "Get comfortable. Face down on the table."

While she obeyed my instructions, I pulled the floor-length curtains closed. They were heavy. They blocked out the world.

"I'm going to slide a blindfold over your eyes now, okay?"

She nodded.

I proceeded, and let the tip of my tongue brush her earlobe just as I had in Panama. It had sent her over the edge there. Today, I wanted it to walk her right back to that final moment before beginning again. Continuity.

I spread Angela's legs enough to restrain her ankles to the back of table. Then, her hands to the front. I turned on a neo soul instrumental track, knowing the playlist would follow me down the tunnel from a gentle, open yearning, to a haunted rapture.

I used my hands and breath first. Caressed her from head to feet. "Breeeathe," I reminded her when I sensed her tensing and anticipating. "Slower....yes...just like that," I talked her through it. "Breeeathe..."

She listened, and I drew my nails down her back. Kissed each ass cheek and then ran the tip of my nose down her hamstrings to the back of her knees. Kiss. Bite. Rub. She melted. I massaged her skin once more and then...

I reached for the flogger, spinning it in the air before going for my first test contact—the back of thighs. *Swish!* She jolted. Shivered. Again, the other leg. *Swish!* She moaned. Squirmed. Immediately after each contact, I rubbed her skin with my hands. Again. *Swish!* Light contact against her ass. A mild sting.

"Oh..." she groaned. "Fuck..." the last word slipped out as a whimper. Angela grinded against the table then arched her back, positioning her glutes up. She wanted more.

I reached for a second flogger. One in each hand now, in a good rhythm, I cycled contacts down her legs, getting much lighter as I left the fleshier parts of her hamstrings. Up and down. Up and down. Up and down.

With one hand now running the flogger tassels against her calves, I swapped the other tool for the raw silk. It was good for building heat and the sound it made against skin was provocative.

Seconds after it touched her, Angela moved like a snake. She tried to use her hands but couldn't. The cuffs clinked.

Pulled against the wooden frame. She whined, but in a good way. Minutes later, I switched to the horsetail whisk.

"Huh?" She responded audibly this time, not knowing where the sensations began or ended.

Good. I needed to break her focus on the restraints and bring her back to center. Contact. She moaned. Contact! Again, she whimpered. Angela shivered as the music darkened. Cain Culto's "Like A Prayer" thundered into the room as I picked up the tempo and alternated what tool hit her skin at different points, so it felt like rain.

My breathing sped up. Deeper. More audible. Intensifying.

Tap. Tap. Tap.

Slap. Slap. Slap.

Swoosh. Swoosh. Swoosh. The sounds were intoxicating.

I moved the very air in the room around us, bringing Angela to a vibrating writhe. Her nervous system was flooded, and we both loved it. This was skill. This was *art*. By the time got to the "just call my name" bridge and "like a little prayer" lines of the song, sweat gathered on her back. It trickled down my stomach. I slowed. Reached for the jade roller that had been in chilled water. Carefully, I placed the smoothed stone inside her thighs, gliding it up and down.

"Ah," she yelped.

"You're okay, beautiful" I assured her, with the impulsive urge to add praise to the session. "You're fine." I repeated. "Now, breeeeathe," I coached her. "Breathe with me."

I then dipped the roller in the cool water again before placing it at the small of her back.

"Whew..."

With firm wrists, I rolled the perfect mineral up her spine then down. Then followed it with a run of my tongue up and down the same wet line.

"Fetlyyyyynne..." her voice quavered.

A bit entranced myself, I answered with a few gentle bites to her skin before finally speaking. "Yes, gorgeous?"

"Mmmmm." She had no words, just a high-pitched moan through clenched teeth.

"Are you alright?"

"Mm hm." She nodded. "I'm good." She huffed the answer out in a heavy exhale, while twisting and struggling on the table.

I thought. Split second. Then asked, "Do you want to be face up?"

Angela debated. "Yes. Please."

"As you wish."

I unfastened her hands and feet and folded her into my arms to guide her to lay on her back. The blindfold was still on. Then, I restrained her again.

Clink.

Clink.

Clink. Clink.

Latches secured. Bound to the table again, she was.

"Are you okay?" I checked in.

"Yes," she breathed heavily.

"Do you remember your safe word?" I teased.

"Fuck, *yes*." She damn near growled. "But I don't need it." Her voice squeaked on the last word.

"Good." I got in her ear and whispered, "Because I'm

ready to please you in every way." I kissed the ridge of her ear again. Then released a long breath.

Angela's body shuddered. Her head fell to one side. Neck exposed. She was so exquisitely open. I continued with the whips and floggers.

Carefully across her breasts and stomach. On her quads. She turned and bucked. Writhed and arched. In a windmill motion, I devotedly whipped her to a peak state. The visual of her blindfolded and restrained while thrashing for freedom mesmerized me. I loved the sound of the soft leather on her flesh. Of the confining metal trembling against wood. Of her lilting moans amidst the table creaks. Angela was the most beautiful creature I'd seen in a very long time. I didn't want to quit admiring her.

But I eventually slowed to a stop.

I had to. My own breath had transformed a heavy pant.

I pulled out a small bowl I'd had hidden under a table that concealed dried, flexible corn husks that I'd soaked in warm water with orange peels and cinnamon sticks. Things I'd picked up at the farmer's market while Jules waited. But this was just for Angela. The root of this 'random' decision went back years to my time in Mexico when I'd experimented with all kinds of plants for various reasons. Out of nowhere, the scent of the husks came back to me while I was in the market, so I grabbed some with her in mind. I tested my idea on myself that night and knew I'd do it today.

Her body glowed under the amber lights, and she gasped through her mouth. This was when I squeezed the husks of water then dragged them across her upper chest, just once. She inhaled with her entire body then twitched. Her fingers curled slightly against the table then released. Angela became still, bracing, but I held. I knew her nervous system was engaging rather than retreating, so I gifted her time to integrate.

"What—what is that?" Angela sniffed. Perked up. Cocked her head to one side, releasing another big breath. The plants had released a warm, spicy scent from the cinnamon and orange soak.

"Something I've never used on anyone else before. Something I got just for you," I told her, and slowly pulled off her blindfold.

She blinked. Adjusting to the light.

"I want you to inhale and exhale into the heat. Let it spread." My fingers gently brushed hair away from her sweaty brow.

I began releasing her, one limb at a time and then soothed her skin with my hands. Worshipping. Honoring.

"Thank you for trusting me." I turned to get warm towels. "I love how courageous you are with me."

"Thank *you*..." she sniffed. "For taking care of me."

A long silence while I cleaned up and retrieved a fresh towel.

"Angela?" I spun around and saw her looking up at me with soft eyes. *Wet* eyes.

She exhaled with a tremor, touching her fingertips to her lips. "I'm fine." Her voice cracked on the word. Angela held my gaze for a trembling second as I placed a linen over her torso.

"Hey..." I reached for her chin. "Hey, hey, hey...you okay?"

A sheen of tears glossed her eyes—the last guard. I sat

next to her. Then it shattered. A soft, surrendering sound escaped her as she broke the look away, turning her face into my thigh. I took her hand in mine. Holding.

"You're safe with me. Always." I reminded her.

"Thank you," she repeated, squeezing my fingers. "I don't even know what to say..." She found my eyes again, then curled herself into my lap. A slow, deliberate collapse. "And I'm okay, Fetlynne. I just suddenly feel so free." Her head fell into me again—as though she were woozy.

I caressed her temple. Held her. Remained silent.

Angela's weight in my lap was a picture-perfect anchor. Her trust was the highest compliment my craft could receive, so was her vulnerability. These kinds of sessions often came with an emotional release, I knew that to be true. But it felt different this time. Beneath my pride, a quieter, more terrifying truth vibrated: I had not just performed a session. I had tended to someone I was actually attracted to. Someone I now *cared* for. Someone I *craved.* Our two waters had mingled, and now I could not separate the sacred from the personal. My rules were destroyed. Proof of it lay weeping softly against me. I didn't want to let her go.

7

REVELATION

"You know," I said as she stepped into the doorway. Her expression was unreadable. "You don't have to pay me to see me, right?" I swallowed. Held the door.

Angela paused mid-stride. Her entire body halted. "What?"

I huffed. "Are you really going to make me repeat that?"

"No—I mean..." A slow blink. Her incomprehensible expression shifted into something more soft and dangerous. "No." She spoke again. "I heard you."

Now *I* was the one exposed. Unsure. The ground felt unsteady. I wanted to run again but braced against the doorframe instead.

"I'd love to see you outside of...this?" she smiled.

I dropped my head back against the wood. "Good." The word was a surrender in a breath. I was relieved.

She turned to go.

"Hey, Angela," I called out. She looked back. "Take care of yourself."

She licked her lips and a small, private smirk played on her lips as she closed her car door.

I tracked her taillights disappearing and a cold clarity—the kind that follows a fever break—settled over me. I'd definitively just shattered my emotional last security gate.

I don't know what made me do it. I'd served hundreds of clients. Explored countless bodies. Held space for women and men across geographical lines. Across time.

It's not that I'd never felt attraction to regulars before. Of course, I did every now and then, but I maintained control. My boundaries formed a fortified line. I kept several rubrics that shielded me throughout all the years of my practice:

Rule 1: Never reveal struggles to anyone—it's unsafe.

Rule 2: Never confide—you'll be blamed for choosing this line of work.

Rule 3, the cardinal: Never succumb to a client—they'll erase your origin story.

Rule 4: Therefore, be a bastion.

I strived to never go around or through this system because it was too dangerous—I'd learned that the hard way for each rule. That's how they came to be.

To thrive in this work, you must become a fortress. People presume you have everything together because you've seen it all and you know more about pleasure than most. It doesn't help that to keep from being stereotyped, women like me polish our exterior until it's blinding. It's hazardous to admit that you ever struggle like any other human being. It's risky to confide in people when something goes wrong because the assumption is you brought it on yourself by rejecting normalcy. It's dicey to fall in love with clients who will almost always forget how they met you when things got serious.

Shit.

It's why I remained a ghost to most. Why I stopped advertising, letting people discover me. That was my shield. It's why I avoided relationships but accepted part-time lovers. It's why I built a religion where I am the only goddess. But... damn it. I'd just made Angela an exception.

Her tears shouldn't have caught me off guard. The work we'd done together covered so much ground. Trust establishment. Heightened body awareness. Pleasure. Controlled pain. Neurochemical shifts...I'd helped her integrate her mind-body system so thoroughly that it created a moment where anything she had pent up felt safe to bubble to the surface. First as a brook, second, like a geyser finally erupting.

I'd explained much of this to her in a phone call the next day. But her tears against my leg. Her warmth about my belly, and my instinct to cradle her beyond what's normal for a session. That, even though I fought the urge, told me that I needed to write my own feelings down and assess what was going on with *me*.

Angela was delicate and I didn't want to ruin her. So, for page after page, I jotted down the exact pressure of her head my stomach, the scent of her hair mixed with cinnamon and citrus. I questioned why that particular combination of trust and collapse felt like a homecoming instead of another professional notch on my belt. And I admitted that I'm not good at relationships—even platonic ones—that's why I run from them. They demand too much maintenance and energy that I don't often have at the end of my days. I habitually forget to text back. If it isn't work, I might take a week to call back. I *loved* dates but disliked them rushing to become more. Hated it, actually. So, I dodged most relationships to protect other people from me while I *designed* the connections I needed to tend to my desires.

There. I wrote it all down. Got it all out. Then, I burned the notes in the basin still in the room from her session.

But two weeks later, Jules was picking me up to take me to meet Angela for lunch. I reassured myself it was a meal between practitioner and a satisfied client. The lie was so thin I could almost see through it to the naked and woman beneath: me.

Angela was there before me—I hadn't planned on being late, but it happened. She rose to greet me.

"Hey you!"

"Hey...sorry, I'm—"

"Don't worry about it," she dismissed an apology.

I smiled. This was already starting off safely. In truth, our conversation flowed easy and light. Moving quickly from an awkward attempt at small talk in a public space to a fun and unexpected mutual quiz.

"What's the worst date you've ever been on?"

"Well, it's been a while since I've had a real date, but I guess you could say the last one."

"Why?"

"Twenty minutes in, she asked if I want to get high after. I told her no. To which she responded, 'You sure? I have a little meth and cocaine in my car, but it's nothing crazy.' I paid the check and left."

"What the f—" I couldn't believe it. "On a first date?"

"Yeah."

We shared a laugh before she picked up. "Okay, my turn: best and worst experience from clients?"

"Easy. My worst experience was getting held hostage for 5 hours by a client who was high on shrooms. Non-violent, but horrible. Best experience...meeting *you*." I grinned stupidly. The words pranced out of my mouth with no shame. And I hadn't even been drinking.

"Don't lie to me, Fetlynne!"

"I'm not!"

She cocked her head. Suspicious. "I mean the shrooms person, I believe. And I'm sorry to hear that. What is it with the fucking drugs?"

I shrugged, not willing to broach that topic further.

"But *me*?" Angela zeroed in on the last part of my answer.

"Why is that hard to believe?

"Because it is!"

"Look I *have* had lots of amazing client experiences. I've met wonderful people from all walks of life. From varying economic levels—blue-collar workers to physicians like you. Even one or two celebrities. But lately...over the last few years... everything has become a very expert exchange. I provide a perfect service, and they receive a perfect result. It's flawless. But after a while, flawless becomes invisible. Not as stimulating as it once was...From the first session, you were more curious than most. You challenged me in that almost sneaky way of yours."

She feigned shock.

"Yes, sneaky," I read her with a smile. "Anyway... it's not that I haven't had inquisitive people before. You were the first person in a long time whose curiosity I couldn't tuck away as a 'client inquiry.' And...I am attracted to you."

She already knew that but still seemed surprised. An adorable blush. "You don't often have clients you're attracted to?"

"No."

"Oh."

"So yeah...maybe that doesn't make you my 'best client.' But it does make you my most dangerous one."

"I wouldn't hurt a fly."

"I know that, Dr. DoLittle."

A smile.

"Well," Angela took a bit of her dessert. "Alright."

There were no more words that wouldn't make things awkward again, so we enjoyed the rest of our meals and chatted about the mundane until she asked: "So, 'just lunch...' How's that working out for you?" A genuine smile warmed on her face.

"Just fine." I giggled.

Our time wound down to a close.

"Hey, do you need a ride home, by the way? I remember you once saying you hate driving."

"Good memory. I don't even have a car! And no, I'm fine. I have a full-time submissive waiting outside."

She nearly choked. Half-shock half-entertained. "You have a WHAT?"

I repeated myself. "But that's a topic for another day. To answer your earlier question more honestly. "Lunch is harder than a session. In there, I know the rules."

8

STAY

"So, you just said it just like that?" Jules asked, pulling away from the curb. She knew from the girlishness in my energy that something was different about this lunch.

"Yeah. It just spilled out. I wasn't gonna lie."

"Of course you weren't." Her tone sounded warm. Almost proud. "I see how you prepare for her. It's different."

"You're not shocked?" I glanced at her, surprised.

"Goddess, please." Jules let out a belly laugh. "I can see it in how you choose your clothes those days…the specific music. You don't do that for clients. You do that for a crush."

I went silent and gazed out the window. The city blurred. Turns out my pet had been my most perceptive witness.

"So," Jules added, her voice gentle. "What did she say when you told her about me?"

"She was speechless. Confused. Shocked. But not in a negative way. I didn't go into details."

"Do you think she could handle it?"

"We're not even close to that mattering right now," I put my hand on her thigh.

Jules dropped her palm to mine and caressed the top before refocusing on the road. The subject was closed. My touch was the period at the end of the sentence.

By the time we got back to my place, Jules and I fell into an entangled nap on the couch. It started with her massaging my feet while we passed a single joint—my request—to unwind. Hours later, I woke up and decided to reward her with a meal. Jules had been a faithful sub for almost a year and a half now. Always seamless. Always of service.

"Broccoli and cheddar or sweet potato and corn chowder?" I offered her.

"Broccoli, thank you."

I expected her to choose that but wondered to see if she'd deviate for once. "The usual. Of course."

I paired the soup with a perfect piece of fish and seasonal vegetables, prepping everything to plate in under an hour. Ladling the bisk into a heavy, glazed bowl we had brought back from Salvador, Bahia, I placed it before her. It was the kind that sat perfectly in the palm of your hand so you could feel its warmth and solidity.

She smiled. It came from one of our first trips together. "I remember this," she said. "From the market with all the street art and live drummers." Jules traced her thumb over the ridge near the base. "The vendor wrapped it in old newspaper."

"And you held it the whole flight home so it wouldn't break."

She shrugged. "It felt important."

"It was." I took my seat. "It is." I nursed my wine, the bowl memory triggering an earlier one. "I still remember the first time I saw you at that munch. Observing while sipping a soda when everyone else downed shots and tried to impress."

Jules cringed a little. "I had no idea what I was doing. Maybe just trying to make friends. Be a part of the community."

"Yes, you did. You were assessing. So was I."

"Well, yeah. I was."

"Me too." I held her gaze. "I think you wanted a role with clear walls. I wanted someone who wouldn't try to put locks on me."

"Think we both exposed ourselves for a bit?" She took a bite of her fish.

"Absolutely."

Her cringe was gone. "You wanted someone who would understand that the structure *is* the freedom."

I set my fork down. "Plus, you never chased me."

"What?"

"We saw each other for a few weeks in a row. You showed up. You stayed. But you didn't reach for me like you were afraid I'd disappear."

Jules thought for a moment. "I didn't know I was allowed to do that."

"That's the difference," I told her. "You are not a bottomless pit of need like most of my clients."

She grunted. “I know.”

We continued chatting about everything from those early days leading up to that evening, and eventually Jules cleaned up the mess I made in the kitchen. But I didn’t want to sleep alone that night. Didn’t want a cool side of my bed.

“Stay...” I told her softly and pulled her closer to me. “I want you to fuck me tonight.”

9

DEEPER THIS TIME

I had no time to dwell on my feelings for Angela over the next six weeks. Duty called. It yanked me out of state first, then, out of the country. I journeyed to Spokane for a teaching gig. Then to Arizona for a high-profile retreat before heading to Colombia for a personal healing trip in the cloud forest. Landscapes. Plants. Medicines. Freedom. I craved the escape. Spring had bloomed and so did my familiar, itchy restlessness.

While I was away, however, I did maintain contact with Angela, Jules, and those keeping my business on autopilot in my absence. Angela remained just as busy wither her life. But she did find time to text me: *"I've been thinking. I want to keep seeing you...as a client. Once a month. And I'll keep paying. I need the container. I think you do, too."*

I understood why she chose that path. If the roles were reversed, I would, too. It was the right thing to do to avoid a mess. Still, her decision stung. Singed, actually. I found myself looking forward to seeing her again more than I should have. In the meantime, I had a steady stream of clients and group workshops upon my return. The latter often brought in groups of at least fifteen. And each time, I hoped Angela would slink through the door. She didn't.

Until the class on Solo Sex Enhancement.

Dressed in all black with tresses flowing from under her wide-brimmed hat, she glided in looking every bit of the beautiful tomboy I'd glimpsed when I first met her. *Why this class? Why now?* I wondered. But didn't question. I greeted her with a hug like every other student that came in—held it a little longer though. Enjoyed her perfume.

Our eyes locked several times over the next hour. Once when I mentioned using a mirror to know what you look like down there in different states of arousal, and again when I talked about CBD lube, shrooms and various toys to enhance your experience.

"I want you all to stop hiding your desire and start celebrating it, unapologetically."

She smirked. Licked her lips. Arrested my gaze. From the combination of my statements and the recall of our shared body heat in sessions, I stifled a shudder.

No one else noticed.

Angela didn't linger after. She floated out just as easily as she had coasted in, though she offered a quick wave. The next day, she booked a Tantric Massage for the end of the week. My whole body tingled when I saw the registration come through. *She's back.*

This time, I realized just how much I fussed over my clothes the day of. Yes, I rotated fresh oils in and fidgeted with my playlists. Put even fresher towels in the client bathroom and new slippers that looked more her size. *Vanilla bean soap today*, I thought, and caught myself.

"Damn it. Jules was right," I chuckled. It was obvious as hell to anyone looking. And...Jules was there. Upstairs.

She came down. "I know she'll be here soon, so I'll take off," Jules yawned like she'd rather stay in my bed. We'd done nothing but cuddle that morning, but she was having the kind of week that meant she never wanted the nuzzles to end. But I had work to do.

"Thank you."

Hugs. Then, departure.

THE SPACE between Jules leaving and Angela arriving was an electric quiet. I stood in the middle of the room with my skin still buzzing from the memory of Jules' warmth and the imminent promise of Angela's heat. The air felt thin. I couldn't tell if I should raise humidity or just wait to see what Angela's presence would do with it.

Soon—six minutes later, not that I was counting—Angela showed up.

"It's good to see you!" She beamed.

"Likewise. Come on in."

She stepped out of her shoes and tossed her jacket on the nearby coat hook. We took longer to get into full-bodied touch than usual. Sharing fresh juice. Nibbling on veggie snacks. Chatting. Petting. Joking. She asked questions. I answered honestly. We showered and I kissed her shoulders after a cloud of soap bubbles slid off it. I couldn't help it.

Angela had inched her body closer into mine the moment we stepped in. "Cold," she said she was.

As the room clouded with steam and desire. I caressed her body with eager yet restrained hands. The ridge of her collar bones. Her neck. Her chest. Her breasts.

She moaned, turning to face me. Angela broke the ritual this time. Now, face to face...nipples to nipples...I felt her breath float down on my lips. My hands dropped to her waist. She mirrored me, cautiously putting her hands on mine, thumbing her soapy fingers against my hip bone while leaning in to kiss my cheeks, my neck. Angela then pulled me in for a complete and warm embrace.

The hypnotic sounds of the water hitting her back and the shower floor entranced me. And in that moment, I felt safe. For a split second, *I* felt held. My shoulders dropped. The air was sweet.

Angela nipped at my earlobe then breathed, "Can we go in the room now?"

I nodded a slippery yes with my face pressed against hers.

THE MASSAGE WAS FOCUSED that day—on her clit. After I toweled Angela off and she lay on her back. I took advantage of her already being warmed up. Giving long strokes to her shoulders and limbs before focusing on her abdomen. Swirling rubs. Delicate caresses. Then I moved to her quads. Fingertip kisses. Nails dragged against soft skin.

"I think today might be better on the floor," I told her, deciding in the instant. "There," I nodded to a pile of pillows.

"Okay."

I splayed several fresh towels over the pillow spray to keep the purity of the moment and then kneeled. I extended my hand. "Please."

She took it and sank down with me.

I put Angela between my legs facing away from me. "Are you comfortable?" I whispered, pulling her into the heat of my core. Belly and breasts against her back.

"Very much..." She inched back, her ass close enough to me that the wetness between my legs could kiss it.

"Oof." She felt it. Backed up more, with a slight arch this time.

"Yes..." I whispered. Eyes closed. Submerging into...us.

This.

Specific.

Moment.

I could sense Angela smiling and biting her bottom lip though I couldn't see it. With my chin buried in the crook of her neck, I gently slid my hands down her arms to her hips. Caressing. Softly squeezing.

I brought my index and middle fingers to her pussy and applied pressure to her clit. She quivered. Feeling the tenderness of her slick skin coat the grooves of my fingertips, I started moving them in circles while still pressing down. Slow. So...incredibly slowly...I rubbed...her clit.

Angela purred, her upper body falling in sync with the firm rhythm of my hands. I pressed in deeper when my fingers hit the top of the circle, a little less at the bottom. Every now and then, I'd add a fast middle finger pulse to the bottom before swiping it up and down at length. She started dripping.

Angela began grinding against me, sinking into pleasure. She placed her hands on my legs, sometimes rubbing, other times clutching. I palmed her pussy like a kiss. Cupping it and cornering the warmth as she pulsed and engorged.

"This feels so good," she moaned, tossing her head back towards me. "So good..." Her voice was mellifluous.

"Mm hm..." I used my other hand to graze her nipples, thumbing her areolas with a feather-light connection. "All you have to do is breathe. I have the rest."

Angela's skin dimpled awake. I still had one hand teasing her clit in one direction while my other rubbed her nipple in the other. It was a twist on mirroring to send her body into a frenzy. Pressure. Just a little. I squeezed her nipple with my left hand while pressing down on her clit with my right. Switched hands then again, to do the same on her other breast.

Her legs shook. Her back collapsed into my chest. I held her close. Kissed the length of her neck and groaned to add vibration to yet another part of her skin. Intentionally. Lovingly. She tasted like nirvana. Angela whimpered, pooling more under my touch. She grabbed my legs again. Her nails dug into my skin. I didn't mind.

"You are so incredible..." I breathed while hoisting her at the hips and tugging her as close to me as possible. I moved her legs, so they draped over mine like two overlapping Vs. Then I opened her up as much as possible. Wide. I wanted her scent to fill the room. I wanted her essence to completely wet the towels. I also needed the air to help me pace her by drying her just...a little. Tempo. Regulation. It was important.

She'd need it to withstand an hour of dedication and receiving.

I enclosed Angela with my left arm while my right hand slowly went back to rubbing her clit and caressing her belly. Putting pressure on her clit with two fingers while a third slipped inside. "Oh fuck..." the words slipped out in a whimper. Angela was a downpour. There was not enough air to slow this flood.

She trembled. So did I. Circular motions. Pressure. Penetration. I found my rhythm and her body danced to it perfectly. Her moans deepened. I knew she was more sensitive when spread so far open. I could feel it in how much bigger she was down there. How much more she rained down on my hand.

"Fetlynne..." she breathed.

"Yes?" By now I had a slow gyration going against her ass. My own clit throbbed against the crease of it.

"Don't stop. *Please*...don't—"

I sped up but with intention. Gradually. Consistently. Carefully. I maintained a pace that would keep her on edge. A steady flow of hedonistic indulgence while I bit her shoulders. My left hand made its way to her chest against, but above her breasts and on her sternum and heart area. I held.

Angela surprised me by placing one of her hands on top of mine. We tuned in to her heartbeat. It banged. Her breath was jagged as she gyrated, grinded, and bucked against me. Then, she pushed my hand to the base of her neck.

More.

More.

Around her neck.

"Are you sure?" I whispered.

Yes. She nodded. She wanted me to choke her. She wanted a little more aggression. More tension. Not knowing how much pressure was too much, I erred on the side of caution and applied the bare minimum. She mewled and relinquished all control. Her body was fluid. Her breathing sped up. I leaned back more to brace us both. *Inside.* I slipped my fingers back in since she enjoyed that so much. Finding that beautiful spongy g-spot texture I rubbed. I rubbed. I rubbed.

"Mmhm. Mmhm. Mmmm. Deeper. Please," she begged. "Deepeerrr..." Her voiced damned near shrilled the last plea out.

Hell yes! Giving was beautiful. I relished this just as much as she did. Only when Angela moved as if the intensity might be too much did I slowly pull out and swipe up with those same sticky fingers. There was no rush to orgasm. She knew this by now. Suspended in bliss was the goal, and we were soaring through a silken sky with no memory of harsh ground.

She breathed. Enjoying the reprieve despite being ravenous for a release. Angela swayed her neck to one side and looked at me with the most beautiful whiskey brown eyes. I kissed her forehead, tasting the tiny salt beads of sweat on her skin. I held her...and I sighed. Such pleasure had to be prolonged.

"I don't even know what to say," she squirmed. "I want more but I also love this pause."

"Your body already told me that before you even had the thought to vocalize it."

She rolled her eyes playfully and smiled. Angela pulled her legs closed and squeezed them together. Mirroring her, I pretzeled mine over hers then wrapped both my arms around her. A perfect envelope and love letter to controlled sexual energy.

The room was thick with it.

Heat.

Scent.

Sweat.

The squelch wet flesh when either of us made any move...it was the beautiful swish of well-lubricated skin. I hugged her tighter. Closed my eyes. Descended into the shoreless ocean of our pleasure...

An array of emotions fell over us in the quiet. But before long, I felt her squirming again. Wanting more. I was actually a little tired by now, my energy more expended on pleasing her than expected, but I didn't let on. I pivoted.

"Come here," I whispered, gently peeling her off me. "Let's get you wiped down. I need to make sure I don't leave you sticky." I rose first, my knees protesting a little bit. Then, I offered her my hand.

"Whew." Angela was unsteady.

I extended my other hand. She took it. "Easy now. Use my weight." I braced myself to allow for her pulling up against me until we were both standing.

She wavered. The room skewed with a second wave of spent energy passing between us before righting itself. I then led her back to the table where I wiped her down with warm cloths. Cleaning the oils. Cleaning the wetness. Cleaning our sweat.

It's hard to describe the joy I got from tending to her. She was so willing to let go with me that I felt a remarkable responsibility to handle her with the greatest care. Angela wasn't a needy client, but she had needs unseen. Barely vocalized. I could hear and read them with every response she gave to my touch. And that unworded conversation between our energies gave me something though I couldn't describe it. I just knew I needed it too. I kissed her temples. The tops of her hands.

"I hope you enjoyed today," I told her.

"I did." She sighed in a mixture of satisfaction and want, incredibly soft spoken. "Thank you."

By the time she left, the equilibrium between us had settled back to normal. With a lingering embrace and not-so-casual, "see you next month," she ambled out of my front door.

A silence. An exhale. Every part of our unworded conversation vibrated in me. I stood in the foyer, still in my post-session robe with the scent of her clinging to its silk. I was still savoring the quiet and pulse in my body when a key turned the lock.

Jules let herself in, a bouquet of flowers in her arms. "Hey, Goddess, I picked up some—" She stopped the moment she saw my state. I needed time. She instinctively grew quiet.

Eyes closed, I reveled in the memory of Angela's imprint on my skin. In my chest.

That's when the doorbell rang.

I knew before I opened it. Not sure why, but I did. Angela stood there with a small apologetic smile on her face. "My earrings," she said, her eyes flicking past me to where Jules stood, holding the blooms. Then back to me.

My mouth fell open a little. Jules looked at me. I looked back at her. Angela stood witness then spoke. "Sorry." She shrank.

"No, it's fine…" I took a quick breath. "I'll go get them." I turned, toward the hall with a quick stride. I couldn't ask Jules to retrieve the jewelry. That would have been a command, and a command in front of Angela felt obscene. I didn't want Jules to serve in that moment. I wanted her presence to be the fact that it already was.

As I walked towards the back room, I felt the weight of two gazes on my back: one curious and soft—Angela, one observant and still—Jules.

"Um, hi. I'm Jules," I heard.

Then a beat before. "Angela."

Awkward silence.

I found the earrings on the side table. I closed my hand around them to feel traces of our warmth still on their metal. When I returned, nothing had moved. Jules hadn't offered Angela a seat. Angela hadn't stepped fully inside. They were two statues in my museum, waiting for the curator to return.

"Here you go." I placed them into Angela's palm. My fingers brushed her skin. It was still flushed.

"Thank you," she smiled at me. "And um…nice…nice meeting you," she told Jules.

And then she ducked out. I glanced at Jules. Jules looked at me. We had survived the breach. My world was still intact. I was sure of it.

10

UNDERTOW

Things didn't turn out as awkward as they could have after the unexpected triangle moment. Jules thought the visual of both of us looked hot. She was turned on. Such an unpredictable little pet. Angela, on the other hand, respected my private life. She did eventually ask for confirmation of who she thought she'd met.

"Was that the submissive who was waiting in the parking lot that day, or...?"

"Yes, it was."

"Oh. Okay."

A silence. The line was dense with unasked questions.

"Hey," I broke the hush before it could thicken any further. "Want to do something normal? No session, just...hit the BeltLine or the High Museum?"

She thought for a moment. "I think so. A bit busy this week but I can do next Friday. Does that work for you?"

"It sure does." I answered without thinking. Without even checking my calendar. "BeltLine or High?"

"High. At...one o'clock?" she suggested. "At the entrance?"

"Perfect, I'll see you then," I responded automatically, then dropped the call. My mind was already prepping for an online class I was scheduled to teach. Both of us had forgotten, or abandoned, her request to only see me for paid sessions.

IN THE BUOYANT, overconfident days that followed, I decided to structure my time even more rigorously. If I could manage this—the sessions, Jules, and Angela in a new orbit—then I could master anything. I was in flow. Handling it all.

But a familiar tightness in my left shoulder kept sabotaging me. From years of massage work and my more recent time back in the gym and pool, it had become a more persistent ache. Sometimes feeling like a pinched nerve. Even CBD salves weren't easing it. So, I did the responsible thing and booked a physio assessment. A one-off for maintenance. I entered it into my calendar. I also took a reprieve from client work, having my assistant reschedule most of my touch sessions so I could give my body the break it was begging for.

I spent the time studying, researching massage schools—never too experienced for new techniques—reading for pleasure, eating for pleasure, and spending time with Jules, mostly-platonic friends and even a little bit with family. I'd generally had my phone off to enjoy being present. By the time my physiotherapy appointment rolled around I was eager to get the tension yanked out. It was not, however, a pleasurable experience. Laser therapy, aggressive heat and cold treatments, deep tissue work and even a little fire cupping work. I grinned through the pain and wished with all my might that it would end soon. Finally, the session climaxed with a precise, brutal manipulation of the joint—a sharp pop that sent a lightning bolt of relief and nausea through my system.

"Geez!"

For a full minute afterward, the world consisted only of the roaring in my ears and the empty space where the pain had been. I was grateful, even if out of it for a second. I wobbled out of the clinic with my body slowly becoming realigned. Jules was waiting at the curb, windshield wipers flinging away rain. I heard her unlock the doors before jumping out to escort me with an umbrella.

"Thank you." I appreciated her attention to detail. Once in the passenger seat, I felt content and relieved. The pain was gone.

It wasn't until we were five blocks away, the city a wet blur outside the window, that a gnarling wrongness pierced the haze.

Friday.

The museum.

One o'clock.

Angela.

My phone, silent in my purse, had three missed calls and two unread texts. The first, sent at 1:15 PM, read: *Hey, running late?*

"No, no, no, no, no. Shit, shit, shit!"

"What's wrong?" Jules panicked.

I didn't respond. I glanced at the time. 2:33. "Fuck, fuck, fuck!" I slammed my fist against my knee. Rain pelted down outside.

"What, what, what?" Jules pressed.

"Angela. We were supposed to meet up at the High over an hour ago. I completely forgot!"

Jules looked worried for me, her face contorting.

Pain was back. In my head this time. Maybe even my heart. I fumbled for my phone, my thumbs slick and stupid. I called.

Ring.

Ring.

Ring.

Voicemail. "You've reached Dr. Angela Gre—" I hung up. Called again.

Ring.

Ring.

Ring.

Voicemail. The same serene, professional recording. I hung up. A third time.

Ring.

Ring.

A click. A beat of dead air. Then, her voice. It was strung too tight. "Fetlynne."

"Angela. My God. I am so sorry. I was at a physio appointment, my shoulder, I lost track of—"

"I waited." Her words were too soft, almost swallowed. "For half-an-hour."

"Ang—"

A deflated exhale. "I called. I... I was starting to think

something had happened." A shaky breath. "Then I went in. Just stopped looking at the door."

Her concern over me was a knife-twist. She hadn't just been stood up; she'd been worried. Jules slowed to a stop at a traffic light. She glanced at me with second-hand ache. Though not on speaker, the call was still loud enough for her to hear Angela's side. I felt horrible. Like a failure. The rain started coming down hard again, loudly banging against the car.

"It's fine," Angela's voice cut through. "I was already there, so figured I'd see the exhibit. It was...it was really good," she tried playing it cool.

"It's not fine. Angela, I...there's no excuse. I forgot, and I should have called. I'm so sorry. Are you still—"

"No. I'm at work." A sound in the background—a cage door clicking shut, the distant bark of a dog. "I have to go."

"Wait," I pleaded awkwardly.

A long silence.

"I really am sorry. I'm bad at this," I confessed. "I apologize!"

She huffed. "Okay," she finally sighed, the word heavy with resignation. "Okay, Fetlynne."

"Can I make this right, please? Tonight, I'll come to you, wherever you are—"

"No." She sounded exhausted. "Don't. I can't process any grand gestures today. I have a surgery in ten minutes."

I drew a quick breath and puffed it out. "I understand. Well..." My left leg bounced anxiously. "When you're ready, *if* you're ready, the offer stands. No pressure." I ran a hand over my head. Flung it back into the headrest.

"Yeah," she whispered. I'll call you." Angela drew a boundary. "I really need to go now."

The line went dead.

SHE DIDN'T REACH out for four days. Ninety-six hours. By then, I'd spent enough time thinking to realize where I went wrong and knew exactly how to explain myself when I got the chance. Otherwise, I had to move on and refocus on work. I couldn't cancel clients two weeks in a row. But something in me had changed. I was still able to be a shelter for others under my care, but something had definitely unraveled. I missed Angela.

I wanted to call her but knew I needed to give her space. I wanted to hug her but knew my touch might be the last thing she wanted right now. I didn't know, actually, about that last part. I hoped it weren't true because that would mean I made her despise the very thing that made her feel safe with me. *God damn it!* But she called...on a Tuesday afternoon, an incoming notification with her beautiful face finally pulsed on my screen.

I answered on the second ring, afraid to seem too needy. "Hey."

"Hey..." A breath. I could hear her settling into the weight of the call. "I've been thinking."

"I've been thinking, too." My throat was tight.

"I—I need to understand," she stumbled. "Was it your shoulder, or was it me?"

The question was a gut-punch. No metaphor. No softening. No nothing, just direct, and it stung. God, I guess I really did teach her to communicate courageously.

"It was my system." I told her the truth before a cowardly lie could form. "My system failed. It treats people like appointments. And you...you stopped being an appointment the moment we first shared lunch together. Even moreso the moment I asked you to the museum. Hell, since the kiss in Panama! My system doesn't have a category for that. It—"

"A *category*," she repeated. Her tone was unreadable. Maybe...*incredulous*? "What category do I fall into now?"

"I don't know." The admission was nerve-wracking. "There isn't one. That's the—"

"Stop, Fetlynne. Please." Her voice sliced through with finality. "Stop talking about your mental filing system because you didn't fail a 'category,' you failed a *person*. Just tell me. Was I important to you? Or was I just interesting...a new...shiny toy?"

Ugggh. I hated being pressed, but I clearly needed to be. Angela didn't deserve bullshit from me. My carefully built explanation crumbled. "You were gravitational pull, Angela. You were the current that made me forget I built a dam. And I'm so sorry I sucked you under when it broke." I paused.

"Can we switch to video?" She filled the gap. "I need to see you."

"Yeah. Sure. Of course." I acquiesced.

Angela was in casual clothes. No scrubs. She sat at a bench in what looked like one of her favorite, "day-off" spots: a state park. A peaceful lake was behind here, and there were no other audible voices.

"Where are you?" I took a chance at a normal question.

"Red Top Mountain," she murmured.

A state park. I *did* know her outside of our sessions. At least a little. "I've never been."

"It's calming."

Awkward silence.

"So...you were saying?" She didn't let me off the hook. "That you didn't purposely ghost me?"

"No! I promise. I *swear*! And you were not just 'interesting' or 'new'," I caught myself. "Okay, maybe in the beginning. But not now. You're not a novelty. You're a gravity," I admitted. "Angela, look...this is all my fault. I knew going deeper with you was dangerous waters, but I was so damned proud of how well I could swim that I got caught in my own current. I lost sight of you. I risked getting personal with a client knowing it was a horrible idea, and I ended up hurting us both. And for that, I'm deeply sorry. I'm not perfect. Far from it."

"I know you're not perfect, Fetlynne. I knew you were a fantasy. That was never the point." Her eyes glistened.

"I can be more than a fantasy. I can be real. It's just—" My breath hitched, a physical stutter in my chest. "I—"

"You are worth the trouble." She silenced me. "That's what makes this whole thing so hard." Angela glanced away from the camera.

Her words unclenched something in my belly. My body loosened. I almost smiled. She looked back up. Her eyes, too, were a bit softer. Deeper. Drilling into mine.

"I appreciate that. I hope I get the chance to prove I can be less trouble," The flirt was a thin rope over a steep drop. I really didn't know what else to do.

Angela rolled her eyes, a smile fighting its way free. “Maybe.” The word was inaudible but I read her lips. At least I hoped that’s what she said.

I hated this part. The clean-up. The apology tour. The accountability for my inevitable missteps and revelation of being a goddess with flaws. Without her magical aura. On the rare times this has happened, I could manage it with charm or distance. This was unusual though. This was Angela. And I wanted more with her. The latter admission made my heart somersault in my ribcage.

“Maybe is enough. I’ll take a maybe,” I responded honestly.

“Okay,” she nodded. “I’m think I’m gonna go now. But uh…I’ll talk you another time.” She stood up. Stretched. Eager to be present in her world filled with nature and beauty.

“Alright. Enjoy,” I sighed. “And Angela?”

“Yeah?”

“Thank you for your grace.”

“You’re welcome.”

The screen died.

The shadow of Angela’s words *worth the trouble* passed over me. She valued me, and I’d devalued her. But I’d try not to make that mistake again. She was too singular. She hadn’t even been scared off by Jules. About the possibility of others. About *me* the person, not the practitioner. And her steadiness in the face of it all wasn’t the shock of a novice. It was the calm of someone who understood that hearts aren’t simple, divided things.

Angela might have been new to lots of the experiences I

gave her, but she was not new to being with multiple partners, and that's what intrigued me even more. She hadn't been repelled by the ugly flaws beneath my perfect practitioner's veneer. That was a warm light. I wanted to bask in it. But I had to get my shit together. I never wanted to see sad eyes on her ever again.

My phone stayed dark, inert. I didn't expect a text. I had used up my allotment of Angela's generosity for the day, maybe for the season. A familiar restlessness crawled up my spine—to move, to do, or to cleanse or clear something with a ritual—but I repressed it. For once, I just sat. There was nothing to do but wait in the quiet and hope for the chance to prove I could be more than trouble.

The End

WETTER THIS TIME

1

WORTH THE TROUBLE

ANGELA

I dropped my phone onto the table like it was hot. My dog, Mr. Pickles, had been gnawing at a raw hide at my feet during the entire call with Fetlynne. He released it when I shifted to get up. Lifted his head and tilted it to the side. The pooch was upbeat and ready to play, oblivious to my ruffled emotional state.

Across the lake, pines stood in apathetic rows. The water was so clear and calm, it held a flawless, upside-down copy of the sky. A postcard view. Until a fish twisted up in a theatrical wiggle before splattering back down, creating a multitude of floating rings on the surface. I wanted to throw a rock into the middle of it. Wanted to kick up fallen leaves. I wanted to sit back down and press my face into my palms and cry.

You are worth the trouble.

I'd said it. It was the truth. But now I had to figure out what to do with a woman who believed in sacred touch and full presence but couldn't remember a goddamn lunch date.

A woman who apologized like she was reading from a holy text yet kept a full-time submissive in her driver's seat. A woman who looked at me like I was a masterpiece, then left me out in the pouring rain.

I knew better than to fall for Fetlynne. Knew better than to become addicted to her. But still...I did. Stupid. Dumb as hell. Stupid as fuck! Damn it!

Mr. Pickles howled softly, a primal sound in his throat. He was ready to chase a ball or run. He was always ready to romp. I wasn't. Not right now.

I looked at his eager, stupid, perfect face. "Fine," I muttered, picking up a stick and hurling it near the shore of the lake. Snorts and all, he gleefully launched after the wood. As he trotted back with it clamped in his jaws, my mind finally snapped free from the loop it was spinning around Fetlynne. It shifted into its default setting: research mode.

I had given her shit about putting me in a "category," but what *was* the protocol here? Do I remain a client after this? Because I didn't want to walk away. What exactly were the rules with someone who had a "full-time submissive"? Jules could live with her for all I knew. Was that a red flag or benefit?

The truth was, I was *not* looking for a deep relationship right anyway. I was happily single and enjoyed my freedom. *But I* could *enjoy a regular lover without heavy strings attached...*

I thought about it.

My lips twisted, brows furrowed—it sounded unnecessarily complicated.

I shot a glance backwards to check on my bag on the

warm bench. I *could* dial Precious to ask about non-traditional relationships, but hers ended terribly and the last thing I needed was a second-hand fear or even judgement on the merits of nonmonogamy. I kept thinking.

Mr. Pickles dropped the sopping branch at my feet, spraying my legs with lake water. He panted up at me, utterly certain of the next move. I envied him and grasped the stick again. I had questions. I needed a neutral voice. But for now, the only answer I had was another throw. *Swoosh!*

Fuck me.

MY PUP SCRAMBLED the moment I heaved him out of my car onto the sloped driveway. He beelined across the sprawling front yard to the front door while I followed at a slower pace. I paused for a second on the flagstone path, looking at the brick face of my home. Solid. 1958. Right in the middle of Capitol View Manor with a huge pecan tree that was definitely older than me. The giant picture window in the living room peeked back at me, the evening light turning it into a dark mirror. I could see the outline of my bookshelves inside, filled with novels, nature guides, and civil rights history texts.

"Hey, Doc!" A neighbor's friendly greeting rang through.

"Hey, Nika!" I smiled back. Nika served as a city worker who was also big on community. Always volunteering. Always looking out, but not in that prying neighbor kind of way. Just good people. "How are you today?" I asked. Though I'd been in my house for nine years, Nika had been on the block even longer.

"Can't complain. Organizing the block cookout for next month. You're on the list for your potato salad, you know."

"Sounds good to me. I'm happy to chip in."

Smiles. Waves goodbye.

I slipped inside in through the front door, tossed my keys in a ceramic bowl on a table in the foyer. *Clink*. Mr. Pickles' paws tick-tacked on the hardwood floors as he made his rounds—checking is food bowl - empty, his water bowl - full, before flopping down with a grunt on a rug in the living room.

I dropped my bag on the kitchen table. It was a big, scarred oak thing, that I'd bought off Facebook Marketplace from a guy who couldn't wait to be rid of it. I loved its textured surface. And for the years I'd had it, it held a history of physical mail, takeout containers from long nights on-call, and a thousand morning cups of coffee where my biggest decision was how much sugar to use.

I scanned the space, cursing my delay in hiring a new house cleaning service. The tables had a thin layer of dust. The dishes needed washing. And I had laundry to fold. *God damn it*. I wanted to plop on the couch but knew I needed to tidy up. Aiming for a compromise, I hoisted my bag and hung it where it belonged. I then took a swig of fresh water from the fridge and popped a few Doritos before pushing myself to start cleaning.

I grabbed another cup and filled it from the tap. The peace lily on the counter was practically bowing from lack of hydration; its poor leaves dull with dust. A good plant mama I was not, but I poured water until the soil soaked it all up and darkened with life. Better.

I can be more than a fantasy. Fetlynne's words landed on me like a wild seed. The question wasn't whether it would grow, but what it would become, and if I had the space for it.

"I don't even know what this is," I mumbled while loading the dishwasher. Plate, fork, glass. My rhythm was automatic. Scrape, rinse, slot. Scrape, rinse, slot.

In the monotony of domestic work, my mind drifted back to the lake. To Fetlynne's face on the screen, looking more exposed than I'd ever seen her. To her gorgeous, gorgeous cheekbones and hopeful eyes.

Focus, Angela.

I flung a detergent pod in the dishwasher, closed its door and started the cleanse cycle. As my hands worked, more questions began piling up in my head.

What does Jules actually do? Is she like a... live-in assistant? A girlfriend?

Is this a relationship, or is it a job for her?

If it's **not** *a job... what might* I *become?*

The questions hovered as I scrubbed the counters and swept the floor. But the answers felt messy. I didn't have the right vocabulary. Didn't know how deep into Fetlynne's forestland I'd ventured and what paths were safe.

"What the hell is a full-time submissive dynamic?" I took a break before mopping. Reached for my phone. I typed it into a search bar. Querying Fetlynne's actual name felt like a violation. Borderline stalker. Instead, I chose to learn more about her world.

A flood of personal blogs, badly written articles—and some good—plus deeply kinky definitions came up as results. This is when I learned the shorthand "D/s." When I discovered a realm of contracts, rules, negotiated protocols, and punishments. Distinctions between ethical power and surrender. The more I scrolled, the more my lips pressed together. The more I rubbed my head and crumpled my brows. One article called it a "conscious dance with our shadows."

I wheezed a little. I was no stranger to adult "lifestyle" choices. I'd done a few parties. Had a few threesomes and an orgy or two. The memory was a quilt of warm skin and polite negotiation, a far cry from the doctrinal texts on my screen. This was different. This wasn't just sex. This didn't even have to *include* sex.

On one hand, it was inherently fascinating. On the other, it sounded like a mission statement for a cult. My eyes skimmed another line: "The power exchanged is a gift, not a theft."

I stopped scrolling. That one landed differently. I thought of Jules' calm in the foyer. Her lack of defensiveness over Fetlynne and curiosity about me. The specific way she'd held flowers, whom I'd assumed were for Fetlynne—not servile, but sure. Like it was habitual.

Maybe it wasn't a job? Maybe it was a genuine relationship?

I closed the browser. The definitions didn't fit the women I'd seen, but I shouldn't have been surprised. It was like my research into "erotic mummification." In Fetlynne's universe, the reality was the opposite of everything online.

Hell…

A loud snort from Mr. Pickles jolted me from the screen. Right. The floor. I hauled myself up, my ankles cracking as I pushed up from the chair. I prepared to mop the kitchen before ordering takeout. *Just call her.*

Absolutely not. My mind was at war with itself as I polished the tiles to a sparkling shine. I had no idea how long the brawl would last or who would win. Or did I? A sneaky smile taunted me, but I suppressed it. I already knew.

Done and finally exhausted, I eyed a magnet holding my one of my favorite takeout menus to the fridge—the Jamaican spot that never skimped on the scotch bonnets or the sweet plantains. It was next to an adorable puppy picture of Mr. Pickles, who was now whimpering again. His legs twitched. The Frenchie was chasing a dream squirrel, no doubt. His wants were pure and immediate. Food, walk, belly rub, sleep. I envied the hell out of him. But envy was a useless diagnosis. I put the mop away and washed my hands. It was time for a different kind of cleaning.

2

PROS & CONS

Hours later, I tapped on the small brass lamp on my nightstand. The overhead light was too harsh. After eating and doing another round of cleaning to get the bathrooms, I was exhausted. Definitely hiring someone else for domestic work soon. A warm shower and firm mattress beneath me were the perfect ensemble to sooth away the day's fatigue. *Fetlynne's touch would be* ***amazing*** *right now*. I could almost feel her lips on my neck, her fingertips tracing every bone in my hand, kissing the top curves of my feet and even my toes. *Damn...*

I missed her. Wanted her.

Being alone in bed was also a combination to unlock. I sat propped up against the tufted headboard with a cool pillow against my neck, knowing I needed to unlock the one thing I couldn't clean: the Fetlynne itch.

"Grrrr." I felt like fucking animal without it. Maybe a rabid one. "Oh, God..." I mumbled and shook my head. I couldn't do anything but laugh at myself and the predicament I walked into with eyes wide open.

My house was finally still, and the only sound was a faint whistle from the wind against my windowpane. Mr. Pickles took his spot just outside of my door in his own lush dog mansion —he snored too much to sleep in the room with me. Like he had a damned job.

My phone glowed on the comforter beside my thigh. I debated picking it up but opted for a notebook and pen instead. I couldn't take any bright screens this late at night, especially after I'd already drawn my blackout curtains. Atop the fresh page, I jotted down:

What do I actually want from Fetlynne? A fling? A dynamic? Just clarity? Because I couldn't keep lying to myself that I was even considering walking away from her. I wasn't. *Clarity first. Then...I don't know. Let's just start with that*, I scribbled. *There's no need to rush anyway. She liked me. I liked her. We could just enjoy that.* I stopped. Thought for a moment. *Easier said than done*, I admitted to the page. *But doable.*

I thought back to the vulnerability she let slip out on our last call. The hug that she, too, needed when we were in Panama. The moments when she was not covered in a goddess mystique but revealed to be an actual, flawed woman—just like me. Just like everyone else. I put down my pen and paper. Glanced at the altar she'd encouraged me to create for myself. A smile. A ripple of a memory of her holding me while feeding me grapes and blueberries in our earliest sessions. The way her fingertips threaded through my hair and massaged my scalp...the smolder of her gaze locking on to mine as she'd licked her fingertips just after pulling them out of me during a deeper session.

"Oof." I squeezed my legs together.

Fuck.

It brought back aftershocks of her holding me from behind while fingering me. Jesus. I shuddered. My breathing sped up. I caught myself. Swallowed. Controlled my air intake to bring it back down to an even pace. Hell, I'd even learned that from her too. "Fucking woman is the type to have you howling at the moon!" I mumbled, grabbing my note pad again. The nerd in me couldn't help but make a damn list.

PROS of staying and engaging:

- *The touch. The unparalleled, soul-expanding touch.*
- *The fascination. She is the most compelling person I have ever met.*
- *The potential. For what? Unknown. But it feels like a lifetime gift.*
- *She sees me. Not just the vet. Not just the dork. The curious, desiring woman.*

CONS of staying and engaging:

- *The categories. I am not just an appointment.*
- *Her "system". It failed once. It will fail again.*
- *The third person. Jules is not a concept; she is a fact. And there might be a fourth or fifth.*
- *The emotional tax from learning the rules of a new world.*

PROS of walking away:

- *Peace. Quiet. Predictable days (eventually, after I shed her imprint).*
- *My dignity. No more getting stood up like a lame.*
- *My sanity. No more decoding texts from a deity.*

CONS of walking away:

- *The regret. The permanent wondering of* ***what if?***
- *The loss. Of her touch. Of our discoveries. Of* ***her.***
- *The admitting that I was afraid of complexity.*
- *The silence. The specific silence where her adoration used to be.*

I stared at the list. The pros for leaving were sane, solid, mature. The cons for leaving felt like a series of small, painful deaths. My eyelids grew heavy. My lungs expanded in the quiet, leading to an open-mouthed huff. And my will to fight my deepest desires simply quit. It was time to go to bed. I'd call her this week. There. Decision made.

Mr. Pickle's yellow school bus pulled up promptly at 7 am the next morning, and he lunged through the door the moment I opened it. Still young enough to revel the ruckus and roar of doggy daycare, he couldn't get enough of attending. As for myself, my first task of the day was mediating a territorial dispute between my clinic's resident cat and our new automatic litter robot. She hissed and clawed and damned near began sparring with it. The feline *hated* it, and we had to relocate the robot to the back with the boarding animals. The cat, a sleek tabby named Shantrell—I hadn't named her—now paraded through the hallway like her personal victory lap, tail held high. She'd won.

The rest of my day unfolded as uneventful and routine. No put downs, thank God, and no life-threatening emergencies. And I went straight the gym afterwards to work my legs and back. A little bit of abs, too. Right after my shower, hair still secured under a shower cap, I'd pinged Fetlynne: *So, about you being "more than a fantasy." I'd like to schedule a test of that hypothesis. Your availability?*

I chucked the phone in my gym bag and soon swaggered out. The day was overcast, muggy and typical of early summer in Atlanta. I made a pit stop to grab potatoes, a few sweet onions and relish. More eggs, mayo and bacon just in case I was running low. Next week was the community cookout for my block, and I, for some reason, I deemed it was a good idea to volunteer to contribute. Not that I didn't want to, but I'd just realized how much work that would be at scale. I could do it though—as long as I didn't leave everything to be done on one day—hence the produce shopping now. Besides, the trip gave me an excuse to indulge in a fancy mango lassi from the Indian café next door. It was the perfect drink to savor on a day where the devil himself asked for a fan.

I unloaded the groceries and neatly put them away. Pantry. Fridge. Cupboards. I swapped my post-gym outfit for a soft shorts and tank. With leftover Jamaican food from the night before, I was set. *Bzzt. Bzzt.*

Fetlynne: *A hypothesis test? I like your methodology. How about Thursday after 7. My place or do you want home-field advantage?*

I blushed. I could that see she was still typing so I held off on responding.

Fetlynne: *Or, do you want neutral ground? I will travel for you.*

Big smile. I bit: *Neutral ground feels like a business meeting. And your place is...saturated with too many beautiful distractions. Let's start with my living room. See you Thursday. I'll text the address.*

A tremble of anticipation. A flash of waiting in the rain. My nervous system was confused, but I hoped for a nice second try. My house. My vibe. Besides, if she meant what she'd said, then it was time for her to come to me.

I didn't know if I was nervous or excited about Fetlynne wading out of her fantasy into my reality. Logic insisted it was the right move, but logic crumbled into a trickier question: what if my world was too ordinary to her?

My bookshelves held veterinary texts and nature guides, civil rights photography books, modern art paperbacks, and novels by Tananarive Due and Octavia Butler. My walls held prints of the Jackson Street Bridge skyline of Atlanta and a salient photograph of a dew-covered spiderweb that I'd taken in Savannah. What would this practicality say to a woman who built temples? Who radiated fantasy and sensuality?

I strolled over to the large window in my living room. Peered out at the pecan tree. A tiny bluejay landed on one of its branches amid the humid dusk. It was an adorable scratch of color that lingered just long enough to tilt its head, peck, and then fly off again. *No need to dwell,* I decided. I grabbed my phone again: *1267...* I started typing my address.

There. Sent. Thursday would come. And she would hopefully come. The silence in the house after the whoosh of the text felt electric. I stood in it for a moment, then went to feed the dog.

3

THURSDAY ALREADY?

Fetlynne arrived on my doorstep at 6:59 pm. A scent cloud of jasmine, shea butter, and sea salt encircled her as she stood there smiling, already tempting. I didn't see a car. Didn't even hear a door slam before my doorbell rang.

"Right on time." I grinned.

"Angela," She spoke deliberately. Eyes locked. "I promised I wouldn't make you wait." Her voice and gaze made me feel like I was the only person in the universe.

My belly was a tumble of butterflies. My heart leaped. "Thank you." I tried to ground my breathing. It had been less than five seconds, and I already felt the Fetlynne effect. "Please," I stepped aside. "Come in."

Fetlynne wore a mint-green romper with a single gold bracelet and dusted gold earrings with pink pearl accents. She leaned more femme than androgynous tonight, and I was pulled in by her presence. She'd shaved her head again, too. Hair gone. Cheek bones popping. Light makeup and beautiful lashes. This woman was a siren's tide, and I had no idea if I'd drown in her current.

"I didn't realize you lived less than 15 minutes away. Twelve, actually."

"Yeah, we're very, *very* close to each other."

"In more ways than one," she murmured, standing a few feet away from me.

Normally, we'd be in her foyer and already in an embrace by now. But things had shifted. There were no established rituals in my home. In fact, Mr. Pickles was down the hall behind a baby gate because I'd forgotten to ask if she had a fear of dogs. Though he wreaked havoc on random packages and chew toys, he didn't have a violent streak with people. Still, I was hyperaware that you never knew what phobias people might have.

"I um..." she started. "I brought you something." Fetlynne reached in her purse and withdrew her hand, cupping something smooth. "A grounding piece," she continued, opening her palm to reveal a river stone. "For your space...or your pocket." She handed it to me. Her hand was cool and dry.

"Wow." It was so thoughtful. So... specific to me. To us. I brushed it over then closed my fingers around it, feeling how silky it was from God knows how many years of water running over it. The stone was solid and surprisingly heavy.

"I hope you like it." Her voice was lower in my home than it ever was at her place. Fetlynne crossed her arms, then uncrossed them and let them fall. Nerves. I recognized the jumpiness.

"I do. Yes, of course I do! I was just stunned at how

considerate it was. Thank you," I smiled, clutching the rock. I liked how it felt in my hands.

She shrugged. Smiled a little.

"Come on in," I waved her deeper into my home.

Just then, a sudden indignant scrap-scuffle-thump against the baby gate, followed by a noise that was less a bark and more a bronchial "Hnnnork!"

Fetlynne's shoulders jumped, but her face broke into a genuine, startled grin. "That," she said, the tension in her posture dissolving into something like relief, "was the most offended sound I've ever heard."

"*That* is Mr. Pickles. He lacks subtlety. And patience." I slid the gifted stone in my pocket.

"Mr. Pickles?"

Arf! Another, quieter whuff-grunt of protest.

"Goofy story. The name just stuck. He's five and too it's too late to change it now." I shook my head. "You don't mind dogs?" I asked, focusing on her

"Only the boring ones." She was already looking past me down the hall. Curious. "He sounds opinionated." Between the nugget in my pocket and Pickles' protest—the ice I was needlessly nervous about quickly shattered.

"Precisely," I giggled. "A stubborn French bulldog is all."

Leave him locked up or let him roam? The question bungee jumped and retracted in my mind. I needed to decide quickly so we could settle in. The former meant listening to him whine and grunt for however long she was there, not to mention caging him in *his* house. The latter was inviting a whirlwind of snorts, barks, and ankle investigations. *Let him out.*

"One sec, I'll let him come say hello," I moved to unlatch the baby gate. Freeing Mr. Pickles was freeing a menace, so I braced.

To my surprise, however, he did not burst forth. He moped out with lazy inquisitiveness, immediately dawdling towards Fetlynne's legs. She stood perfectly still, letting him conduct his audit. She'd already slipped off her shoes. *Pretty toes. Fresh polish.*

"He's confirming you're not a threat," I announced, watching her watch him.

"Or cataloguing my flaws," she quipped. A soft smile played on her lips as he finally finished with a conclusive snort and sat, leaning his weight against her leg. "I think I passed." She crouched down to give him a small scratch behind his ears.

Mr. Pickles threw his head back dramatically. "I think you did, too. Come on, let's..." I grinned and gestured toward the living room. "Can I get you something? Water? Tea? I have wine, but that feels..." I paused.

"Like too much too soon?" she offered, straightening up. "Water is perfect."

In the kitchen while filling two glasses, I listened to the easygoing pad of her feet as she ambled around, the soft thud of Mr. Pickles sauntering after her. I turned to see Fetlynne standing at the large window. She eyeballed my backyard. Her stare followed the slope down towards my firepit.

"It's so peaceful," she vocalized, not turning around. "Like a private park. It's perfect for you."

"Thank you."

I brought the glasses in. She took hers with a nod of gratitude. Then, the moment hung—where to sit? My L-shaped sofa was wide. I chose a corner of the sectional. After the briefest pause, she took the other leg, turning slightly to face me.

Mr. Pickles circled once, twice, on the rug between us, then settled with a huff. He chose the sofa base, resting on Fetlynne's toes. Damn. The dog already picked a side. I took a sip of water. She did the same. Her eyes never left my face. The pleasantries were a burned-off mist. The air was clear now, and terribly still.

Silence stretched like caramel over a candied apple. Our eyes deadlocked on one another. Holding. Breathing. Three seconds. Maybe four. She leaned forward. I scooted towards her an inch. Sighing. The feet between us felt like a gulf. But the quiet felt more like an assessment than discomfort. We were reading each other's energy in this new space, the ghost of every touch in her studio pacing between us. My thumb found the stone in my pocket, its smoothness a comfort.

Fetlynne's gaze finally dropped to her hands, then at the dog on her feet, then back at me. "You asked me here for clarity." Her voice sounded more like old times in her parlor. "So… Ask me the first question. The real one. I'm an open book, Angela. And I hope you're interested enough to want to read every page."

"Okay." I took the first punt, grateful for her taking the lead. "What does *she* get from it—Jules? What does she get from giving you that kind of control?"

Fetlynne exhaled and put her glass on a coaster. "She gets certainty. Relief from surrendering the weight of endless choices. She also gets care she in a way she hadn't had before."

"I think I get that," I mumbled. "But when you say 'full-time,' do you mean she lives with you? Is it a job? I'm just trying to get a handle on this."

Fetlynne chuckled. "It's definitely not a job, and it's not literally 24/7. No, she doesn't live with me, but she does have a key. 'Full-time' in this sense is just a distinction from those who lean more kink or keep submission to solely to the bedroom."

I pressed the heel of my hand into forehead. Dragged in a mouthful of air through my mouth. "But you do sleep together. Is she your girlfriend?"

"Sometimes. Yes. And no, she's not."

"Are there others?"

"Not really. I mean, I have connections. Intimate, but part-time. No traditional partners or relationship. Honestly, I spend most of my time alone, Angela. The partnerships I do have are very customized. Infrequent. Don't even live in the city."

"I see. So, it's not relationships you dislike. It's... the script."

"Correct. I dislike the default. The assumption that love has to be possessive. And that curiosity is betrayal or considered a lack of love for others. It's not true. And I am too old and don't have the energy to argue with a paradigm that feels so small." She ran a finger over her left eyebrow, parting it with her nail. "It's easier to design the life I want. Less cruel than trying to fit cages built for other creatures."

"Mmm," I grunted, soaking up her words. "I get it. Decisive of you, too. I've never really thought about curating my life that."

"Believe it or not, I was actually married once.

I gasped.

She relaxed. "It lasted 29 days. Had it annulled before the mistake could cause any more damage."

"You said it like you just changed a pair of shoes!"

She chuckled. Shrugged with both palms up. "At least I didn't drag it out! My life isn't compatible with those structures."

"Okay. Ok, ok, ok, ok." I rushed through the words. "You designed a life that protects you. I respect that. And it's honest. I really admire that. But what does it want now—from *me*?"

She looked me in my eyes. "All I know is my heart hurt when I realized I'd let you down. That my days were off kilter during the hours we were out of touch. Crazy, because I usually only see you once a month and am just fine. But that's because I knew...or at least relied on the knowledge that you'd always come back." She moved closer to me. Mr. Pickles popped up from his daze then laid back down.

My body warmed, but I leaned back slightly. "What does that mean right now, though, Fetlynne? Does your life have room for someone who isn't looking for a cage, but isn't sure she can handle you?"

Fetlynne didn't smile. She swallowed. Her forehead wrinkled just the slightest and her eyes transmuted into dark pools. "It means that I want to take you on a proper date. And another. I want to cook for you in my kitchen and see what makes you laugh when you're not on my table. It means... I have feelings for you, Angela. A specific, resonant frequency that only your presence seems to tune in me." She paused. "I hear it in your voice. I feel it in your gaze. I sense it in your touch." Her speech tremored. She went silent. A slight melancholy settled in the space between her words.

I was at a loss, but I tried. "That all sounds amazing. So beautiful. But...but I don't know if I can—"

"You don't have to *do* anything. Honestly, I would love for you to feel free to just *be* from moment to moment." Her voice was gentle but firm. "You wondered if you could 'handle' me. You can't. I don't think anyone should handle another person. But you can choose to trust or not trust my actions." She came right next to me now. Touched my hand. The air pulsated with her proximity, her sweet scent. "The last time, I failed that trust. I own that. So now, I'm asking for the chance to build it back—one date, one conversation, one moment of undivided attention at a time. I'm hungry for that."

Her words made me squirm. Made me turn my body more towards her so our knees touched. "Fet..."

"Yes?"

"Do you mean that?" I fiddled with the stone in my pocked. Pulled it out and placed it on the table in front of us so it sat like the tip of a triangle.

"I do." Her voice was a bare whisper now, a confession in the quiet room. "I want to discover the depth and the joy with you." She came closer. We shared warmth. "Without so much damn space between us." Fetlynne let the words hang. Then, with a slowness that felt like a question, her fingertips grazed my shoulder—a point of contact so light it was almost ethereal. "That's the clarity I have tonight."

Before I could form a thought, her touch drifted into a feather-stroke along the underside of my jaw. The caress made my pulse drop. "I see." My words drifted out as air, not sound. The softness of Fetlynne's fingertips threatened to put me in a trance. Slowly, I reached for her hand and pulled it back down. It wasn't that I didn't want it. I just couldn't think with it present. My mind went completely white and my body went slack.

Her words were a poetic dream. I wanted to wake up to them. To put them in my pillow and sleep with my head on them. But I was scared. What if I couldn't do this with falling too deeply in love? What if she broke me?

Fetlynne didn't touch me again. She let her hand remain where I'd placed it, but her gaze was soft. She scooted back a micro-inch. "You're holding your breath," she spoke. "It's okay. We can just sit here with the idea for a little while. It doesn't need an answer tonight. Just breathe. Please."

I exhaled. Stifled a nervous laugh. She'd seen right through me. "Sorry, I think...I think I need to change the air. And my mouth is suddenly very dry." I pushed myself up from the couch. "Earlier, I was going to offer wine earlier and thought better of it. But I'm rethinking. And, well...I have a firepit out back. It's a nice night. Would you like to see it?"

"Absolutely."

"Perfect. I can get it set up quickly. Wood's already chopped."

I pulled two textured Afghans from a nearby storage

bench and slipped a small vial of citronella in my pocket then I set them by the back door. It should have been past the hour where mosquitos ruined outdoor experiences, but I'd had in my mind to protect her shoulders and arms if we weren't. And of course, the fire and smoke would repel them.

"Red or white?" I perused my wine inventory in the kitchen.

"Surprise me." Fetlynne's smile was in her voice. She'd followed me. "But let me carry something. The blankets?"

"Sure, but..." I shook my head, debating. "Actually, just follow me. The good stuff's already down there. Come."

"And him?" She nodded.

Mr. Pickles had followed the herd. "He'll be fine. He has his own door and will follow if he wants to. Now, *come*."

I led her out the back exit, down the gentle slope to a tidy, shingled black shed tucked against the tree line. Purplish-blue hydrangeas bordered the outline of unit along with two barely visible speaker rocks. Unlocking the tiny cabin, I pushed the door open and reached in.

Soft golden light immediately bloomed to reveal a wooden jaguar sculpture on a small pedestal. A tightly woven, mud-brown rag rug carpeted the floor. And a low, woven-seagrass stool sat tucked in the corner. The room was just big enough for two people to comfortably stand inside. One wall held a perfectly stacked cord of dried oakwood. The scent was rich. Clean. Crisp. And a sleek 12-bottle wine cooler dominated the other wall. Above that, was a single rustic shelf with two crystal glasses, upside down. The last indigo shreds of the sky seeped through the room's sole window.

"Wow!"

"My sunset spot," I said, the confession leaving me in a rush. "I come down here to think. To have a good glass or two and listen to the owls. The wood's always dry." I opened the cooler, feeling the chill kiss my face. "So... red or white? I have a Gamay that's all rain and damp earth, or a Viognier that tastes like apricots and honey."

Fetlynne hadn't moved from the doorway. She still clutched the Afghans. Mouth slightly ajar, her gaze moved from the precise woodpile to the sculpture to my face, back to the glasses and wine. "I... I gotta be honest. I don't know *that* much about wines, but oh my."

"What?"

"You," she said, her voice thick with something like awe, "are a series of perfect, hidden rooms." She laughed in disbelief. "Apricots and honey? Would have never guessed you be a wine aficionada."

I smiled. A slight bite to my bottom lip. The night air stood still. The choice of beverage suddenly felt less important than the decision she was acknowledging: I had just shown her a very private, cherished heart of my world. "Just a little," I simpered.

"I'll take whatever you think is best," she told me. And while I got us set up at the nearby firepit, I felt the weight of her gaze on my back. Just as tangible as the Afghans she finally laid across the chairs.

4

APRICOTS AND HONEY

The fire had eaten its way down to a cradle of pulsating coals. I'd turned on a mushroom heat lamp above us. And our third glasses of wine sat half-forgotten on a small table. Fetlynne and I had talked ourselves out.

Mr. Pickles was a snoring lump in the shadows. The only sounds were the creek-sigh of the cooling wood, low instrumental R&B from the speaker rocks, and the thrum of my own blood in my ears. Forgiveness was a finished thing. The future was a shapeless mist. All that was left in the clear night was the undeniable fact of our two bodies sitting a careful twelve inches apart on a smooth log. That we shared warmth from the wool Afghans.

I stared into the embers until their patterns burned onto my retina. My right hand lay limp on the rough bark of the wood between us. Without thought, without a plan, I closed my eyes and drew a breath. I turned my grip over, so my palm lay open to the sky—a pale offering in the dim light. I wasn't asking her for anything. I was just... open.

I felt the exact moment she saw it. Opening my eyes to just thin slits, I watched Fetlynne deliberately...I mean like a slow, tectonic reorientation of her whole posture, turn toward me. She lifted her left hand from her lap and brought it across the baby canyon between us. She held it there, palm down, an inch above my open one.

I shivered out a high-pitched, open-mouthed breath.

Her heat spread against my skin. Distinct. Noiseless. It was a question in a language older than words. *Do you want this? Now? Like this?*

My body melted like candle wax. Shoulders relaxed. Stomach concaved. Head tipped forward and hanging low. My breath was a slow-building pant. Heart, a gallop. Every professional, and healing... devastating touch we'd ever shared swirled in that inch of air between our skin. The pressure of her hands on my back, the scratch of her scalp against my stomach, the careful tracing of my scars. The drip of my tears onto her thighs after submitting to her dominance. This was none of those. This was a blank page.

Trembling, I nudged my hand up. Simultaneously, she slowly...oh, so slowly, lowered hers. But she didn't clasp. Instead, Fetlynne let the back of her knuckles—the smooth, elegant ridges of them—graze the center of my palm.

A spark shot straight up my arm. A live wire. Her knuckles began to move in a faint, deliberate exploration. They traced the line of my lifeline, the mound of my Venus, the callus at the base of my thumb. She was reading me.

My fingers shook but I didn't close them. I let her read.

And then finally, our hands interlocked and a simultaneous moan escaped us. Palm squeezes, and me only slipping free to toss one more log in the pile before pulling her into my arms.

I'D NEVER KISSED someone in front of a roaring fire. I'd never held someone so tightly who wasn't the definite start of something monogamously romantic rather than a sensual experiment between two aware adults. I'd never felt my heart thud so hard toward a scary unknown while enjoy every wallop. Entangling with Fetlynne felt like being slowly drawn into the sky from the ocean. Magical. Warmer with each elevation towards the sun. All I could see were clouds. And though I knew soft water was beneath me, I also realized it could feel like concrete if I crashed back down too fast. I was scared shitless. But I didn't want to stop.

"You know..." I later teased when we finally started disassembling things. "It's been almost a year, and I still haven't orgasmed with you." *Why did I say that?*

Her eyes popped wide with a guilty smile that tumbled into belly-chuckle. We'd made out endlessly but were both still fully clothed.

"Because that's not the point of the work," she quipped, sliding our two wine glasses in my sink. We were back in the main house now.

"So, I'm still 'work' to you?" Drunk talk. The zesty words spilled out on their own. Messy.

"Absolutely not." She yanked me closer to her. Kissed me

again. Her kiss shifted, deepening, a hungry press that seamlessly drained my breath. She was serious now.

"Mmm..." I reciprocated. Stronger. More passion. No regrets or over thinking.

We kiss-walked and staggered over to my sofa. She fell backwards first. I crawled on top of her. Hands roving. Knees on the outside of her hips. Arms eventually sliding forward to slink down into a downward dog position. I kissed her chest, her stomach, her arms, with each peck bringing my back further up until I anchored over her on all fours, nails clawing into the sofa.

Fetlynne raked at me through glassy, tender eyes. Slow-motion blinks. And even slower, more subtle body waves. She let her head loll back and reached up to cradled mine with both hands. Closed her eyes again. She moaned.

Fetlynne caressed both my ears between her thumbs and index fingers.

The touch coaxed a soft exhale out of me. "Whew." In that instant, though, I wanted to stop *and* continue. Sudden nerves.

"What's wrong?" she breathed.

"Nothing." I couldn't hide anything from her.

"Liar."

I laughed. "I'm nervous."

"*What*? Why?"

I pushed up more, now towering over her. "Well, normally, I don't have too much performance anxiety, but this is different. This is *you*."

"This is *you*." She mocked me. "What is that supposed to mean?"

I looked at her like she was stupid.

Fetlynne burst out laughing. I mean, a deep, guttural laugh. "Come ooonnn, Angela. Don't be like that!"

I blinked.

"Okay. Fine. I get it." She inched up on her elbows. "Step one: stop thinking of it as a 'performance.' Step two: Understand I am *not* your bodyworker right now. I'm just a woman under you, wanting you." Slow blinks and licked lips. Yearning eyes. "Can you just meet me here?" Fetlynne's hips pulsed upwards as she grabbed me at my wrists.

"Yeah…" I relaxed. "I can." I smiled.

She pulled me down for an embrace. I had no time to retreat. My face found a sanctuary in the crook of her neck. I didn't just breathe, I *drank*. Her scent was layered terrain with top notes of jasmine and natural salt. Beneath that was a sub plain of shea butter. And woven through all of it now, was a draft of our evening…whispers of woodsmoke and cooled wine, the ozonic atmosphere of night air. *Heat*. The fire was in her pulse, and it enlivened me.

I inhaled through my nose, and through my mouth. Breath sometimes steady, sometimes not. Audibly. Hungrily. Deliberately—to focus sensation on one, single, spot. Closer, I inched closer. Drinking…and I felt the shift in her body before I heard the sound. A sharp, silent intake in her chest. Then a shudder of unraveling. Fetlynne's head fell to one side, exposing more throat. She whimpered. And her hands, which had been holding the curve of my waist, plummeted open. *Surrender*, a slow splay of it.

I paused, gently resting a hand on her solar plexus. "Do you want to go to my bedroom?"

"Mm hm." A soft, definitive nod against the cushion. *Yes.*

We untangled and I stood. "Come on." I offered a hand to pull her up. I led Fetlynne down the hall, past the closed door of my office, and to the entrance of my bedroom. I didn't turn on the main light. "Bathroom's through there," I told her, pointing to the en suite door. "I'll use the hall one. Meet you back here."

"Thank you."

I winked and blew her a kiss. No other words were needed.

In the guest bath, I moved on autopilot: water, mouth-wash, a glance in the mirror at the woman who was bringing *Fetlynne* to her bed. Back in my room, I drew the blackout curtains and killed all but one light.

The door to my bathroom opened. She stepped out, a striking contre-jour outlined by the warm light behind her. We faced each other in the hushed dark, and the air between us reset, crackling with fresh tension.

"Now I get to marvel at you."

A hair shorter than me and fully nude, I circled her. Running my fingers over the curve of her hips, the swell of her ass, until I faced her again and dragged my palms up the planes of her thighs and torso before pulling her in for another kiss. Against the door frame. Against the wall. To the center of the room. To the *other* side of the room where, for no reason but feeling, I cut the last light in the entire space—the one in the bathroom had already shut off from a timer.

The darkness was a velvet void without even the metronome of music.

Jagged breaths and smacking kisses. Murmurs, mumbles, grunts and groans. Footsteps stamping. Heartbeats hammering. All that was left was the tremorous truth of two bodies devouring each other in the dark.

We tumbled down on the bed, and I flipped her to be on all fours instead. Legs spread.

I kissed the arches of her feet first, slowly. She shuddered. Then her heels. Ankles. Up her calves and inside her thighs. She moaned. I kissed her ass, lingering. Caressing, biting, squeezing. I eased her down, and we rolled to one side. Face to face. Breathing. Kissing. Rubbing. Until I rotated her to her back and climbed on top.

A high-pitched "ah" trolled out of me when our dripping pussies *finally* made contact. Wet. Hot. Slippery. And stacked. We oozed into each other after my mount gave way to a grind on her at an angle. *Squish.*

Squish.

Squish.

We were scissoring. Gliding. Fetlynne grabbed me at my hips, her body thrusting upward to match my rhythm. We moved as one ocean. One current. A squelching dance of intense pressure and release. I used my fingers to open myself up more. To feel her clit against mine more. I waited a fucking year for this.

"Yesss…" Fetlynne sighed beneath me. So did she.

The sticky smack of her pussy bumping into mine made me speed up a little. Grunt and groan a little. I put my left hand on her right knee to steady myself and kept moving. Kept sliding. We continued until a sweat built up before I repositioned us, so she was on top.

Fetlynne put my legs up at ninety-degree angles and widened them just enough to wedge herself between them. On her knees—spread to an upside-down V—she began to pump and grind and fuck me. Long, strong, slow strokes that pressed her dripping wet pussy into mine.

It felt so good. It felt so good. It felt so GOOD.

The swish and swoosh and mini splashes of her wetness onto my flesh made me grab her head. Made me clutch the back of her neck. The room was still pitch black, but I could *feel* the unblinking intensity she'd have locked on me were it not. I could *feel* the strength of her want with each soaked thrust into me. And I could *feel* the sway of her body as she rolled her head—deeply into our session.

Soft moans over bed creaks.

"Angela..."

"Fet..."

I extended my legs. She laid down full missionary. The grind continued, but with her clasped in my arms now. With her face pressed into my neck. More gasps and groans. She bit me. She licked me. She kissed me. Fetlynne overwhelmed me in the most transfixing way. Eventually, we shifted and I pulled her onto my face. I wanted her to ride it.

Fetlynne did not flinch. She let go. Rode my face like a fucking champion. Slow at first to let me eat it, then fast to dominate. Slowed down again to let me lick it. Then bouncing on my tongue to rule and remind me who the fuck she was. I braced on the headboard. I held on to her hips, lapping her up with minimal breath. She was so turned on that her juices trickled down my cheeks. Dropped down my neck.

"Right there," she instructed. "Keep your tongue right. *There*," she commanded. And bounced and grinded on it until she screamed and shrieked in orgasm. *Yes!* I could hear her nails grate as she dug them into tufting of my headboard. Her body melted.

I gasped for air. Smacked her ass. Enjoyed the treacly glaze she left all over my lips and face.

Fetlynne eased off me, hard breathing into my chest. I held her. Sucking in more air of my own. *My God*...I didn't dare say it, but this woman! She inched in closer to me. Soft moaning in post orgasmic bliss. She used her index finger to quietly trace random patterns on my chest. She kissed me. Kissed me again.

With just a few more moments passing, we rolled over into spooning position with me being behind. But I rotated her fully on her stomach and climbed back on top. Spread her ass cheeks open enough for me to press my throbbing clit between them. The warmth was a pleasant jolt. And with no words, she arched up into me. Letting me tribb. Almost ten-thousand nerve endings rubbing in a hot wet hole. *I* lost it. Faster. Faster. Harder. Harder. I pumped. I banged. I thrust myself into Fetlynne until I reached an explosive climax with a slight gush into her.

"Ahh!" my voice squeaked, still tightly clutching her shoulders as ecstasy shot through me.

We both trembled and sighed. I collapsed. And for a moment, Fetlynne and I were nothing but a collection of satisfied moans. Eventually, I peeled myself off her and returned to my "big spoon" position, pulling her in and felt her take a deep, full-body sigh. Her muscles were liquid. She arched back into me and purred a little. Nuzzling into the pillow just a tad. I kissed her shoulder, thinking. Wondering. But before I could over-analyze, I found myself hearing the faintest, most delicate little snore I think I'd ever heard. Almost like a child's toy boat puttering across a path. *She fell asleep?* I froze.

Then, a smile. Huge smile. A helpless wave of tenderness nearly drowned me. The woman who commanded rooms and who curated touch like a renowned composer, was asleep in my bed, snoring. And in the next second, I decided to kiss her once more near her ear. "Good night," I whispered.

She became alert—a subtle stiffening and slight inhale as she located herself in the dark, in my arms. Then, with a surrendering murmur, Fetlynne wormed into my embrace. "Good night."

Carefully, so carefully, I pulled the sheet over us both. For once, I wasn't nervous with her at all.

5

THE CURVE OF HER

The AC kicked on in the basement. A slight rattle and mechanical yawn in the early morning hour. Friday. The coolness droned in for my morning shift. Awareness returned with the air-conditioning. The solid press of another body along my spine. A warm knee fitted behind mine. The smell—trace remnants of my bath soap mixed with sex—anchored in the thick air.

Fetlynne.

Behind me, she shifted in her sleep. A deep inhale stirred the hair at my nape. Her arm, slung heavy over my waist, pulled me back an inch into the curve of her. I lay still in the absolute dark with my heart beating a steady tock in the quiet. *Okay*, I thought. *Now what*?

Just as more thoughts came to mind and the first idiot bird began its serenade, I felt a kiss between my shoulder blades.

"Good morning," She was awake. Her left hand coasted

down to my breast for a delicate caress. One more gentle peck.

I smiled. Relaxed. "Hey..."

"What time does your morning require?"

I squeezed my eyes shut, then reopened them. "I have to be at work by 7:30."

A beat.

"Okay. Give me 12 minutes."

Incredibly precise. Fetlynne slinked out of bed and tiptoed into the bathroom. The loss of her warmth was immediate. Through the shut door, I heard the soft splash and shuffle of her washing her face and dressing. I sat up. Couldn't just lie there.

I flicked on the warmest light and tugged on a long t-shirt and soft sweatpants. Commando just for the moment, already hearing a soft jingle come from down the hall. Pitter-patter. Pitter-patter.

Fetlynne emerged shortly after, dressed and looking as put together as one could be the morning after. Pitter-patter. Pitter-patter. Mr. Pickles was ticking outside the door with morning excitement.

"He thinks it's walk time," I told her. My voice still husky with sleep. I opened the door gently, trying to curb his enthusiasm.

She braced, then I heard the rapid-fire investigative sniff of her ankles again. "Hey buddy," she whispered. "It's just me."

He gave a decisive woof and padded around us before squatting with his back to the door. A stubborn sentry.

"Coffee?" I offered.

"Sure, thank you."

We moseyed to the kitchen in a comic procession: Mr. Pickles leading, Fetlynne in the middle, me bringing up the rear. The predawn dark faded to a charcoal grey gradient at the windows. I went through the familiar ritual—grinding beans, the gurgle of the machine—while she faced the opposite direction, watching. Fetlynne peered into the front yard, admiring the pecan tree that was a deeper black against the lightening sky.

"That's a solid tree."

I handed her a mug. "It's a messy tree. But I like it."

"I might steal one on the way out," she giggled. "A souvenir." She sipped her coffee and briefly closed her eyes. "Mmm. This is good." When she opened them, she was looking directly at me. "I should call a car."

No Jules? A little reality unexpectedly bit me. Already.

As if reading my mind, she said, "It's better that way."

The sentence landed between us with the gentle finality of a period.

"You can… finish your coffee first."

She nodded. We drank in a silence that was a bit weighty with everything unsaid. Mr. Pickles, having deemed the excitement over, sighed and flopped onto his side. *Ruff!* With an attitudinal grunt. Fetlynne retrieved her phone and called an Uber. A minute later, it chimed, "Four minutes."

She set her half-finished mug in the sink. "I'll wait on the porch. I need the morning air."

I hadn't expected that. Didn't know what to do. Didn't know what to say. Fetlynne collected her things and made the too-short walk to the front door. The dream was ending.

Already. She turned, and I expected a kiss, a hug, something. But she reached out and gently tucked a stray curl behind my ear, her fingertips just brushing my temple. The touch was tremendous in its tenderness. My knees weakened.

"Thank you for your bedroom," she whispered. "For you."

Then, the quiet click of the door.

I stood in a stupor. The suede-like texture from her fingers lingered as I watched her crouch to grab a single pecan and pocket it before slipping into a car. Still mischievous. Still mysterious. Still enchanting. Still...delightfully debilitating. *That's a solid tree.* I heard her voice in my head. In the silence. I sensed her presence on my skin. The coffee was still warm in my hand, but I shivered.

Nails on hardwood. Mr. Pickles again. Shit. I glanced at a clock. I had one hour before I had to become Dr. Green. The treading began.

6

AND EVERYTHING BEFORE IT

At 7:34, I shifted my car into park and shouldered my way into my clinic's back door. It squealed and clicked shut behind me, muting the rush-hour hum. Fetlynne had been long gone and safely home, but I still managed to lollygag out of my house.

"Doc G! You're late." Lewis was decked out in graffiti dog patterned scrubs, grinning as he hefted a fifty-pound bag of litter onto his shoulder. The morning banter was on.

"By four minutes, you clock-watcher. I was admiring the sunrise."

"Sure you were." He disappeared into the kennel corridor.

The sterile air bit my nose—alcohol and bleach mixed with the wet-earth smell of kibble from the storage room.

"Morning, everybody!" I called out, marching into my office. My voice was a decibel too bright.

"Good morning, Dr. Green!" came the chorus from

various corners—Ashley at reception, the murmur of the techs in treatment.

The clack-clack of steel trays on stainless steel and the rising hiss on the autoclave wafted out of the surgery suite. Carl's shaved head appeared in the doorway. "Morning, boss. The spay schedule is on your desk. The 9:15 dental—you want pre-op bloods?"

"Always," I said, pausing. "And please add a clotting profile to the schnauzer's pre-op panel. Just being thorough."

"You got it."

I passed the treatment wall and heard a low whine from kennel three. The frantic scritch-scritch of claws on polyurethane. Buster, an old boarder, let out a wet, hacking cough. I kneeled down and tapped the grate. "Hey, buddy. Ashley will get you walked soon." His eyes were exhausted.

My office. I flicked the light switch. The fluorescent bulb buzzed to life. I dropped my bag and dug my hands into my pocket. For whatever reason, I'd brought the river stone from Fetlynne. Slowly rolled it around in my palm. It was smooth. Cool. Solid. But then I withdrew my hand as if it burned. The Post-it on my monitor glared back: "8:30 – Diabetic recheck, Cornelius. Owner anxious." in Ashley's loopy script. Right.

"Got it, got it, got it," I sang to myself.

The chatty Chihuahua. I took a steadying breath, focusing on my long list of tasks. But in the same instant, I felt the ghost of a warm perfectly knee fitted behind mine. *Mmmm.* A mini moan escaped me. *Focus!*

"Dooooc!" I spun to see Carl. "You didn't hear me?"

"No, what?"

"Needed to confirm which schnauzer because we've got two coming in."

"Oh. Gretchen. She's the 9:15 dental."

"Got it. You okay?"

"Yeah. I'm good. Didn't get much sleep, but I'm fine."

"Alrighty!" He shuffled off.

By 11:00 I'd wrapped up two minor surgeries. My hands knew the work, even if my mind wasn't completely in the room. As the day marched forward to noon, I had one more patient before my break. A routine exam with a geriatric labrador and it's too-nervous owner. It should have been quick. Should have been simple, but the dog's trusting collapse into me reminded me of a different kind of trust. Apricots and honey and an exposed throat. I suppressed a shudder.

Finally, I strode to my office and settled into my chair. Lunch.

As I mindlessly stared at patient records—seeing nothing—my phone rattled in my pocket. Fetlynne: *The pecan is on my altar. Thank you for the coffee, and for everything before it.*

My whole body jumped at the message, nervous system overriding thought. My eyes widened. Breath deepened. I gulped. Clenched my thighs. *Jesus. Shit!* I couldn't reply right then. Couldn't risk another flashback of her thighs squeezing against my cheeks. I pocketed my phone with the stone.

My altar. The words boomeranged. She'd placed a piece of my world into her sacred space. I smiled. Then shrank. Then stood so fast my chair wheeled back and hit the wall with a thump. "I gotta get some air," I announced to no one, striding past the front desk.

Outside, the Atlanta sun was a hammer. I leaned against the warm brick of the building, catching a tiny patch of shade. Seconds later, I pulled out my phone again. I needed someone to talk to later. But whom? I had no siblings. Would never talk to staff. Had reservations about my friends. I scrolled my contact list. No one. There was no one in the well-ordered grid of my life built for this... this ambiguous, breathtaking collision. I bumbled back inside. Folded my body back into my seat and ate quietly, alone.

The afternoon was a slow, precise torture. By 3:47, I was finally signing off on a discharge when Ashley popped her head in. "Doc G? You busting out early yesterday? You better be living it up this weekend. Got a little *sump'n-sump'n* lined up?" Her grin was all knowing mischief; the kind shared between Black women who've clocked a certain kind of distraction.

But the question landed like a key turning in a lock. It was the permission of being seen, however vaguely. My smile felt wobbly. Real. But bashful. "Now, you know I'm not answering that."

"Ha! You just did!"

I was in my car by 3:59. The engine purred to life, sealing me in a quiet, private pod. And I sat there with the AC blowing the weight of the entire day back into my face.

That night, I decided to call Precious. The only person I knew who had been in an open relationship. Though hers didn't last long, it was the only line I had. The phone rang once. Twice. I was already wound down from the day. Just waiting for the call to connect.

"Heeey, friend!" she answered giddily. "The hell's going on with you calling on a Friday night? Everything okay?"

"What's wrong with calling on a Friday night?"

"Girl, you never do it! What's up?"

"So...I don't remember where I left off, or what I told you. About the intimacy coach I was seeing."

"Not much to be honest. Just how much you were learning about yourself and how much fun you had in Panama."

Of course. I'd kept everything to the vest. "How much time do you have to talk tonight?"

"Shiiit...with a preamble like that, I have all night! Spill the deets, bitch, I ain't doing shit!" She cackled. Precious was always going to be Precious.

Her laugh was infectious. I ended up telling her everything—the canceled friend date, Fetlynne's confession, the research, the text, the invitation to my living room, the stone. But..." I hesitated.

"What?"

I held.

"Girl, Angie! What?"

"When I saw her again. Yesterday... it wasn't for a session."

A silence.

"She spent the night at my place, actually. It was incredible. Out of this fucking world, honestly. But...I don't know what this is and I'm nervous. And I—"

"Okay. But wait. Wait, wait, wait, wait, wait. Back up. The

mystic actually showed her hand? That's what you're telling me."

"Yes. She was honest about her feelings too."

"Mm. Okay," she paused. "That's new."

"I wasn't totally surprised. Our chemistry is insane. But now, I just... I don't know what this is."

"What did you *agree* it was?

"Nothing. I agreed to nothing. There was no pressure to agree or give her an answer to anything right now. In fact, it was the exact opposite. She left a wide-open space for me to walk into or leave, and I decided to do what felt right in that moment: stay. Enter. But I know what this is not and what it will never be," I explained. "That was clear long ago. She does not do traditional relationships. It's how her life is designed."

"And can you handle being in a non-traditional one?"

"I have no idea."

"Do you want to try?"

"I don't fucking know." A beat. "Yes. I do."

"Let me think," Precious exhaled. "So, you have a stunning, confusing, no-label thing with a woman who has a full-time sub. What do you need from it to feel sane? A weekly text? A monthly sleepover? You have to define your own rules, because she might not give you a playbook," Precious said. "I don't know. Maybe she will. But you should make your own, Ang. And you need to talk a *lot* more," she advised. "If there's one thing I learned about these kinds of set ups, is you will talk way more than you do in regular settings."

"Yeah, I can see that already."

"From what you've told me about her so far, though—

observant, patient, nurturing, and trustworthy to the best of her ability, with no intentions to hurt you—it might be worth a try," she said. "I could tell you to run as far away as possible because my ex did me dirty, but that wouldn't be fair to you. That was on *him.* Each person, each relationship is different. But whether it turns into a fucking mess or not is highly dependent on the intention of the people involved. And she doesn't sound like someone out there just trying to sleep with everybody she can."

"Not really a sex worker problem. Not one like her." Admitting her profession out loud made me wince.

"She's probably seen and heard enough to understand the gap between what people say and the fucking mess they really are. Because all of us are some kind of mess, chile. Even her."

I nodded. "Mm hm. I think she just wants to enjoy being together without typical pressures. And without feeling like she can't love anyone else."

"And how does that make you feel?"

"Hadn't thought about it much, really."

"You should. You better. Because shiiiiit...if she's as magical as you say she is, you *will* fall in love. And baby, love in a situation with no rules is just a fancy name for agony with better dick. Or kitty cat in this case," she giggled. "You need rules, Angie. You need even more clarity. You need to talk and not leave any gray areas."

I smiled. "You're right. I don't think that'll be a problem with her. She's excellent at communication. Verbal and non-verbal." Then, more to myself than Precious, I mumbled "She did break a boundary with me but—" I froze. *She also stood you up.* My mind jabbed me. To the head. To the ribs. On the chin. I felt flush. Felt unsteady. "I don't know," I finally spoke again. "I'll talk to her."

"Please do. This can either be beautiful and a great life experience—with you having freedom too—or it can be a slow torture where you're the only one bleeding," she paused, hesitated. Then she finished. "Because loving someone who's designed their life *not* to be possessed can be like trying to hug a beautiful knife." A little pain was still in Precious's voice.

"I hear you," I whispered. "I hear you."

"Yeah..." her voice trailed off before perking back up again. "And does Jasmine know about all of this? Should I keep my mouth shut, or..."

"Not much. Not about anything that recently happened and...yeah, I think I need to sit with this myself before I bring Jasmine into it."

"Say *less*." Precious' voice was all understanding. "Your business is your business. Just keep your eyes open."

"Yeah."

A beat.

"You gonna be okay, Angie?"

I puffed out a breath, a flash of the kiss before the fire playing behind my slow blink. "I have no idea, but I'm gonna try to be."

We wrapped the call with me thanking her and promising to get more clarity since the dynamic had changed again. That night I finally texted Fetlynne back: *I can still feel where your knee was. Can we talk?*

7

THE CONTAINER

"Pick a letter," Fetlynne's voice carried through my car speaker. "F or S."

I was halfway to her place, the Saturday evening sun warm on my left arm. "What? Why?"

"Humor me," she added. I could hear her smiling.

We were going to a drive-in movie theater. Her idea. I hadn't known Atlanta still had one. "It's a little gritty, but it can be fun," she'd confessed. "Haven't been in years. Now, pick a letter."

"Um..." I had no idea where this game was going, but I wanted to play. "S."

"Okay."

"Now what?"

"Now we see if S is really what you want."

I was still perplexed when I pulled up to her curb. She was waiting on the porch, a small cooler at her feet, mini backpack slung over her shoulder, and a smile like she held a delicious secret.

I'd worked half-day earlier, but it was a breeze. Much easier. Much softer. The talk with Precious was exactly what I'd needed. More than Fetlynne, or perhaps just in a different way, it pushed me to define what I actually wanted. What I required. And now we were heading to Starlight Theater almost an hour before the show started so we could settle in early.

"You look beautiful," she complimented after sliding into my passenger seat.

"So do you," I reciprocated.

A shared smile.

"Thanks for thinking of snacks. I hadn't even considered it."

"You're welcome. Figured we'd avoid the greasy French fries and lukewarm burgers—unless you were looking forward to those."

"Not at all," I chuckled. "I appreciate you thinking ahead."

The lot was mostly empty when we arrived. The giant screens still silent, revealing their sun-bleached skin against the dusky sky. Fetlynne directed me to a spot near the back. Under the skeletal branches of a large tree.

"Better sound, and we can recline without headlights in our eyes," she explained. Fetlynne was an expert of comfort even here.

I killed the engine and dropped us into a crunchy silence of cicadas, crickets and the trolling tires of other cars rolling in over gravel. The darkness felt illicitly private, a delightful microworld of our own.

I fidgeted with the radio dial to tune-in for the film while she popped open the cooler. An array of unexpected snacks was contained within. Somehow, she managed to arrange them all on the center console, making the best use of the cup holders.

"Let's get the libations sorted before the previews," she said. Her voice was a firm contrast to the staticky babbles springing from my speakers. Fetlynne handed me a cold glass bottle of brew, then a small dropper of orange bitters. "Your dosage?"

I reached for the dropper, feeling our fingers brush in the transfer. *Wham!* A memory of her riding my face in the dark. My breath skittered. Stomach dipped.

"Angela?"

"Just two," I told her, holding up two fingers.

She squeezed the drops into my cup and then hers. The ritual of it was unexpectedly intimate. A tiny, shared ceremony until... *mmm...oh fuck!....ahhhA* slithered through my mind. Deep breaths. Obscenities, wet slaps, and pitched moans from the night before crashed into each other as she poured the dark liquid over the bitters. The sweet aroma of it wafting up as we clinked metal cups.

"To being out of our usual habitats," she raised her drink.

"I'll toast to that."

The first sip was bitter. Bright. It cut the dusty evening air. On screen, trailers began flashing, painting her profile in fleeting colors. We had until the movie started to make small talk. Or we didn't.

"What's on your mind, darling?" She quizzed me. Her voice had a slight rasp. Fetlynne offered me a fresh cherry before I could answer.

Disarmed and enchanted by her feeding me, I tried my best. "I was just thinking..." I chewed. "That last night was absolutely incredible..."

"But..."

"I think I need more clarity?" My words came out more uncertain than I wanted them too.

She offered me almonds. "I know we'd need to talk more." Ate one herself. "Because situations like this with no guides often end in carnage. And I don't want that for us." A piece of dark chocolate next. She kept feeding me.

Us. The word warmed my entire body. I took a teeny sip of my brew. Relaxing. "I don't know what this is," I peered at her.

"It's fun. It's freedom. But it can be challenging."

"It's the last part I'm concerned about. Maybe the freedom too."

"We can start with free—"

"Well, wait," I cut her off. Thinking aloud. "Let me make sure I'm clear on what you want—me, Jules, and whoever else? Correct? And what you're offering—fascinating dates, earth-shaking sex..."

"My absolute honesty. My complete attention when we're together," she filled in. "And my best and most sincere attempts to never hurt you." She paused, hand trembling in her lap. She looked straight ahead to the movie screen. "Is that something you still want?" She glanced down. Then, slowly, too slowly, over and up at me with vulnerable eyes.

How the fuck could I ever say no to this? I couldn't speak.

She continued, a nervous bite to her bottom lip. "The request isn't 'be mine,' Angela. So much as it's 'be with me, in the space I can faithfully and beautifully maintain.'"

"What about me?"

"What do you mean?"

"Do you expect me to only see you?"

"Oh, God no!" A mixed emotion laugh erupted. She leaned more towards me with a smile. Her voice morphed into a neutral register. "I expect you to see other people. I *want* you to. And I'd never ask you not to." She took a sip of her brew. "Whatever happens between you and me...I want you to choose to stay because being with me is additive to your life, not because you feel you can't explore other options. That means you *should* see other people. Date. Discover. I am not, and cannot be, your everything. And I wouldn't want to be—nothing to do with you at all—but I wouldn't be able to sustain the pressure."

My flabbers were gasted. I had never spoken to anyone so honest in my entire life. "Hm," was all I could grunt quietly. A quick reel of her in my house replayed in my mind. Her interaction with Mr. Pickles. Her carrying the Afghans down to the firepit. Her coaching me out of my own self-consciousness and performance anxiety. Her actually drifting off to sleep instead of ducking out after sex. This was a woman who could have demanded exclusivity or ownership but offered liberation, and I was humbled by that. "Okay," I finally spoke up. "I see."

"How does that sound? How does that make you feel?" There was no eagerness or stress in her voice.

"Intrigued." I popped an almond in my mouth just to do something. Sipped my drink and just sat. Eyes forward. This was a lot. "I want this!" I blurted out.

Immediately, she giggled. My words came out with so much force it was comical. "I'm glad," she confessed. I sensed her own relief in the near darkness. "Because I want this, too, Angela. More than I've wanted anything complicated in a long time."

Butterflies.

The main feature film began. There were pictures, but no sound at first. Late-comers rolled in with blinding headlights. "Pretty sure we won't even be able to watch the first movie," Fetlynne said.

"I don't even remember what it is."

The sound crackled on. We reclined our seats, neither looking at the screen. The space between us had become charged with a new, giddy certainty. But the cooler and snacks on the console were a minor fortress between us.

"This is in the way," I said, my voice low.

"It is," she agreed. "But…" a spark flickered in her eyes. "The solution is in the back." A quick head nod behind us.

It wasn't even a question. With a single, synchronized and wordless move, we opened our doors. The interior lights flashed on, then off as we shut them again. They closed with a thud that rippled up my spine. Now enclosed in the deeper dark of my backseat, the world outside the windows felt miles away. There was nothing but trees behind us.

Her thoughtful spread of snacks sat half-eaten in the front—still there if we needed nourishment—but more of a live vestige from the conversation we'd just left behind.

"Come here." She reached for me.

I reached for her.

There was no more space, no more console, not a thing besides the soft give of the seat and the hard press of my body against hers. Fetlynne's fingers skimmed up my thigh, leaving heat and havoc in their wake. I kissed her with fierce tenderness that said everything I had no words for. A collision of relief and desire, tasting of bitters and promise, she hungrily kissed me back. Lots of tongue. Her teeth delicately tugging on my bottom lip.

I squirmed. Moaned. Melted. Slipped my hand under her shirt. Caressed her belly. The fan of her ribs. Leaned in closer. Kissed deeper. Light from the big screens played over our faces as every atom of my awareness sank into pleasure with her. Deep, deep pleasure. I felt the glide of her thumb over my knuckles, the shift of her body as she angled toward me. It tasted of cold brew and orange and the sweet, dark potential of the night ahead. It was slow, and deep, and a silent seal on the contract we'd just negotiated.

When we finally pulled apart, breathless, the world had narrowed to the front seat of my car. The movie was an irrelevant dream. A wash of random images and barely-there sound.

"So," she whispered, her forehead resting against mine, "about that letter S..." Fetlynne gently pulled one my hands in between her legs.

I felt a bulge. Startled. Smiled ridiculously. "WHAT IS THAT?" *Was this woman really wearing—*

"A strap," she bit her bottom look in a cocky swagger kind of way. "Technically a pack and play but whatever."

"Shit..." I lost my breath. Groped it. Gently squeezed. Felt my body swiftly lubricating. "Wh—what? Why? I mean?" I couldn't speak.

"Just testing. Just seeing how you'd react. I already know you like penetration." She spoke so matter-of-factly. "I had this in a drawer untouched. Got it at a sex convention months ago, but didn't have anyone to use it with."

"And you thought tonight was a good night to try?" I asked incredulously. My whole body wanted to laugh.

She shrugged like a naughty teenage boy. "Figured I'd take a risk. Worst case is you recoil and I make a fool of myself. We'd laugh about it later. But best case is that surprised and hungry look in your eyes right now. I know you want it—" She gyrated upwards.

Fucking right I did! I was climbing on top of her before she could finish speaking. I didn't even know what a pack and play was, but knew it was close enough to the dick I hadn't had in over a year. And I wanted to learn more. Right now. Fetlynne reached in her pants and quickly adjusted its position, so it was against her belly instead of packed down. Seeing the medium-brown tip of it against her skin is an image I never want to forget. Perfect color match. Cut. Firm.

The car fogged completely up. I rubbed her head. She held me at the waist, then slid her hand up my sides. We kissed. I felt the stiffness of her new addition at just the right angle for me to rub against it. Fetlynne moved her hands back down. Anchored them on my hips.

"I love the way you move. Damn." Save for last night, she was used to me on my back. Used to me being more passive.

"Yes..." she whispered, looking up at me while palming my ass.

"I wish I was wearing a skirt."

"Me, too," she giggled.

I mirrored. Cackling and slumping down into her neck. A quick kiss. For whatever reason, those last lines injected a vein of laughter to the moment.

"Angela, would you like to come back to my place?" she asked.

"Yes."

I couldn't have returned to the driver seat any faster. Ever carefree, Fetlynne took her time. She repacked most of the uneaten food back in the cooler and tidied up while I tried to figure out the best way to creep out of the lot without blinding people. She even slowed down enough to peel and feed me a lychee that she'd forgotten in her snack box delight.

"Mmm. That is really good." Tasted like a strawberry and sugar cane had a baby.

She winked.

"Let's get out of here!" I cackled.

Brake lights. I followed the low luminosity of red and eased out.

Back on the road, Fetlynne moved her hand towards my chin, but I intercepted, pulling it to my lips instead. We were only seven minutes from her house. I pressed a soft kiss on her wrist bone. Licked and nipped at her skin a little. Ran my tongue over the top of her hand. Eager to taste any part of her I could.

"If this thing was real, it would be a *lot* bigger right now," she laughed. "And leaking."

I dropped my right hand to her lap.

Shoved it in her pants and stroked it anyway. Excited, she gyrated. She reached over and squeezed the back of my neck. Grabbed a little bit of my hair so my head jerked back. "I am gonna to fuck you so good tonight."

8

IT WAS HER HANDS

We dropped everything in the foyer. Stumbled out of shoes and shuffled upstairs. Fetlynne led the way—pulling me by my hand one moment, by my shirt collar the next.

The room was dim. Foreign yet...hauntingly unfamiliar. But there was enough light to see each other. My eyes adjusted. Her personal space was shockingly simple, but one shelf held rows of small, clear jars filled with sand, soil, and tiny dried blossoms. Labels in her precise script: Puerto Escondido, Playa Morillo, Atlantic City, Puerto Rico. And among them, not in a jar but placed deliberately in front, the green pecan from my tree. Next to it, a river stone like the one she'd given me. She'd had its twin. I gasped. This was the room of a woman who collected places she'd left, and maybe pieces of people too. But here, now, were two pieces of *me* displayed. My throat tightened.

She shoved me onto the bed. Tore off her shirt. Refocused my attention and quickly showed me the gentleness was gone. I had zero problems with that. Fetlynne shed the last of her clothes. Her packer looked insanely realistic in the low light. She cupped and stroked it with her hands. Retrieved a bottle of lube. Played with it some more, watching me watch her. My pussy started aching with want. It had been too long.

Fetlynne climbed on top of me like a midnight jaguar. Her breath was a hot gust against my neck, ragged and rhythmic. My body shuddered, sinking into the sheets. Every shift of her hips was a deliberate, rolling wave. I watched her, my breath hitching at every turn. She bit my neck. Nipped at my cheeks. Kissed and pulled at my lips. She thumbed over my nipples. Squeezed them a little. She ran her palms up my inner thighs, testing me.

"Very wet."

"And very wanting," I whispered back.

"Yeah?"

"Yes. *Please*," I begged.

My hands found the hard wing of her shoulder blades, her muscles bunching and sliding under slick skin. She wedged my legs apart with her knees and slowly, watchfully, rubbed the tip of her dick against my clit. Up.

Down....

Up.

Down....

Around.

Tap. Tap. Tap. Tap.tap.tap.tap.tap.tap.tap. Ruuuuub.

Up.

Down...

She teased the head in. Pulled out. Rubbed my clit up and down. Again. She dipped the head in, a little deeper this time. Pulled out. Rubbed my clit in a circular motion.

"Mm hm," I whimpered. My nails dug into her back.

She pushed in.

"Ahhh...oh...*fuuuuck.*" My entire body rocked and expanded. Needing. Wanting. Accepting. Calling. The splish slosh sounds got louder as she sank into me. "This feels sooo goooood." I buckled. She could do whatever she wanted me. I needed this.

She worked the fuck out of her hips. Carving something distinctly Fetlynne inside of me. Eyes LOCKED. She barely blinked. In and out. In and out. She stroked me to a dripping, pulsating, throb while clutching my shoulders. "You like it?"

"Yes."

"Say it louder."

"Yes!"

Her body leaned more to one side. She used her knees to push me open more and then repositioned to slide in at an angle. Deeper. Wetter. More rhythmic. She rolled and twisted her hips and body. Fetlynne pushed and she drilled. Fast. Hard. Dominant. Owning. She rocked the bed. It was perfect. Almost too much.

"Uh uhn. Don't run, Angela. Use your words."

I opened my mouth but nothing came out.

She searched my eyes. Gave my left arm a soft caress, before saying, "I got you. You're safe with me." But she didn't let up. Fetlynne heated up the room.

She flipped me over and fucked me from behind. Dragged me to the edge of the bed and did it again. Hard.

Strong. Consistent. Building. She reached around the teased my swollen clit with her fingers. Slowed down.

"I wish you could see how beautiful you look. The way your ass just shakes when I'm fucking you. Damn, you're beautiful, Angela."

I moaned so, so loudly.

She slowed down.

Slowed down, slowed down, slowed...down... Fetlynne allowed me time to collapse and breathe. She held me. Catching her own breath as well. Then she repositioned us on the bed. On her back this time.

"I want to watch you ride. I *have* to see that again."

The request made me smile through the exhaustion. I nodded. Wordless. And then climbed on top of her in reverse so my ass was in her face and my eyes were on the wall ahead.

Slowly, at first, I gave her a show. Circular moves. Then a sultry, deliberate up and down...all the way up so she could see the dick pop out and then back down on it. Fetlynne spoke through gritted teeth. It was inaudible. She grabbed my ass. I slid back down on it. Faster now. Bouncing now. Getting my juices all over it and her legs now.

We moved in a shared, wordless cadence—the creak of the bed, the slap of skin, the choked-off gasps we couldn't swallow. I repositioned. Mounted while facing her now. She reached for my hips again. Clamored for my breasts. I closed my eyes. Steeped deep in pleasure now. I let go. I rode. I fell forward, bracing myself on her while still riding. Sweat dripped off me on to her. She pushed up into me. Dug deeper. Fetlynne fucked me from below, shaking me. Rattling me. Her stamina was otherworldly.

The air grew thick with the scent of us, of salt and brew. She drove us forward with a relentless rhythm. With endurance. Her unflinching gaze narrowed us to a frantic, perfect sync that tore out orgasms and raw screams. I was out of my mind in ecstasy. She huffed heavily. Juddering beneath me.

"Oh my God…" the words slipped out.

She heaved a breath. "He's not here."

"Mm hm." We laughed. I crumpled into her, not even remembering falling asleep.

I

Was

Done.

My nose twitched. I sniffed. Stirred. My eyes squeezed shut then peeled open. I squinted. Confused. I closed them again. Inhaled and recognized something buttery. Something honeyed, with a dark, nutty roast underneath. I opened my eyes again. Morning. It was morning.

I glanced around.

I was curled in a fetal position in a gigantic bed, tangled under weighted sheets. The near-blank wall. The shelf with sand and artifacts. *Fetlynne.* I remember now. I could smell her skin under the rich scent of browning butter and caramelizing sugar that wove up the stairs, a golden thread pulling at the hinge of my jaw. My mouth watered. An involuntary twinge.

The bedroom door was ajar. I passed through it.

The kitchen was warm. Well-lit by morning sun. I paused in the doorway. Fetlynne stood at the counter with her back to me. She was dressed in a soft grey Henley, drizzling something from a small saucepan in a slow, deliberate spiral over a golden, puffed bread. The aroma was divine.

But it wasn't the food I saw first. It was her *hands*. The absolute, unshaking steadiness of them. I knew that saucepan was heavy. The syrup was a thick, molten rope, but her wrist was fluid. She had total, unhurried control. This was the same focused exactness that had, hours ago, mapped pleasure across my skin. Seeing it now channeled into something as simple as syrup was beguiling. This was her in her purest state: creating beauty with unwavering attention.

The syrup pooled. She set the pan down with a soft *clink* and turned. A faint smile touched her lips, but her eyes were soft, open.

"I wondered when this would wake you," she blushed.

I stepped into the kitchen. "What is *that*?" I asked, nodding at the glorious, golden puff. The warmth and scent wrapped around me.

"Pain perdu," she said, a little French softly rolled off her tongue. "The lost bread. My grandmother's version. I gave it a little lift." A small, proud shrug touched her shoulders.

"It's stunning." *And so are you*, I didn't say.

"Please, sit." She gestured to the table and returned with two glasses of orange juice.

There are no words to describe the delight in my mouth

when I took the first bite. When I damn near licked the plate. Fetlynne could not have offered a more enticing morning after. We chatted. We laughed. We dreamed up a few dates. We revisited clarity and agreed some things. Others, we'd address when the timing made sense. I learned she spoke a little Spanish. A little French. Told her more about my love wine and the outdoors. For animals and for travel.

By the time I was gearing up to leave, I felt like my feet were off the ground. Fetlynne had me levitating. Hearing trumpets and choirs, and shit. I was seeing beautiful prisms in everything. Under spell, whether she called it witchcraft or not! Or, I was simply under the intoxicating peace of needs being fully met. But... that peace surely had an opposing twin. I just hoped it didn't show up any time soon.

9

NO PRESSURE

The next few weeks were the most delicious I'd had in years. Work was compassionate and fun. I journaled more. Cooked more—was ready for that neighborhood cookout after all—sang and dance for no reason more. I took Mr. Pickles up to Amicalola Falls State Park to sniff something new. To enjoy waterfalls and natural wonders with me.

I eased off the gas with Fetlynne to pace myself. She also had to get back to work anyway. I'd felt so energized after our time together that I got a bunch of old clothes donated and volunteered for a neighborhood clean-up. The sun was BRUTE that day, though. Hot enough to fry an egg on the sidewalk, probably. I had second thoughts the moment I stepped out of my car, but I stayed.

I'd tied my hair up, and my tank top was sticking to my back. Mr. Pickles was at doggy daycare for this exact reason. He could run amuck indoors while I, and others, hauled soggy carpet and collapsible metal garden carts from the Sandy Creek bed. Real glamorous stuff. My arms were burning, but in that good, honest way. I'd just wrestled a waterlogged metal utility bucket free when a slightly winded but warm voice cut through the grunts around me.

"Need a hand with the world's worst souvenir?"

I squinted up. A woman was on the bank above me, offering a gloved hand. She had a strong, capable build. Locs pulled in a ponytail through a faded trucker's cap.

"Actually, yes, because I think it's winning," I said, bracing my foot against the creek bank.

She climbed down, her boots stamping the mud with a slight splash. She didn't just take over; she matched my effort, finding a grip on the opposite side. "On three," she instructed. Her voice had a calm, carrying quality. And on three, we muscled it up the slick bank in one heave to dump it on the pile with a wet, final thud.

"Whew! Thank you!"

"You're quite welcome." Her smile was easy. "Hell of a grip you got there. You a mountain climber or something?"

"Hardly. But I sort of wrestle animals for a living?"

Her eyebrows shot up.

"A veterinarian," I assured her.

She nodded and chuckled. "Gotcha. My name is Alana," she added, sliding her glove back on. "I teach biology over at Carver High. And this," she nodded at the creek, "is my weekend classroom. Nothing like pulling a shopping cart out of a watershed to make the nitrogen cycle feel personal."

Nerd level 10. Noted.

Alana gestured to the now-clear stretch of bank we'd just

worked. "See that? Instant lab. Much better than a textbook. And the surprise teaching assistants," she said, glancing at me with a wry smile, "are notoriously strong." She smiled. A constellation of freckles decorated her nose and cheekbones.

It took me a second to see what she did there, but I admit it got a smile out of me. I went back to working. So did she. But soon, the cleanup was winding down. People were packing tools into trucks. Alana found me again and pulled a card from her back pocket—simple, matte, just her name, Carver High School, and an email.

"If you'd ever consider doing a guest lecture...My students are doing a unit on local ecosystems—I think they'd get a lot from someone who actually works with the animals in them." She held it out. "No pressure. It was good to meet you Dr..."

Her voice trailed off, waiting.

"Green. But that's way too formal. My name is Angela." I took the card. Our fingers didn't brush. She was careful. "It was nice meeting you too, Alana."

I pocketed the slip. It was just a card. A piece of paper. A tiny, weightless counterbalance to the heavy, beautiful certainty waiting for me at home. I tossed it in my purse and drove off.

THE STONE FETLYNNE had given me eventually found a home on the windowsill above my kitchen sink. My eyes brushed over it every time I washed the dishes and tidied up. I smiled, thinking of even the low-intensity times we'd since spent together. In her garden. On my porch. Back in her bed, but with no sex. Rather *holding*. Rocking. Cuddling. Swaying. Mutual caretaking. I savored all the un-asked-for moments that we still managed to find our way to, and I felt peace. Lots of it. So did she.

Fetlynne and I had built something that felt safe, which is why when the universe decided to test that safety, it didn't send a monster. It sent a beagle named Brownie into my clinic. His appointment was for a lump removal. A simple, benign mass on the flank of a middle-aged pup. We'd scanned it. It looked contained. Routine. But what was actually inside was not a lump. It was a web, wrapped around a deep vessel. My scalpel found the edge of it, and the vessel gave way like a rotten seam.

"Shit." My own voice raked flat in my ears. "Shit. Shit, shit!"

The blood welled up, a dark, fast flood, swallowing the gauze faster I could pack it in. Damn it. Fuck. No! *Too much blood, too much blood.*

"Carl, retractor. Now. Lewis, more laps, please. Four-by-fours. Go!" The words flew out automatic, a script written in my spine. My world constricted to the red well, my fingers searching for the torn seam in the slick, hot darkness.

"I can't see it," I spoke through gritted teeth.

"You will. Suction. Right there." Carl's voice was a firm bass note under the panic.

Brownie's heart rate on the monitor ticked up. *Too fast.*

"Pressure's dropping. Sixty over forty."

My hand didn't shake. That came later. "I see it! Got it.

Clamp." I slid the clamp onto the pulsating nub of the vessel. The flood stopped. The well became a puddle.

But the monitor screamed. A long, flat tone.

No, no, no, no, no no. "Pads!" I yelled. "Pads, pads, pads, pads, pads!"

Carl was already moving. The gel, the jolt. "Clear!"

Brownie's body joggled. The line stayed flat. It was a one-in-a-thousand thing. A statistic. *Oh, God, no. No. No!* "Epinephrine. Now! Lewis, compressions. **Go**." My voice was somebody else's. My heartbeat bolted. Sweat beaded on my temple. On my spine. But my hands did what they were trained to do. *One. Two. Three. Four.*

"Come on, come on," I muttered. "Come on, come ooonnn, Brownie. Wake up!" I begged, fighting tears.

A jolt. A blip. A stutter. Then the beautiful, ragged sprint of a heartbeat finding its way back onto the screen. *Thank God!* I shuddered in relief. Ninety seconds of controlled chaos. The silence that followed was the loudest sound I'd ever heard. The steady, thready beep of the monitor was an answered prayer.

My head dropped. My shoulders buckled. My breathing came in uneven gulps of the panic-stricken air. Brownie would live. He'd need ICU, and a transfusion, but he'd live. We'd pulled him back from the line. My body was shaking though I tried to hide it.

"Good work, team." I gave next steps orders. Saw to it Brownie was situated and comfortable in ICU. I felt the grounding coming back to my voice. A miracle.

I stripped off my gloves and gown, moving on autopilot through the post-op ritual. Cleaned up. My hands were unsoiled, but they wouldn't stop trembling. In my office, the energy was off. The fluorescent lights and the echo of the flatline in my head made me ill. With my adrenaline drained, I now felt a cold, odd vertigo. I crossed my arms over my chest, trying to reestablish steadiness but I couldn't. I was distressed. I didn't need a hug. I needed someone who who would see the fracture in me and not look away. Someone who wouldn't just say, *"but he lived."*

I needed Fetlynne.

I pulled out my phone without thinking. I just typed the raw truth into the text bar: *Almost lost a patient today. We brought him back, but I feel hollowed out.* I clutched the phone in my hand while staring at it in a daze. I'd never had a day like this before.

Threet dots appeared in my chat with Fetlynne. She'd seen it. They pulsed forever. Well, maybe a minute...then they vanished. No reply. I went back to work. Took a break. Cried a little. Thirty minutes passed. No text back. I pulled myself together. Soldiering through the day. She could have been in a session. Two hours went by. Nothing. Three. *Is she with Jules? Or not prepared for me being needy? AM I being needy? Or does she just not know what to say?*

"Get yourself together," I said aloud when I left for the day. "Brownie made it. Just go home and wind down in the yard." I slid my seatbelt over my chest, sniffled and drove out.

The lack of response from Fetlynne shouldn't have felt like torture, but it did. She had her own life. Her own business. Her own "system." And we still had no definition. I had no right to feel like I could demand her time on a dime. She was not my girlfriend. Not my partner, not my wife. I didn't know what she was. Right then, though, I felt inconvenient. Like something she'd wave off to deal with later. And that hurt.

I remained in my car in my driveway. A flash of lifeless Brownie made my stomach clench. He'd lost too much blood! My phone rang, drawing me out of my harsh flashbacks. Fetlynne. I stared at the screen—a ball of emotions rolled into a lump in my throat. I almost didn't answer. But I swiped accept. "Hey."

"Angela," her voice was husky, stripped of its usual honey. "I'm here. I'm sorry it took me so long to get back to you. Talk to me."

I opened my mouth, but not a single word came out. Only a ragged breath. I closed my mouth. Deflated. A sniffle. "Today was so hard," I finally managed. My voice cracked. "I'm in my driveway."

"Okay." A pause. The sound of her settling in to give me her full attention. "Just breathe. I'm right here. I'm not going anywhere."

And for the first time in hours, the screaming vibration in my in my bones softened, just a fraction, but enough. She'd hadn't fixed anything, but because she was finally, actually, there.

"I'm right here," she whispered once more, and I could almost see her eyebrows furrowed in care and concern. She *was* present.

I talked. Haltingly at first, then in a rush. I kept going while slipping out of my car an into the house. Told her everything. She listened. We stayed on the phone until my breathing matched the quiet of the yard. It helped. A lot.

When Fetlynne and I hung up, though, loneliness rushed back in. Ugh. Thirty minutes later, however, a courier arrived with a small, wrapped package. Inside was a beautiful ceramic mug. It was heavy. Deep oceanic blue. Shiny. Along with it was a tin of loose-leaf ginger-turmeric tea, and a note in her precise script: *For the hollow places. Wrap your hands around this. Think of me. –F*

I heated water, smiling and relaxing the way I needed to. Mr. Pickles would be delivered from daycare any minute and I couldn't wait to hold him. The little snorting lead-weight of uncomplicated love. In the meantime, however, I wrapped my hands around the mug to feel its warmth on my palms. My fingers found the grooves she'd chosen for me to hold. I thought of her. Drank it all.

The week that followed was a steady wave of contrasts. Fetlynne's texts were attuned and perfect. She checked in, sent a song, read me a poem. But they were interruptions in my day, not companionship. She lived twelve minutes away yet our connection was a series of beautiful, deep, discrete dives. I hadn't seen her. And the space between them was just... space. My space. I slowed my responses to protect myself. Just in case. She'd had me too wide open.

By Friday, the shock of everything had calmed down. But it left a dull, familiar ache. I was kind of bored. Kind of lonely. Of course, I had shelves of unread books. And yes, I had enough streaming subscriptions to feed a hundred-hour binge. I could have gone down to my firepit to and uncorked a new bottle of wine—a gift from a globe-trotting client, still in its bag. But none of it intrigued me. None of it was the serene sharing of empty minutes.

I was staring at a slow drip from the kitchen faucet I'd been meaning to fix for a month. The *plink... plink... plink* in the empty house felt like a taunt. This was the life I'd built: solid, independent, full of love that arrived in packets. And I was mildly irked. Restless.

I grabbed my purse to fish out a hair tie. My fingers brushed against cardstock. I pulled it out. **Alana Jordan, Biology Teacher. Carver High School.** Oh.

Well, well, well...

"I didn't throw this away?" I eyeballed her email address. There was no phone number. I flipped it over. Blank. *Hmph.*

I didn't care about traumatizing teenagers with parasite lifecycles. But I was mildly curious about the strong woman with the neat locs and wry smile who'd called a creek bed a classroom.

I stared at the card, and a clear memory surfaced: her calm command, *On three*. The solidity of her on the other end of that bucket. And the effortless, uncomplicated collaboration. The way our breathing had synced as we heaved. I opened my laptop. Started typing.

To: AlanaJ@CarverHigh.edu

Subject: Following Up

Hi Alana, it's Angela Green from the Sandy Creek clean-up. I've been thinking about your offer to speak to your class. If it's still on the table, I'd like to take you up on it. I'm free to discuss details whenever you have a moment.

The cursor pulsed as I hovered over "Send". The card was just a card. But the action felt monumental. It wasn't betrayal, was it? It was just exploration. It was, for the first time, testing the freedom Fetlynne had so gracefully offered. I shrugged. And I clicked. *Sent.*

10

AT DAWN ON SUNDAYS

Alana's reply hit my inbox at 7:04 the next morning.

Angela, great to hear from you. I'm buried in lab reports this morning but could use a break. If you're free for coffee around 11:15 to chat about the lecture, I'm at Black Coffee on Jonesboro. I'll even spring for a scone. 😉 –Alana

It was efficient, warm, and present. A concrete offer for *today*? As I was staring at it, my phone rang. Fetlynne.

Her voice was low and focused. The honey was back, but it was a deliberate, warm pull. "Angela. I'd like to see you tonight. I have an experience for us. Your living room. I'll bring everything. Don't make me negotiate."

Damn.

The two asks landed in the same moment of silence.

I sat up straighter. "Tonight works," I told Fetlynne. The words were automatic.

Experience? Shiiit!

My thumb drifted over Alana's email. "Fuck it," I thought

aloud. I hit "send" on my reply: *See you at 11:15. I never say no to a scone.*

I had just accepted two dates for the same day. One represented freedom I was exploring. One with the woman who represented the ground that freedom was built on. Them both being on my calendar personified a choice that had until now, only been a theory of liberation. The math now just got terrifyingly real.

BLACK SKINNY JEANS ripped at the thighs. An oversized Braves t-shirt that slid off my shoulder at an angle that highlighted the sleek line that peeked out, drawing eyes to my athletic deltoids. Comfortable sneakers on my feet and a baseball cap with an emblazoned *A* covering my tresses while protecting me from the sun. I arrived at Black Coffee at the suggested time.

I didn't spot Alana at first. The shop was energized. Chatty. Music, weekend readers, and always-working influencers filled the space. But then, my sightline led me to a corner table with a spread of paper, medium cup, and woman with glossy, cascading locs pulled back in a ponytail. She glanced up. Looked around aimlessly. Then back down. I walked toward her. She peeped back up again, and then, our gazes met. Her eyes glimmered and a shy smile spread across her face. Bashfully, she waved me over.

Grin reciprocated on my face; my feet followed the welcome.

"Hey there." She stood.

"Hi!"

"Thank you for coming." She gestured for me to sit.

Feline green-gray eyes. *How did I* ***not*** *notice those before?* Beautifully arched eyebrows. A handful of aesthetic jewelry pieces delicately clamped round a few strands of her hair. Alana looked strikingly put-together under the cafe lights. Away from the creek's mud and work gloves.

"It's my absolute pleasure. I must warn you though, I don't know much about children."

She leaned back in her chair with a light chuckle. Raised her hand to tuck a stray loc behind her ear, then absently scratched at her upper arm where the aggressive AC vent made her skin prickle. Her fingers traced over a nautilus shell tattooed there. My brows furrowed slightly. Head tilted slightly. The art was barely visible under the sleeve until she shifted—its chambered spiral quickly disappearing again beneath fabric. *Interesting*. But I didn't comment on it.

"That's perfect," she said. "They're feral anyway. My goal is just to survive with my credibility intact."

I giggled.

Alana stood, gathering her cup. "Let me get you that scone I promised. What can I bring you to drink?" Her voice rose and sped up on the next few words, "They do a meeean dirty chai here," then lowered, deepened and slowed with, "if you're into that." She stifled a smile.

I cackled this time. "A dirty chai sounds amazing. Thank you!" I laughed so easily and so hard a baby tear formed in the crinkle in my right eye.

Alana confidently moved towards the counter. She didn't even looking back. When she returned with my drink—and two blueberry scones on a plate—I felt a warmth. An unexpected sense of nurturing.

"Thank you," I told her. "You really didn't have to though."

"I wanted to. Now, about the guest lecture..." She settled back in her seat with bright and focused eyes. "I was thinking, to keep it low pressure, we could frame it around how animals adapt to urban environments. Like the coyotes in Piedmont Park, or the red-tailed hawks nesting on skyscrapers instead of cliffs."

My eyebrow lifted. On one hand, I couldn't think "cliffs" without being reminded of Fetlynne in Panama. On the other hand, Alana became instantly more fascinating. This wasn't just a frilly idea. Oh *no*. It was damned thesis delivered by someone who had clearly thought about it for a while.

"Whoa. That is a fantastic angle," I gushed. Alana had immediately transformed from a high school biology teacher to a scholar teasing me with a scone. I leaned in. "I like it. I mean, for the animals...it's literally their backyard."

Her grin broadened with a flash of pleasure and pride. "Right? It makes ecology feel urgent."

"Not abstract."

"And it lets you talk about veterinary medicine as a form of urban wildlife negotiation... Maybe? Not just neuters and spays and domestic pets." She spoke with her hands, ending with them palms up. Her shoulders too, a tiny shrug.

"Yeah, that could work. It's all a compromise. We all need each other. Have to live together without doing too much harm to one another."

Alana relaxed. "Yes..." her voice trailed off and a crooked

smile crawled on her face at a snail's easy pace. She took a sip of her coffee.

"Maybe I *can* do this," I thought aloud, my mouth slightly open with the thought.

"You look like someone who practices what they preach about coexistence."

A silence. A lingering gaze. I watched her chest rise and fall with a big breath.

"You know, I just had a flashback to you and that metal bucket at the creek. You have a hell of a grip for a teacher."

"For a teacher?" she laughed. "I was a rower in college. Still scull on the river sometimes. It's my church."

And with that, I took a bite out of my scone. My leg bounced a little under the table. I hoped she didn't notice. I sipped my dirty chai. Alana smiled, letting the gap in conversation stand. She peered at me over her thin rim of her cup. I exhaled.

"I can't even swim," I finally admitted. "Well, I at least know how to not drown—I think. But rowing? I don't know what "scull on the river" means but I'd love to watch you do it." Shit. The words fell out. I clenched my teeth. Buried an embarrassed laugh with a bite to my bottom lip and gulp. My eyes felt tense.

She threw her head back in laughter.

Yup. The old goofy Angela is still in there, I thought to myself. "I'm a nature girl myself," I tried to recover. "At a state park at least three weekends out of the month."

"Which one's your favorite?"

"Tough choice...maybe Providence Canyon, but I still

haven't visited Talulah Gorge yet, so...might be a toss-up once I get around do it."

"I haven't been to either, but I love the random deer you can spot on the trails at Amicalola."

"Get out of here! I was just there with my dog!"

"No way."

"Yes way," I kidded.

"Nice. I don't get around to all the parks as much as I'd like, but I try when I can," Alana said. Then she pivoted. "Anyway... back to the lecture. This was really great. Take some time to think about it. Again, no pressure. Either way... I'm glad you emailed me."

Back to professional talk again. Okay. Great. I think. Not really?

A silence with a shared smile. Alana looked a little flustered for the first time.

"Me too," I spoke up. "Glad I emailed you." I stole a quick glance at my watch without taking my eyes fully off her.

The time had dissolved. I needed to get going. Alana might have caught the whipped time check, as she gathered her papers, signaling she was done as well. "I should let you get to your weekend," she told me, though she made no move to stand before I did.

We walked out together into the Saturday sun. At the curb, the professional pretense fell away again.

"And, Angela?" she called as I pivoted to walk a bit further toward my car. Alana had opened her door, then paused, looking back over the roof at me. "If you ever want to see what 'sculling on the river' actually looks like... I'm usually on the Chattahoochee at dawn on Sundays. No swimming required. You can just watch." She gave a final, friendly smile, slipped into her ride, and drove off.

I stood there dumfounded with the sun now on my back and the taste of chai still on my tongue. *At dawn on Sundays* replayed in my mind like the opening of a secret door to a parallel, simpler life. One with schedules you could set your watch by and promises that didn't need to be decoded.

I ducked into my vehicle. I had a few hours before Fetlynne would arrive with her surprise "experience". I was curious and excited to see her, but now my feelings were coated with a new, subtle tension. It felt like preparing for a masterclass in intimacy, while the coffee shop had been a study group with a possible crush. One now felt like it required my full and focused reverence while the other simply felt like play. By the time I neared my block, a little fear set in. I was afraid of what Fetlynne might see in my eyes. Yes, I had freedom, but how would it look like on me, especially so freshly tested?

11

EXPERIENCES

I didn't owe Fetlynne anything, certainly not an explanation. It wasn't a date. It wasn't a betrayal. And it wasn't even about her. But I still felt guilty. I still felt the sticky-sweet residue of a good time another woman. And I still walked into my house wearing it like a perfume I had no right to.

In my *own* house, I now felt like this? I had not expected that.

I brushed it off. I was overthinking. Likely overreacting.

This was all new, of course there would be kinks to work out. Besides, it was *not* a *date*. I lied to myself. It was just a chat over coffee about a possible lecture. That's it. Right. Now, I needed decided to tire Mr. Pickles out with a long walk before Fetlynne arrived because a tired dog was a good dog.

After that, and showering, shaving, and styling my hair in an updo to get it off my neck—damn hot flashes decided to add their own jitter to the static in my veins, as if I needed that tonight—I was ready.

Wink. Showed myself some love in the mirror because I knew I looked great. Smelled good too. I made a mental note to pull my hair up more often. Twas a completely different vibe than my default casual ponytail.

By the time Fetlynne arrived in a pearl-gray SUV, my mood had been reset. I'd turned on some music. Had a glass and a half of white wine. Gave belly rubs to Mr. Pickles. All of it was enough for me to not flinch at the realization that Jules dropped her off. Lord. This was my life.

"Hey," I opened the door with a big and genuine smile.

As usual, she was a vision. But a comfortable-looking and inviting one this time. Fetlynne was draped in a deep moss green linen shirt. Oversized, with the sleeves rolled. She sported wide-leg, high-waisted cream pants and sliced geode pendant on a leather cord that gave her an effortless elegant look. I loved it.

"Wow," she glanced up at my hair. "*Hello*, gorgeous..." Her gaze went from my head to my feet. Slowly tracing back up for a linger on my eyes. She smiled. "How are you? How was your day?"

"I'm good. Busy day. Ran some errands, took a breather for some coffee." I stepped aside to let her in. "You? Oh, and I *love* that neckpiece," I flowed.

Fetlynne quickly ditched her simple leather slides. Mr. Pickles trundled forward for his usual inspection—jangling collar around his neck adding its own layer over the Jill Scott I had softly playing in the background. I had to admit though, having her back in my space felt good. Felt grounding. Felt...reassuringly familiar.

"Thank you. Found it at an arts festival last week. I couldn't resist the way the light hit it."

"And I don't think I can resist the way it lays against your chest." The liquor was already talking. I was too old for liquid courage. But I'd needed it to relax earlier.

A flashback to Alana and the rowing comment. *Maybe it wasn't the wine.* Maybe it was the confidence I'd grown since walking into Fetlynne's studio. I had no idea. My mind was just as scattered as the crystals on her jewelry.

Fetlynne just smiled. She'd brought with her a small, beautiful wooden box with strips of handmade paper.

"So...I'm on edge about this experience you have planned. What is it?"

"Certainly nothing to be on edge about, darling." She sat close to me. Caressed my knee with a slight slide then squeeze.

An internal *mmm* flooded me. My body relaxed even more.

Fetlynne retrieved two pens, a small bottle, and a single candle from her bag. She put them on the coffee table but didn't fuss with them. First, she took my hands—one in each of hers—then turned them up.

She paused, then spoke in a whisper.

"So much *will* in these." She glanced at me. "Strength. Determination. Courage. Life..." Fetlynne thumbed over my palms. "And power." She inched closer to me. Pulled my hands, one at a time, to her lips and pressed a kiss into the center of each with closed eyes and an inhaled as if she could siphon any trauma still embedded in my palms and metabolize it into care. She turned her head and breathed it out.

The move sharply took my breath away.

"You're an incredible doctor, Angela. And a disarming lover, too." She smoothed a finger over one of my eyebrows. "I missed you. And I'm glad to be here tonight."

Warmth. It felt like she'd lit a small candle inside my chest. "I missed you too," I whispered. *Should you have really met up with Alana this morning then*? My mind immediately chastised me. *Not now. Not **now**.*

"You okay?"

Shit. She sensed everything. "Yeah. Just... a little overwhelmed is all."

"I know you had a rough week last week."

"I did, but I'm good now," I recovered.

"You're better than good, Angela."

I leaned into her. Let myself soak up everything she was offering. Fetlynne felt intense but in the most perfect way possible. I didn't know if the whole hands kiss and affirmations were a part of her experience or just her, but in that moment, it didn't matter. I accepted the gifts. I loved them.

She gave my arms slight compressions. Kissed the crown of my head. Swaddled me. Nurtured me. It was intuitive, a return to our old energetic dances where she was the only one moving while I lay on her table. It felt like an aura hug.

I smiled. "I missed you, too. And I'm glad you're here too," I confessed, hugging her back.

We held for several moments. Savoring the embrace.

Eventually, I glanced at the table. "So...you're really not

going to tell me what this is?" I sat up. "And do you want something to drink?"

She chuckled. "Gosh, you're antsy."

"Well, hell! I wanna know what's in that damn box, woman!" I laughed and headed to the kitchen. "Water, juice, or wine?"

"Water first. Maybe wine later."

Fetlynne lit a real candle this time. She then suggested we sit cross-legged on the floor before guiding us on a brief meditation on where we were in the moment. Nothing but the present. Bizarrely, I'd opened my eyes to Mr. Pickles quietly in our little meditation space. *What kind of family is this?*

"One of these is to release a fear," Fetlynne said, gesturing to the paper slips she'd brought. "One is for a hope you want to nurture. And one thing that you love about what we—you and I—are exploring," she added. "You don't have to show it to me. It's just for you to express and offer."

She picked up her pen and began writing with absolute focus. I stared at my blank strip. The candle flickered. *A fear to release.* My pen delayed. I thought of earlier at the coffee shop, the easy laughs, the glance at my phone when Fetlynne called. I wrote a single word. Folded it before the ink could dry. *A hope to nurture.* This was harder. I scribbled a phrase, quick and sure. Folded it. *One thing you love.* That one came easily. A gorgeous memory surfaced. I smiled as I wrote it, a private gift to myself. I folded it into a tight square.

We threaded our papers into the small glass bottle in silence. The only sounds were the crinkle of sheets and Mr.

Pickles's soft noises from below. Fetlynne sealed the bottle with a cork and held it between us.

"Now," she said, her voice low and resonant. "We give it to the future."

"And what does that mean?"

"That we'll revisit it in six months, and...see where we are."

"Six months, huh?"

"You'll still be here, right?" She spoke a little too fast.

"Yes."

The word landed with a thud. Certain. Without hesitation. Something about what we'd just shared felt so intentional and sacred that I couldn't see me *not* at her side six months later. The experience felt durational.

She smiled and closed the box. Fetlynne didn't move to blow out the candle. She looked at me with her eyes reflecting the flame. "Every ritual needs a seal."

Just then, she leaned in and gently turned my head. I gave zero resistance, and the next thing I felt was her lips pressed to the pulse point at the base of my throat, holding them there for three long heartbeats. A long, trembling breath rattled out of my open mouth. The kiss felt less like passion and more like a brand—a claim, a blessing, and a taking of oath all at once. I whimpered. My face contorted. My body cascaded like a falling feather. When she pulled back, her breath was warm against the damp spot she'd left on skin.

"There," she murmured. "Now it's real."

My throat was vibrating all night. Fetlynne stayed over again, and while we fell asleep in a tender spooning position, I kept blinking awake. Kept thinking of the possessive, yet reverent feeling of her stamping my neck like that. Her lips. Her breath. Her tongue. The heat of it all. Fetlynne held me from behind now—the big spoon, and I felt owned but knew I wasn't. I also felt cared for but knew I was.

I stirred. Shifted. Struggled to sleep. What *was* this? She shifted and kissed the back of my neck. I inched back.

She pressed forward. I moaned. She *bit* the back of my neck. I wormed. She clutched me tightly. Sucking. Kissing. And biting more of my skin. Tonguing it.

My body trembled. I felt her hand slip between my legs from behind. I opened them wider. My pussy started to pulse. Started getting wet. She touched it and moaned... pushing my panties to the side and rubbing two her fingers over my clit.

"Everything about you feels like a gift," she moaned, hot in my ear.

And we were off. Fingers and tongues. Thrusts and bucks. Grunts and groans. From behind. Sideways. Missionary. Completely entangled.

Gripped sheets. Unmuffled screams. Sliding. Gliding. Tribbing. Bumping and grinding. Sheets torn off the edges of the mattress. Comforter crumpled on the floor. Face riding—me on her, her on me. Penetration.

Fingers again.

Tongues again.

Rimming in the dark. She went there. Circled and stuck her tongue in there, a little finger pressure—just fucking right. I screamed. She grabbed my hips and held me still. She gripped my soul. Licking, lapping, sucking and fucking. We continued until spent...until we were a pile of sweaty, post-orgasmic loose limbs. We both probably snored that night.

God damn.

12

CHASING THE OTHER'S TAIL

We cooked together. Or rather, I cooked, and Fetlynne was my charmingly lost assistant dressed in a pair of my sweatpants and tees.

"Spatula?" she asked, opening the drawer full of towels.

"Other side. Second from the top, to the right of the sink."

She found the utensil and held it up like a trophy. "Success!"

We fell into a rhythm. I chopped peppers and she grated cheese. Our hips brushed as we passed at the stove. It was effortless and ordinary. Felt like another kind of dance.

"Small plates are in there," I nodded.

Fetlynne stopped to taste test. "Needs more pepper. And maybe a kiss."

"You're a terrible sous chef. But you have great ideas." I gave her the kiss. Lots of tongue. She pulled my closer by my shirt. Deeper tongue.

"Whatever. Just keep doing more of that," she grinned.

Good energy. We were buzzing with it.

"You know what." I stopped, standing hip-cocked while thinking. "Let's get out of here," I continued. The omelets were finished. "The backyard. We can pretend it's a French café."

Fetlynne looked surprised but grabbed two plates. "Ça me semble bien," she switched languages on me. I had no idea what she said, but it sounded sexy as hell. Then, back to English:

"Lead the way."

We settled in under an umbrella. Our conversation was an easy ebb and flow of chatter and silence. At one moment, I pointed my fork at her wrist. "I've wondered about that since the first time I saw you in your parlor. What do the fish mean?"

Fetlynne glanced at her inner arm then rotated it, so the tattoo faced me fully. A soft smile played at her lips. "They're koi," she began. "And they're swimming in a circle, each chasing the other's tail. Basically, my spin on yin and yang—life's duality. Harmonious partnerships. Everything exists in relation to something else, never on its own."

"Why fish?"

"I just love the water." She met my eyes with a steady gaze. "And for me, it's also reminder that you can't have any experience without its opposite. Light needs shadow. Stillness needs motion." She paused to think. "The fish's movement reminds me that my strength will have to sometimes bend. That my discipline for one thing can become a cage if it can't make room for surrender. That's the whole point—

one defines the other. They're not opposites, you know? They're a single, moving whole."

Her words turned inside me like a key. *Surrender. Bend. Make room.* They made my mind wander back to Alana, my first sincere attempt at living inside the new world I'd willingly decided to dwell in. A wild hope surged in my chest. Could I really have this otherworldly relationship with Fetlynne while exploring different paths with someone else? Sounded way too good to be true. Probably was.

But there was only one way to find out. Besides, shadows made light more fun. More real. The thought was a physical thing, a warmth in my gut. The reality of it all made me flush. I needed to get up and move. To get us into an element. "It's too hot to just sit here with all this wisdom," I blurted out, standing up. "I have passes to the new aquatic center a few blocks away. Want to go be lazy in the pool?"

"I didn't know it was open already!"

"It isn't. But I have passes," I winked. "I can swing by your place so you can grab whatever you need. You down?"

"Absolutely!"

We were in and out of her place in five minutes. At the pool, she entered the water the same way she entered a room—with ease. Confident. Like she belonged. She floated on her back, eyes closed to the sun, completely at peace in the liquid silence. Her comfort was comforting, and I watched her from the steps, the water lapping at my legs. Eventually, I stepped in the water beside her, allowing myself to enjoy this blue afternoon without guilt. Without shame. I commanded my mind to be quiet.

That was the best weekend I'd had in a long, long time. It set the tone to balance the busy but bearable work week that would surely come afterwards. When I'd dropped Fetlynne back off at her place, Jules was in the yard fiddling with the flower bed. She waved hello with a smile. I returned the greeting, grin and all. It was all still weird—sharing Fetlynne—but I was getting used to it. Didn't even feel jealous.

Fetlynne had been with *me* all weekend and was intensely focused. I couldn't really have asked for more attention. But one thing was still nagging me though, so I did question her for a definition.

"What do you even call me when you talk about me," I asked.

"My lover." She reached over and laced her fingers through mine with a grounding squeeze. "My lover," she repeated in a softer tone. "Is that alright?"

I thought. "I think so." I had no idea, but it was something, I surmised. "I think so," I whispered, and watched the left right of her beautiful ass as she walked towards her house.

Fetlynne stopped to give Jules a swift hug but didn't let it linger. She knew I was watching. As I eased my car back in drive, a glance back at the yard reveal Jules stealing a look at me from under her brimmed hat, and then at the trail of Fetlynne's footsteps. Then, she went back to her flowers.

When I got home, I took my phone off DND and saw an email from Alana. She was wondering about a non-lecture meetup. "The BeltLine?" She suggested, careful to keep her wording neutral. I couldn't process it right then. It was too soon after Fetlynne's skin was just on my skin. Too fast after I'd just been staring at her ass. Too much after feeling a flashback of her long-kissing my throat. But I did enjoy Alana's company, so I saved the message as new to remind myself to come back to it later.

I responded to her the next day while in a lull between patients in my clinic. I was sitting, elbows on the desk, chin resting on my folded hands. My thumb tapped nervously three times against my knuckle. Then I typed the three words, my exhale sharp in the quiet room.

Let's do it. Name the day.

She wrote back later that afternoon, perhaps after her students had gone for the day: *Next Saturday at dusk? By the way, my cell is below—texting might be more efficient than email.* 😉

A silly grin spread across my face. I pressed my lips together to trap it, but my shoulders shook with a silent laugh anyway. God. The professional line evaporated. We were arranging a first date without naming it and I figured she didn't want traces of this on her work account. The thought jangled my nerves. Lit a little spark, too.

"Don't overthink it," I told myself. I forced my focus back to work. There was a damn pet monkey eating a taco in my waiting room.

Alana isn't anything but a new and interesting acquaintance until one of us makes it otherwise, I thought, unable to help myself as I stood. I headed towards the hallway. She was attractive. Intelligent. Seemingly more rooted in a traditional way—a vibe I was picking up, anyway. If this BeltLine walk leaned even more personal, then I'd have to come clean. It was the right thing to do.

SATURDAY CAME. I got there a little early, which felt like a rookie move. Couldn't help it though. Punctuality was baked in my DNA, especially after getting dressed to the rolling bassline of Outkast's "So Fresh, So Clean." The track's confident thump still bounced around my skull as I hunted for parking. That is, until "Ms. Jackson" slid through the speakers next. Then I was really enjoying myself!

My eyes darted around. Searching, while bobbing my head and shoulders from left to right. "I'm sorry, Ms. Jackson. Oooh!" I sang a lil' bit too, off-key but whatever. The song's rhythm synced with the steady stream of runners and bikes flowing past.

I found a spot.

Amid the graffiti bleeding neon characters into crumbling concrete stood The Krog Street Tunnel. The air was that warm-soup summer evening kind, just starting to cool. Alana was already there. She leaned against a pillar of spray-capped brick—the tunnel was an uprising of color. When she saw me, she pushed off the stone with a smile that was pure, undiluted *hello*.

I waved.

Alana's stare did a quick, appreciative sweep. "Well, look at you. That slate-blue is the only relaxed thing in this whole circus. Very nice."

I glanced down at the soft cotton tank I'd thrown on. "What, this old thing?" I played it off, but I could feel my earlier grin threatening to come back.

"Mm hm." Her eyes twinkled. "It's good to see you again."

"Same. Thanks for the invite."

We fell into step inside the tunnel. The roar of a passing car momentarily swallowed us, then faded into an echo chamber of footsteps and distant bass. Art exploded on all sides—a ten-foot-tall cartoon heart on one wall, a photorealistic portrait of a forgotten civil rights hero, a single, beautifully rendered "FUCK ICE" cube in dripping silver on the ceiling.

Two joggers zipped by. An old man with mis-matched socks and a happy, scraggly dog.

"It's like walking through a brain," Alana noted. She'd been drawn into textured stickers next to a random phone number painted in green.

"A very angry, beautiful, caffeinated brain," I added.

The tunnel was a visual scream—liberated layers of tags, murals, and temporary declarations. Outside the far end, a cute food delivery robot named Devante scooted past, its little dome light blinking cheerfully at a steel sculpture of a fox.

I stopped and pointed. "That's a black ass name for a robot," I hooted, rubbing my hand over my head. "Damn."

Alana snort-laughed. "Definitely. And only in Atlanta."

We walked. We talked. Alana pulled out a version of me that was easy-going and silly, unguarded in a way that required no philosophy, just a good beat. Not any better or worse than with Fetlynne, just different. *Fetlynne*. I hadn't mentioned her. Didn't know how to without making it weird. We hadn't even deemed this a date although that's exactly what it felt like. For a few minutes of our talk, my mind wandered to when I'd be honest. Soon, I knew that, especially if the afternoon ended as beautifully as it started. Going out a third time without sharing was a choice I wouldn't make. *I wouldn't want it done to me,* I thought. *Tell her. Or at least ask what she's looking for.*

I shelved the thoughts and refocused on Alana as she pointed out a mural of a giant, grinning possum holding a slice of pizza. "Now that's art," I giggled.

The evening light gilded the railroad tracks as we moseyed along. And it was promptly eclipsed by random bursts of Ludacris or Usher thumping through passing cars. Summer in the A was a mixtape you walked through.

I ducked into a pink-colored sweets shop and emerged with two peach ice cream cones. One of them was already leaning to the side.

"This one is yours," I cackled, giving her the crooked cone.

"You're terrible," Alana laughed and took it.

"You like it."

Playfully, she touched my arm and mouthed *whatever*.

It was stupid, flirty fun.

We paused to let a rollerblader whizz by, then to watch a heron lift off from a nearby creek. Eventually, we stopped right under the glowing sign of Ponce City Market. Laughter and bass-heavy music spilled down from the rooftop bar above us.

"You should have gotten more napkins," she teased, wiping a little cream from her bottom lip.

"Need help?" I asked the question faster than I wanted to.

Alana locked eyes with me while letting her tongue catch another straying drip. "I think I can manage." She didn't look away. "But the offer was noted." Alana's stare lasted a second too long. Warm. Charged. Piercing. And on the heels of her tongue slow-lapping up the cream.

I blushed. Smiled broadly. Then, averted my eyes to look past her and break the trance. That's when I saw them.

Fetlynne. Glass in hand, at the railing. Her gaze suddenly fixed on me, a direct line through the crowd. I thought I saw the rise and fall of her shoulders in a huge breath but wasn't sure. Jules was beside her but turned away. Fetlynne was perfectly still, casually *watching*. The distance between us was too far to read her eyes, but I felt the focus of it like a spotlight.

The smile I'd just had with Alana cracked and crumbled but from a sudden exposure. She was seeing my easy joy with someone else. I was watching her witness it. Did I look too happy? Was it a non-issue? I was overthinking again. Or was I?

An extended beat passed. Then, Fetlynne's head tilted. Her expression shifted into a cool, composed acknowledgment. She raised her glass an inch in a slow, silent toast. At the same moment, Jules, noticed her focus. She turned to look down at me and Alana, then back at Fetlynne. Jules took a micro step back then they both turned away.

"Wooow," Alana let out a low chuckle. A smirk was on

her face as she glanced from the rooftop back to me. "Someone's got an admirer. She barely looked away from you."

My voice was stuck in my throat.

"Friend of yours?"

"Ssssoooorrt of." The words leaked out like air from a balloon. "Yes." I dragged my eyes back to face her.

"But?"

Fuck.

My stomach plummeted. "She's... more than a friend." I took a shaky breath. "I never wanted to be one of those 'it's complicated,' people, but...consider this the visual aid for the conversation I was planning to have with you—if warranted."

Alana's smile didn't disappear, but it settled into something more neutral. Observant.

"I see."

"I'm sorry. This isn't how I wanted to tell you."

She nodded slowly. Her glare flicked back to the space where Fetlynne was, then back to me. "Okay." She spoke carefully. Her voice was light. "So. Complicated."

"Yeah." I looked her in the eyes. My shoulders tightened as I held myself together. "Maybe we should find somewhere to sit."

Alana glanced at the remains of her ice cream cone. "Sounds like a good idea. I'm all ears."

We found a nearby bench in the shade. I suddenly wondered if I were still in Fetlynne's eyesight or long gone from her mind. Next to me, however, was a freckled-faced beauty waiting to hear what the hell just happened.

"Okay. Before I start though," I said. "Promise me one thing, *please.*"

"This is getting weird already."

"No. I just want you to promise me I won't be the joke in your group chat," I laughed. It was dry and nervous. But I was trying. "Just let me be a normal, awkward human for a minute—no screenshots later?"

"Okay, fine." A real smile touched her lips. "Your secret's safe. Now...feel free to share."

So, I told her. I kept Fetlynne's profession out of it. I just said we'd met a while back, but things recently turned more serious, but that she lived a very...open life. A life without traditional boxes. I told Alana that I was trying it on to see if it fit. That it was thrilling and confusing, and that yes, seeing her up there was as much a surprise to me as it was to anyone.

The whole time, I felt like I was explaining a complex board game I still didn't fully know the rules to, using pieces from two different boxes.

"So, you're not exclusive," Alana surmised. Her voice was even. It wasn't a question.

"No," I said. "We're not."

She nodded slowly, looking out at the passing crowd on the BeltLine. "And you're okay with that?"

I thought of the circling koi tattoo. "I'm trying to be. I believe in the idea. The practice is..." I gestured vaguely at the space between us, at the whole evening. "Messier. I've never been in this situation before. And every day I learn something new about what it requires."

"What did you learn today?"

"That insane fact that this can only work if *all* parties

want the same thing. That I can't mix non-traditional and traditional." The statement came out like a lightning bolt.

Alana's eyebrows lifted slightly. "And you think I'm traditional?"

That was a question I'd been dancing around. "I… get that vibe. Yeah," I told her. "And of course, there's nothing wrong either, I don't think." I waved a hand between us. "I honestly wasn't sure what your angle was, but I knew I was going to ask you tonight either way. Just got pushed into it faster than I wanted to is all. So…" my voice trailed off.

"You're a good reader," she said, her smile warm but final. "And there's nothing wrong with *either*, I agree, but it's not for me. I'm looking for my person—*the* person. And I need simplicity. A clear label. A shared calendar." Alana reached over and gave my right hand a brief, solid squeeze. I covered her hand with mine, my thumb brushing her knuckles in a tiny, unconscious caress. "I think you're fantastic, Angela, but I'd be a complication in your experiment, and you would definitely be a heartache in my plan."

"*Definitely*? God," I chuckled, the sound thin. "So harsh."

"Didn't mean it that way. Just being honest. You're intriguing. Smart. Funny. Beautiful. A heartbreak waiting to happen if I had to share somebody like you."

My heart jumped. "And I definitely never want to be responsible for that." I looked down at the pavement then back at her. "I think you're amazing, too, Alana. Even more so now. Wow." Her lack of judgement was a gift.

She watched me. Her expression softened from curiosity to something closer to compassion. She let the silence sit for a breath.

"Okay," she said again, slower this time. She leaned back against the bench. "So. You're… exploring."

"Yeah," I said, the word a puff of relief. "Exploring." It sounded so much more deliberate than I felt.

We lingered quietly for a few more moments before I spoke again. "Alana?"

"Yeah."

"Thank you."

"For what?"

"Not making this more uncomfortable or weirder than it had to be," I explained. "For your kindness."

"Thank *you* for your honesty. Says a lot about you."

We shared a soft glance and warm smile.

Alana stood, brushing a stray loc from her shoulder. "I should probably… let my students off the hook for that lecture." She gave a small, genuine smile. "For obvious reasons."

"Yeah," I said, following her lead to rise. "Probably for the best."

She stepped into my space, but not for a hug. Alana's hand came up and rested warmly on my shoulder. Then, she leaned in and pressed her cheek to mine. It was a slow, deliberate gesture. I felt the warmth of her skin, the faint scent of peach ice cream and a summer night. She held it for a breath —a full, somatic imprint.

For a second, just a flash, I saw the woman from the coffee shop—the one with the wry smile and the "dirty chai" line. Then she exhaled. Pulled back. She let her hand slip from my shoulder. I closed my eyes, noticing the cool air left on my cheek from where her skin had been.

"I hope things work out for you," Alana whispered, her smile a little sad, a lot final.

"Thank you."

13

JUST FALL

The embers in my firepit pulsed like a slow, tired heart. The night air carried the scent of damp soil and woodsmoke, but it was the recall of song lyrics from earlier today that filled the space between my thoughts: "*You can plan a pretty picnic, but you can't predict the weather.*" The words hit differently now. I wasn't cruising down DeKalb looking out for Alana now. I was planted in my backyard facing a blaze alone, a forgotten glass of wine sweating on the small table in front of me.

My mind kept spooling the same tape: Alana's giggles in the tunnel, her suggestive ice cream lick, the warm, fleeting press of her cheek, the clean severing of her "not for me." Then a jump-cut—the rooftop, Fetlynne's silhouette sharp against the skyline, the deliberate, silent lift of her glass. A toast that felt like a question mark burning in the dark.

I finally took a sip of my wine, thinking. I rubbed my head. Squeezed my knee. Glanced at the sky, then down at my slightly bouncing left foot. I sighed. Rowdy tree frogs sang their hearts out for mates only added to the mild cacophony in my mind. My awareness was heavy, and I wanted to put it down, but I couldn't.

My phone buzzed against the wooden slat. A seam ripper, splitting the thin veil of the night. Fetlynne. I noted the time: 11:11. The sound felt inevitable. I watched the device shiver for one more second, then picked it up. The fire popped, sending a spray of sparks upward.

"Hey," I answered. The word was soft against the persistent crickets and night critters.

"Hey," her voice lifted in pitch the instant she heard mine. She was speaking through a smile. "I can feel you already," she whispered. Sounded like she could have been sitting up in bed—against her headboard rather than lying down.

Now I smiled. Just a little. "What does that even mean?" I leaned forward, elbows on my knees, left fist against my cheek while the phone hugged the other.

"It means the space between us just shrank to the width of a soundwave. And I needed to hear your voice in the quiet, not in the crowd. Are you alone?"

I sat up straight. Released my tense limbs. Rolled my neck...processing. Fetlynne had a habit of packing so much in a few words that kept me present to the second. "Yes, I'm alone," I told her, and reclined in my Adirondack. "So... what's up? Can't sleep?"

"Couldn't wait til morning."

"To?"

"Recalibrate our frequency. Hear with my own ears that

you're okay. I—I couldn't see your face clear enough earlier, but I saw you go from feeling free to constrained."

"And I saw you go from observer to participant." A beat. "How are *you*?"

"Equilibrium is slightly off, but generally speaking, I'm fine. Swimming."

"Up or down stream?"

"Whichever direction the current is moving. I'm just trying to remember how to breathe in it. But I didn't call to talk about my axis." Her voice was a deliberate shift. "I called because I need to see you. Tonight. May I come over?"

So Fetlynne, I laughed to myself. "It's late..."

"I know but...*please*?"

"Sure."

"Thanks," she whispered, and the line went quiet.

Twenty minutes later, she was on my doorstep in a heather-gray hoodie—a little frayed at the cuffs—and black leggings. I'd put Mr. Pickles deeper in the house with music to mask her entry—wasn't in the mood for his ruckus tonight. I smiled when I saw her. Really big. She smelled amazing and looked surprisingly bright-eyed. This woman was perfectly perplexing.

We settled in quickly. Chatted about nothing—the ride over, the night air, the missing dog and unusual clatter-free entry of my house—a gentle warm up. Then a fat silence wedged itself between us. Fetlynne pulled her feet up underneath her and eventually spoke again.

"What happened early...between you seeing me and me seeing you," she began. Her gaze was steady but open. "If you want to tell me about it, I'd love to listen. Because my reaction took me by complete surprise. I'd like to understand both."

"Seeing me or watching."

"The latter wasn't intentional. I spotted you just a few moments before you saw me, but when I saw your face...I couldn't look away like I could with anyone else. Like I *should* have. And for that, I'm sorry. I didn't mean to come off as entitled to your private life. Definitely didn't mean to make you uncomfortable."

"But you yourself were?"

She exhaled. Pursed her lips, then curled them under and in and bit them. "Yes. Surprisingly. Yes, I was."

Her honesty was arresting. I looked her directly in the eyes. "But why? I don't understand. This whole freedom to see each other people thing was your idea."

"I know."

"So only you can have other people, not me?" I got a little defensive.

"No." She answered emphatically. "It's not like that at all."

"Then what is it, Fet? What *was* that?" My heart was in my throat. So many emotions. Fear. Sadness. Uncertainty. Desire. Guilt. I thought about Alana...so graceful. So kind. And then I felt lost. Just lost.

"I think," Fetlynne began. Her eyes twitched and her brows quickly furrowed. Then her next words rushed out in clarity. "I think I know what it is."

"What?"

"Her."

My face scrunched.

"Not *her* specifically...but just it being a 'her.'"

"What does that mean?"

"It means that if I'm honest with myself. A part of me thought that when you dated other people...they'd be men. Not other women."

My eyes flew open. Belly, too—filled with a gasp of unexpected air. I clutched my chest. Almost chuckled disbelievingly, but I stuffed the desire down. She was being forthcoming with me, but I was astonished at the lightbulb moment. "Why?" It was the only word I could utter.

"I don't know."

"What difference does it make?"

"I don't know." She looked at her hands. "I don't know, Ang. There shouldn't be a difference."

"I mean, I am attracted to men. Sure, but..." my voice trailed off. Unsure of what to say next. "Are you more threatened by other women?" I picked back up.

"I didn't think so. I shouldn't be."

"But you could be."

"Maybe. Clearly."

"Oh, that's rich," I stood up. Paced a little. I thought about Jules. I thought about everything.

"Wait, wait...please." She got up after me. "Yes, I felt a twinge today. A tax, I suppose, for designing a life without cages. I don't know why I thought your freedom might look like a man or why seeing it look like her tasted like a bitter shade of my own medicine. But it did. And it doesn't matter," she said. "I was just...processing out loud. This changes nothing. I'm not asking you to not see her. Jealousy is a normal human emotion and I'm willing to feel it for you to experience freedom."

"But the freedom isn't free if it comes with the cost of your pain—"

"Temporary discomfort, not pain. I'll get over it."

"She's gone anyway."

Fetlynne flinched. Then stilled. "Gone?"

"Yes, but I don't want to talk about that. Or…maybe later." Oddly, my own desire flip-flopped in me like a fish flung out of water. On one hand, I didn't want to talk about Alana with Fetlynne. On the other, I wanted comfort for my brief grief. Shit was weird.

She looked disappointed in herself. Or in everything. "You don't have to. I'm here for *us*."

"Well, *us* needs some more rules. We need clearer lines, especially about public spaces," I declared.

"You're right. And that's on me. I haven't had anyone in my life…like you…in a *long* time. I neglected crucial steps of this and left you to figure it out as you went along. Again, my fault. I apologize. I was wrong." She touched me at the waist. Tenderly. Her fingertips made my entire body shiver. Made me weak.

I felt the urge to cry. Felt like I had a volcano on the verge of eruption inside. I'd never experienced—or been aware of —so many conflicting feelings in me at once. "I'm scared," I blurted out.

"That's normal," she comforted.

"I don't know what I'm doing! I'm terrified," I admitted.

She pulled me in from behind and squeezed. I shook. A few tears slipping out despite me trying to bar them inside. Fetlynne turned me to face her. Looked up at me and caressed my chin. I felt a graze from the cuff of her hoodie as she traced my skin.

"You know what I feel? Nervous, too." She met me half-way. Her eyes were slightly glazed. "Earlier, I felt this... contraction. Like an animal snarl. The part of me that wants to claim what brings it joy and hide it from the world." She dropped her hand. Took a baby step back and paced. A dry, humorless laugh escaped her. "I spent twenty years building a philosophy to outrun that feeling. To make it irrelevant. And there it was today. Waiting for me at the fucking Ponce City Market with a dripping ice cream cone."

She did not cry. She'd seem almost dissociated, observing her own agony with a clinician's distance. This agitated me. I didn't know what to do with my surge of feelings and she was in some kind of intellectual freeze.

"What am I to do with your reaction, Fetlynne? What is this? If you're not yelling or demanding I stop seeing other people, does that mean you don't care as much as you said you did? As much as I thought you did?"

She halted. Pulled down her shirt sleeves. Fetlynne peered at me with the most intense eyes I'd ever seen. They could burn, but not in a destructive way. More like smoldering. Or worrying. I had no fucking clue. "Angela," she began. "I am standing here, allowing myself to feel my heart break in real time. I'm not running from it. Not transmuting it into a client session or Jules's devotion. I am choosing to feel it shatter and spread shards all over my chest. It is the direct, inescapable consequence of the joy you bring me. That is the math. I accept it." She looked at me with aching eyes. "Angela..." she swallowed. "I'm in love with you."

I cracked. Felt woozy. I needed to sit or I'd fall. My mouth went agape and my bottom lip trembled. I staggered back to the couch.

"And if being with her, or *anyone* else...if having a simpler love is what you truly want, then you should have it. Not because I don't care, but because I love you enough to not be the one who tries to limit and constrain you. I want to be the one who makes you feel *free*... in every way. So you can keep *choosing* to come back to me." Now, she cried. Now, she burst. *Now*...she fell into me.

I held Fetlynne so tightly I could have suffocated her. We melted into each other like lava finding ground to cool. My hands, which had just been clutching my chest now moved to soothe her back.

I moved the hoodie out of the way so I could touch her skin. My other hand cupped the base of her skull, my palm cradling its smooth, warm curve.

"Shhh..." My fingers traced the shell of her ear, then the tense line of her jaw. Fetlynne held me back tightly, and I felt a hot dampness of her tears on my collarbone. We rocked. We cried. My right hand curved, pressing a straight line of my nails into the crease of her spine. "Shhhh...alright. Alright..." I was at a loss for words. I scratched and rubbed and swayed. Soothing.

Fetlynne clutched a fistful of my shirt while her whole body trembled with release and faint whimper.

Silence. A long, heavy, sacred silence settled into the bones of the room. We breathed. We softened. We unspooled. Then, I kissed the center of her forehead and whispered. "Let go of the ledge, Fetlynne." I sniffled and tightened my hold. Pressed my lips more into her skin before releasing to continue. "Just fall, baby. I'm right here."

Her body gave way without words.

We held.

Eyes closed. Hearts open. We *held*...for...I don't know how long before shifting from the couch to the bed, the shedding of her frayed hoodie and my thin tee, a compassionate negotiation of limbs under sheets with no words but plenty of breath. Plenty of energy exchanged until the eventual slowing...to the peace that comes ceasing to fight the feeling.

14

FRESH SNOW

I woke to the solid warmth of another body in my bed. The settled weight of a shared aftermath. Fetlynne lie awake too. Under the sheets, she quietly found my hand. No words. No words. No words. The feather-light scrape of her fingernails against my palm. Quiet.

I blinked.

She breathed.

I felt my body micro shifting to get closer to her. She mirrored. We were skin to skin. Shared energy fields. Soon, one breathing organism once again. Just like we'd started.

Dawn light sieved through the blinds, striping the rumpled sheets and the clean, smooth line of Fetlynne's leg where she draped it over me. Though our inhales had synced, I could feel a faint, residual tremor in the muscles of her hand when she interlocked her fingers with mine. We had cried ourselves into a stupor, and now we were here.

The domestic silence felt enormous.

Gently, I slipped out from under the covers. The hardwood was cold under my feet. Quickly, I let Mr. Pickles out then put him back at bay. Then, in the kitchen, I filled the kettle. The click of the stove burner was too loud. I leaned against the counter and watched the gray light strengthen in my backyard. It was starting to hit the gifted river stone from Fetlynne on my windowsill.

I heard the soft pad of footsteps before I saw her. Fetlynne stood in the doorway, wearing last night's hoodie. She looked younger, and utterly tired.

"Good morning."

"Morning," I smiled, taking down two mugs. Fetlynne still had salt-tracks of dried tears on her cheeks. The sight rattled me.

I poured the hot water over the tea bags. The scent of ginger and lemon bloomed in the space between us. I handed her a mug. Our fingers brushed. She looked into the steaming cup as if it contained an oracle. "I'm so bad at this. Should have never even..." her voice trailed off for a moment. "I apologize, Angela. I am afraid I've made a terrible mess," she said. The words were so quiet the dawn light seemed to swallow them.

I set my mug down. Looked over at her staring down into her mug. "Then we'll clean it up," I told her. "Together." I reached for her hand across the counter. "Because...Ms. Fetlynne Cadet...I love you, too."

She looked up in a breathless reprieve. Her eyebrows raised and wrinkled. Fetlynne's lips pursed. Then finally, everything relaxed.

"I mean it." I looked her in the eyes. "And I'm just as

afraid you. Maybe even more so. But I know what I want, and what I want is with you.

"In all my complicated glory?" she asked bashfully.

The word 'complicated' sent a swift flash of my conversation with Alana flying through my mind. I hoped she'd find someone better suited for her. I refocused on Fetlynne. "The entire puzzle of it."

She studied me. Picking up on even the nano second of a drift. "I'm so sorry about yesterday. Truly, I am. I didn't mean to ruin your—"

"It wouldn't have worked out anyway. I'm learning as I go. But thank you for the apology."

We finished our tea with more words of affirmation and slight touches of comfort. Fetlynne eventually took an Uber home, and I spent the rest of day both lounging and doing laundry. I needed the monotony. Needed the nothingness before my work week started.

By Wednesday, I found myself at Fetlynne's place after work. Nothing serious. We were in her backyard. The same stone bench where she'd first taught me how to be held sat under the same magnolia tree, its leaves now rustling with a different kind of anticipation. The fountain murmured its old song. We were just... being. She was complaining about her nosey neighbor one moment, pointing out how the late sun gold-plated the edges of climbing roses the next.

This time, her fingers gently tilted a bloom toward the light simply to share its beauty. Some ambient, wordless track drifted from the kitchen window. I sipped raspberry lemonade she'd made me. The easy silence between us was a present I was still learning how to hold.

The metallic scrape of the side gate latch cut through it. Jules strolled into the garden toting a reusable grocery bag hooked on her wrist. She looked settled in a way I hadn't seen before.

"Hey," Fetlynne's voice was a perfect, neutral chord. She didn't move from her spot beside me, but her entire focus sharpened toward Jules. "I didn't think you were coming by until tomorrow."

"I know. I was in the neighborhood." Jules's smile was small but genuine. Her eyes flicked to me. "Sup, Angela?"

"Hi, Jules." My voice lilted a little too bright. I felt like I was sitting in someone else's favorite chair.

"I just came to drop off your bowl. The one for the salad." She pulled a ceramic container from the bag and set it on the small patio table. "It's washed."

"You could have kept it," Fetlynne smiled. She moved toward her but stopped a few feet short. A careful distance.

"Nah, it's too nice. And I know you have a whole system for these things." Jules paused with a smirk. "Probably categorized by diameter and emotional resonance." She turned to me. "Have you seen her kitchen?"

Fetlynne let out a soft, surprised laugh—a real one—and spoke before I could answer. "Guilty."

And with that, the air loosened for a second. Jules looked back at the garden, at the rose Fetlynne had just been admiring. "It's looking beautiful back here."

"It is," Fetlynne agreed. Her voice remained soft.

A slightly less agonizing, but still profoundly weird, silence settled. The fountain babbled. The neighbor's dog barked.

"Welp," Jules announced, clapping her hands softly together. "I'll let you two get back to it. Good seeing you both."

She let herself out the way she came. The gate didn't scrape this time; it latched with a quiet click.

"Well," Fetlynne said after a beat, her voice regaining its usual timber but not its earlier ease. "Where were we?"

I reached for her hand. "Right here."

She laced her fingers through mine. "Right where?" She smirked and bit her bottom lip.

"Here." I pulled her in for a kiss. Deep. Engrossing.

She froze for a fraction of a second—then kissed back, deeper. Her hunger unlocked.

"Mmm." I only pulled away to ease off the bench and into the grass. I didn't get on my knees like she did the first time we'd been in her yard. But I did pull her down to earth with me to continue. We resumed kissing. Rolling playfully in the grass like young lovers. The cool blades tickled our skin.

The fountain gurgled. Music wafted. The rose was forgotten. The only thing outside of ourselves that mattered was the crush of grass beneath us and the heat of her tongue. Fetlynne's eyes were bright with joy when we pulled apart. I was on top of her by then—back to the sun, eyes lovingly locked on hers.

The weirdness had dissolved into the taste of her.

TWO DAYS LATER, Fetlynne called. I was stuck in traffic, the world a blur of brake lights, utterly unprepared.

"Jules is stepping away from the dynamic." Her voice was a flat lake, but I knew there was a cold fracture beneath it. "She needs something for herself that I can't provide."

Oh boy. I grabbed the back of my neck and squeezed. Huffed out an exhale. "Um. Wow. Okay." I gulped. "How—how are you?"

I heard her breath catch before she explained. "I am... respecting her choice." A pause. Her unsaid words were a scream in the quiet. "And I don't know what to do with my hands right now. They feel useless."

Her confession was so raw it seized my heart. This wasn't about her systems or philosophy. This was a woman who had created a specific way of loving watch one of her subjects march out of its frame. My chest ached for her. And beneath that, a treacherous, shameful little current of relief hissed, *More of her for you.* I shoved it down.

"Where are you?" I tempered my voice.

"Home."

"I'm coming over."

"Angela, you don't have to—"

"I know." I cut her off, my signal clicking as I changed lanes.

The truth was, this wasn't my win. It was just evolution. Jules was claiming a chapter for herself. Fetlynne was swimming in a new kind of grief and learning, through grace, how correct her "single, moving whole" theory was indeed correct. And I was the one now driving toward it, my own relief a silent, shameful passenger. "Just be there. I'll be there."

I hung up.

We ended up on the floor in the corner where she first fed me grapes and surrounded me with touch. Where I'd thought I was an idiot for paying $300 to cuddle until she showed me what being nurtured and feeling cherished as an adult truly felt like. This time, I held her. This time, she had one last cry. This time, in the quiet that followed, my own uncertainty bubbled up.

"So... how does this work *now*?" My voice was just a flicker in the dim room. "What are... our rules?"

Fetlynne took a deep, settling breath. She wiped her cheeks with the heels of her hands. "No big guarantees." Her voice regained its grounded tone. She sat up in my arms and faced me more directly. "But I can promise you this: I can be as gentle as I can with your heart. Even if it's ever broken someone else," she paused. "And I can honor the love I have for you, here, now, with everything I am in this season."

"Because people change."

"They do. We all do." She reached for my hand. "I can also promise you freedom and radical honesty. That doesn't mean there won't be hiccups. It doesn't mean I'm not human and won't feel unwanted emotions sometimes—that comes with the territory of boundless living. You'll feel them too."

I nodded, fully grasping what I was choosing. What I was co-designing. I laced my fingers through hers. "I can promise you intense presence," I told her. "And spontaneous fun. And respect for your feelings."

She smiled wearily. "As you're already doing right now."

I mirrored her tired grin. "Yeah...I guess so. Feeling any better?"

"I am. Thank you. Thank you so much...for just being you."

My body warmed. "You're welcome."

Fetlynne and I also agreed to continual, gentle re-negotiations. We acknowledged that our bond must be flexible enough to hold changes. Strong enough to withstand the growing pains or necessary endings.

We sat in the silence of our new understanding. The words settled around us like fresh snow. Then, Fetlynne shifted. Slowly. Deliberately. She took my right hand and brought my palm flat against her chest, just below her collarbone. Her skin was warm. Her heart was thudding. She covered my hand with both of hers, pressing down with a gentle, unwavering weight. My fingertips felt her vitality—steady, alive, trusting me with its rhythm. We didn't speak. We did not need to. We just breathed, my breath beginning to sync with the pulse under my palm, in the new, uncharted country we had just vowed to build together.

The End.

EPILOGUE

ANGELA

The best part of my week is the moment her key turns in my lock. The scrape, the heavy *thunk* of the deadbolt, the pause where she toes off her shoes... By the time she rounds the corner into the kitchen, I already know, from that symphony, what kind of night we're about to have.

It took a lot to get here. Not so much hard work as the constant and gentle strain of intention, trust, and communication. *Never-ending* communication. I've talked more with Fetlynne about stranger, truer things than with anyone I've ever shared a bed with. Anyone at all, really—probably more than my best friends. She knows about the darkness behind my light. And me, about hers as we keep going.

We discussed how we might distribute our attention. We pondered the bitter aftertaste of pain as a consequence of bliss—the ebb and flow of it all. And we dreamed up dripping wet scenes that included a third or fourth. But we haven't delved into group play yet. We needed the three months after Jules' departure to define and design our world. To fortify it against old ghosts and insulate it from our own insecurities—the urge to clutch, the fear to voice fragile needs.

We also dissected the theory of "security," concluding that it's beautiful fiction. A forever promise can shatter just as easily as a negotiated agreement. The security I used to crave was a noun—a static thing to possess. I needed a verb. With Fetlynne, I found one: the conscious, continual *act* of choosing. Over time, the idea of us became less a petrifying knot in my stomach and more a beautiful excavation of a site we'd decided to build. A place that no one else had to understand.

My front door opened. The symphony began. I didn't turn from the stove, but my shoulders dropped an inch.

"I'm in the kitchen," I called out, a smile already in my voice.

The frantic *tick-tick-tick* of Mr. Pickles' nails across the hardwood added a syncopated snare to the music of us. Fetlynne crept up behind me. Arms slipped around my waists. Lips quickly stealing a peck from my neck. I threw my neck back into the safety of her shoulder and the welcome of her kiss.

"Mmm. Hey, baby."

"Hello, darling," she whispered, and kissed my cheek.

I arched my back into her. Felt a surprise line of cool links against my spine. "Ayye, what is that?" I turned around.

Fetlynne donned drapey gray halter and ultra-soft, wide-leg sweatpants. The latter sat low on her hips, allowing a chain to ride and decorate that beautiful ridge of skin. "A dotted line." Her voice dropped a register as she ran a finger along the chain at her hip. "Suggesting where to sign."

I was already sinking down. "Can I use my tongue instead of a pen?" I nipped at her skin. Ran my lips against it.

Fetlynne braced herself on a counter. "You can use whatever you want," she breathed, cupping the back of my head and bringing it closer to where she wanted it.

I kissed her through her pants. Breathed on her through the fabric. Grabbed her at the sides of her thighs and scraped my nails down her legs. She closed her eyes and surrendered to the devotion. Her head dropped forward, then rolled slowly to one shoulder, back, and around in a complete, releasing circle. Then she opened her eyes to peer down at me on my knees.

"Mmph. You look amazing from this angle."

"Nex time, wear a strap so I can suck your dick."

Her eyes snapped open. A shocked smile. A stunned laugh. "Maybe I'll leave options here."

"Please do. I have my own, but I'd love to wrap my lips around one that's yours—chosen for me."

She got serious. Looked at me in pleasurable amazement. Fetlynne helped me off my knees and pulled me into an embrace. "Where have you *been* all my life?" She whispered in my ear.

"Waiting for you to show me this version of me?" I confessed. The words came out soft. A little vulnerable. But true. "You gave me pleasure that changed how I showed up in life."

She melted. Eyebrows twisted and uneven. "Angie..." Fetlynne slow-blinked and shook her head with a smile. "I am so in love with you my body just shakes when I'm in your presence."

"I know," I said, holding her tighter. "I feel it shaking in me, too. It's the best feeling in the world." I rest my head on her shoulder and she rubbed my back.

This was us.

This was our design.

And this was our freedom.

ALSO BY CHERIL N. CLARKE

Kinky Cabins: A Halloween Novella - Featuring Angela from THIS book

Trick or Treat: A Halloween Quickie - Featuring Angela from THIS book

When the Road Softens: A Novella (Sapphic fiction)

Hard to Hold - The Keyhole Chronicles Book 3

Before I Am Erased - The Keyhole Chronicles Book 2

What the Mountains Remember (a companion story featuring Mariana and Nyla) - The Keyhole Chronicles spinoff novella

Reservation Under My Name - The Keyhole Chronicles Book 1

Rift: The Sensual Portal Book 2

Trip: The Sensual Portal Book 1

Whiskey Dungeon

Corsets and Cognac

Sweet Dark Rum

The Edge of Bliss

The Beautiful People: New Orleans

The Beautiful People: Las Vegas

The Beautiful People: New York

Losing Control

Candle Wax

Bite the Pillow (Poetry)

Oxygen (Poetry)

Spoken Word albums by Cheril N. Clarke (as C. Nicole):

Honey

Drip

ABOUT THE AUTHOR

Cheril N. Clarke is the author of nine novels, two stage plays, several short stories and poetry collections, and numerous children's books. She has been featured in *Curve* Magazine, *VoyageATL*, About.com, *Out IN Jersey*, *Burlington County Times*, as well as Phillyburbs.com, among others. Her creative writing website is CherilNClarke.com. Clarke is also an executive ghostwriter and the woman behind PhenomenalWriting.com. She has written for Fortune 500 executives and entrepreneurs worldwide.

www.ingramcontent.com/pod-product-compliance
Lightning Source LLC
LaVergne TN
LVHW020702110826
845149LV00012B/2078

* 9 7 9 8 9 8 9 5 2 2 5 7 6 *